THE
ROSIE
BLACK
CHRONICLES

EQUINOX

THE ROSIE BLACK CHRONICLES

EQUINOX

LARA MORGAN

WALKER BOOKS
AND SUBSIDIARIES

LONDON • BOSTON • SYDNEY • AUCKLAND

First published in 2011
by Walker Books Australia Pty Ltd
Locked Bag 22, Newtown
NSW 2042 Australia
www.walkerbooks.com.au

The moral rights of the author have been asserted.

National Library of Australia Cataloguing-in-Publication entry:

Morgan, Lara, 1971-
Equinox / Lara Morgan.
ISBN: 978 1 921529 40 5 (pbk.)
Series: Morgan, Lara, 1971- Rosie black chronicles; bk. 2.
For secondary school age.

A823.4

Cover image © Shutterstock.com/aggressor
Typeset in Adobe Garamond
Printed and bound in Australia by Griffin Press

10 9 8 7 6 5 4 3 2 1

The paper this book is printed on is certified against the
Forest Stewardship Council® Standards. Griffin Press holds
FSC chain of custody certification SGS-COC-005088. FSC
promotes environmentally responsible, socially beneficial
and economically viable management of the world's forests

For Fay, Simon and Serena,
for the love, frustration and laughter.

*"To the outside world we grow old.
But not to brothers and sisters. We know
each other as we always were."*
Clara Ortega

Rosie took a steadying breath, licked her finger and touched it to her eye. The identification-distorter lens stuck to her skin and she lifted it off her iris. First one, then the other. Then she swallowed them. Gross. She gagged and leaned on the sink. They always tasted foul, like rotten fish scales.

She was alone in the shuttle station bathroom and the harsh sounds of her coughing echoed off the pristine tiled walls.

"That's three minutes." Riley's voice came through the receptor in her ear. "Put the new ones in and get out of there." Rosie didn't bother replying. He couldn't hear her anyway; they never used reverse coms for a job because the signal could be tracked. Helios thought

Riley was dead, and he wanted to keep it that way.

Rosie rubbed her eyes. The disintegrating lenses made her nauseous, no doubt affected by the message capsule she'd swallowed earlier. She ignored it as best she could, her hand only a little shaky as she carefully slipped the replacement lenses on. Now any ident readers would clock her as Bridget Faraday, a scientist's daughter. The lenses had a microscopic camera in them as well, so when she looked in the mirror above the basin Riley could see her. She blinked, speaking slowly so he could read her lips.

"Are they working?"

"Vision's clear," he said. "Get out of there."

She tossed the Central dress she'd been wearing in the rubbish disintegrator, ran the decolouriser over her hair to strip out the blond, and chucked that away as well. She ripped her clothes out of her bag and dressed in her own pants, black singlet and white over shirt. She gave herself a final once-over in the mirror.

"Rosie, get going." Riley's tone was sharp.

She resisted the urge to mouth something rude at him and turned to the corner above the bathroom door, pointing the jammer at the invisible surveillance hub. The jammer flashed once. She had ten seconds before the shuttle station cameras kicked in again. Rosie slipped the device in her pocket and headed out.

It had taken her four minutes and fifty-three seconds to change this time. Was that a record? She pretended to be idly checking her personal com as she walked back down the corridor to the street.

Outside Central shuttle station A, the sidewalks weren't as crowded as usual. Instead of the habitual mass, only a thin stream of pedestrians passed her. It left her feeling exposed.

The station was the hub for the city's cosmetic alteration parlours and, because it was so busy, Riley often used it as a pick-up point for messages from his contacts. A good crowd made it easier for Rosie to become just one of the masses. Today, she'd met a Central party girl called Sharia in one of the enhancement cafes. She had disguised herself as a Central and it seemed to go okay, but she couldn't help being nervous. Plus what the girl had told her was doing her head in. Hadn't anything they'd done on Mars made a difference?

After she'd leaked Riley's parents' files about the MalX to the news wavers and they'd gone global, she'd thought they'd dealt Helios a massive blow.

Now everyone knew Helios existed. More importantly, everyone knew Helios had created the MalX. They'd heard how MalX-infected mosquitoes had been accidentally sent to Earth in a shipment and how they'd escaped, spreading the disease. The Senate and Orbitcorp had publically denounced Helios, calling them enemy number one. The Mars Enclave was gone, blown up. She'd seen it happen – made it happen – and damn near died in the process.

But now Helios was at it again. If the message was right.

She increased her pace, going straight past the elevator tubes shooting people up to the suspended station. It was depressing to know Helios hadn't been destroyed, but deep down she wasn't surprised. Only low-level operatives had been caught in the manhunt the Senate and Orbitcorp had run, and most of them had mysteriously died in custody. Hardly a shock, given the moles Helios had in both the Senate and Orbitcorp. Riley said it was likely some of them were still there, despite both organisations' much publicised declarations that they were rooting out any Helios supporters in their ranks.

We won't rest until our corridors are once more places of safety and hope for the people, was the latest sound bite from the authorities.

Security and hope. Rosie snorted. She and Riley had blown a damn base up and Helios was still around. Clearly the invisible puppetmasters behind Helios were as strong as ever. And the problem was no one knew who they were. Not even Riley.

It was ferociously hot and she was suddenly thirsty as the sweet scent of engineered berries from a juice bar assailed her. She wondered if she could risk stopping for a drink. Maybe not. A group of Senate guards was strolling in her direction. One was talking nonstop into a com and they all had one eye covered by opaque shields. Scanners. Rosie slipped alongside some fat guys in noodle franchise uniforms. Helios had impersonated Senate guards before.

It didn't hurt to be too careful, even with the ident-distorter lens. She forced herself not to turn around as they passed, keeping close to the noodle guys, who were bitching about a club they'd been in the night before.

"Take the Rim line." Riley's voice came again in her ear. "Central West C just had a quarantine scare; it's closed for UEDC."

United Earth Disease Control. That was the third MalX scare in Central this week. That explained the sidewalk space. Rosie changed her direction, dodging past the noodle guys and swinging towards the sky street crossing.

It was a long walk to the closest Rim station, and by the time she got there the nanos in her over shirt were struggling to evaporate all the sweat. Rosie looked up at the entrance scanner and made sure it clocked her fake ident as she went in. She'd passed more guards on her way and was jumpy with nerves. Somehow Riley must have picked up on her nervousness. He spoke softly, "Calm down. The message capsule has another seven hours at least before it disintegrates."

Easy for him to say; he wasn't the one who'd swallowed it. It sat in her gut like a lump of congealed starch. She threaded her way through the busy station, looking for the next shuttle east. She had to go through a convoluted shuttle switching process – one of their security protocols – before she headed to where Riley was.

Rim South station was more crowded than usual

thanks to the Central line closure and it took her almost ten minutes to push through and find a shuttle. The shops that lined the station projected loud advertisements for their wares, and huge floating screens hovered above the commuters, showing news wave after news wave. She stood in the line for a shuttle and watched as she waited.

The latest quarantine news flickered silently on one screen, alongside a list of shuttles delayed due to the detection of disease carriers. Yet another displayed vision from the southern Asiatic States where the MalX had taken the strongest hold. There was also a constantly changing tally of the dead in glowing orange numbers. It was now just over five million.

"Can you believe that?" A short man in a brown coat that stunk of rancid oil pushed up next to her and nodded at a news wave about the Oceanus mission. It showed images of a deep space freight ship with debris drifting from a massive hole in its hull.

Oceanus colony ship hull breeched. Leviathan *breaks apart*, scrolled along the bottom of the screen in big black type. *Five hundred dead. American Republic claims United Earth Commission delays on the wormhole project to blame.*

"Sons of bitches," the man murmured, staring at the wave. "I was going to sign up to go."

Oceanus was one of the projects Aunt Essie was now assigned to. It was a recently terraformed planet in the Gliese system, twenty light-years from Earth, and the UEC had been calling for colonists. It took months to reach it on the current ships. The United Earth Commission had been promising to build a stable wormhole to cut the distance, but so far nothing had eventuated. The planet had become the shining hope for people desperate to escape the MalX, especially now Mars was closed to colonists since Helios had been exposed. Oceanus was a water planet with pristine new growth, touted as some kind of utopia, but getting there was risky. Ships didn't always make it – maintaining power and shields all that way was difficult. There was plenty of space junk out there waiting to tap a hole in the sides of ships, and all the money in the world couldn't stop a hull breech in space.

Rosie could understand people wanting to take the risk; she might live in the Rim now, but she still felt like a Banker. She knew the odds, and at the moment they were stacked in the MalX's favour.

As she stood watching, the news wave vision suddenly blurred. A high-pitched beeping cut through the noise of the station and a new piece of vision began streaming along the bottom of the Oceanus news wave. Bold black letters cut over the now frozen picture of the *Leviathan*.

Not gone, not forgotten, they said. An image of the Helios logo of the horse and rider over a sun flashed on the screen, followed by pictures of people dying of the MalX, their limbs wasted, skin red with the rash. *What will they do next?* The black words proclaimed. *What will you do to find them? Stop Helios. Save our world.* An image of a man in silhouette, one raised hand brandishing a sword, appeared, followed by the words, *Rogue Waves. You can't stop the fight.*

Rosie's eyes filled with tears at the pictures of the dying people and she looked quickly away. It reminded her too much of her mum in the final days before the MalX took her. Around her, people were exclaiming and staring at the screens.

"Tell it, Rogue!" someone shouted.

"Bastards!" someone else called.

It was a common reaction when one of the anonymous broadcasts cut through. They'd been happening more regularly of late.

"Well-timed distraction." Riley's voice was soft, and tinged with pride. He wouldn't tell her, but Rosie was sure he knew who was making the broadcasts. Maybe he was making them himself.

"Shuttle," someone called. The crowd surged forwards and she had to fight to stay on her feet. She ended up pressed up against the brown-coated man as they crowded though the doors.

Rosie rode the shuttle system for the next two hours, switching lines four times until she finally got on the North Coast route. It was her last change. The shuttle reached the river and paused at the bridge checkpoint where the Senate scanned the carriages for any MalX carriers. Everyone was terrified that the MalX would mutate and start transferring from human to human, so now infection scans were everywhere. Anyone infected was taken away to a Senate-run hospice, usually by force. Some of them were never seen again.

The cabin was half full and Rosie had been lulled into a relaxed state by the low hum of conversation and wasn't prepared for the sudden screeching alarm. It split the air like a blade scraping down metal. She jerked up, heart racing, and immediately felt ill. Her vision blurred. The sound was disorientating, designed to make you dizzy to reduce resistance. The doors burst open and two men in full disease-control suiting came in.

"Everyone sit down!" the first one shouted, his voice amplified by his helmet. They were dressed head to toe in white, and one carried a small case and scanner. The first man had a pulse gun and was plainly the soldier escort for the medic. Fear rippled through the carriage like a contagion.

The woman next to Rosie shrieked, clutching at the child on her lap. She wasn't the only one. At the other end, a man started to kick desperately at the plasglass window.

"Stop!" The soldier ran towards him, people scrambling out of his way. The alarm abruptly shut off. Rosie's vision cleared and she heard the unmistakable whine of a pulse weapon charging.

"Stop!" the soldier shouted again.

"I'm sorry! I'm sorry!" the man cried, but he was

still trying to kick through the glass. The soldier fired, the sound a concussive whump in the confined space. Everyone screamed and Rosie ducked down behind the seat in front of her.

The pulse hit the man in the back. He slumped down, head lolling. The red rash of the MalX on his neckline was exposed as the soldier pulled him backwards by his shirt. Rosie had seen it that bad before. If the shot hadn't killed him, the man would be dead in a few months.

The cabin of the shuttle was still with shock and suppressed fear: everyone thankful it wasn't them, terrified one day it might be. It was barely a comfort for Rosie to know she was immune to the MalX.

She wondered if the man had a family. He was around the same age as her dad. The guilt hit her hard. Helios had taken her dad, tortured him and infected him with the MalX. And Pip had saved him. This man wasn't going to be so lucky. Unlike her dad, or her aunt, and even her, the MalX cure in Pip's blood wasn't something this man could get. He would die, as would thousands of others, and there was nothing she could do about it. Pip was gone and she had no idea where he was.

"Rosie. Rosie!" Riley was calling her name.

She blinked. The medic was now pushing a shot of something into the fallen man's neck and she realised her hands were curled in fists.

"Rosie, are you all right?"

She forced her hand to uncurl and raised it in front of

her eyes, forming an O with her thumb and finger. Okay. There was an audible short breath. "Good," he said. "You know what to do. I'll see you soon." The com went dead as he cut off its signal.

CHAPTER 2

Rosie slouched down, picked the wafer-thin disc from her ear and ground it to dust under her boot. Now she had no contact with Riley, but she couldn't risk the earpiece being detected by the soldier.

The soldier was scanning everyone's idents. She sat up again as he came to her and waved the machine over her eyes. He surveyed her through the panel of his helmet as the machine beeped.

"I'm just going home," Rosie said.

The soldier checked his handheld and Rosie worked on keeping her face neutral. Riley had put her image in the ident system so there shouldn't be a problem. It should read her as Bridget.

"Been in the Banks the last week?" he asked.

"No." Damn, she'd answered too quickly. She sounded jumpy.

The man's eyes narrowed a fraction and the woman beside her shifted nervously.

"Raimes," the medic called. "The team's at the doors."

Outside, four more suited agents were waiting to be let in. The soldier gave Rosie a last look then walked away.

Rosie let out the breath she'd been holding. She'd been certain that he'd been about to consider a DNA scan and that would have been a real problem. Not even Riley could fake DNA.

The other agents came in and took the unconscious man away in a disease capsule and Raimes finished scanning the rest of the carriage without bothering to go back to her. The woman who'd been sitting next to Rosie made a point of moving to another seat.

Rosie just turned and stared out the window. She was starting to feel really ill now from the message capsule in her gut.

The shuttle finally started moving again over the bridge. The north side of the river was a patchwork of research stations and residential estates for the scientists – all Senate owned and controlled – and beyond that were acres and acres of farms.

Rosie got out at the next stop. A road continued on past the small shuttle stop towards the research stations. On either side of the road were the estates. High walls and code-controlled gates delineated them.

Riley had taken over a derelict house in a section of the estates that had been shut down. There'd been a MalX scare the year before and the Senate had closed down a whole estate on the western side. It was a perfect spot to hide. All the surveillance tech had been dismantled and the only thing to worry about was the occasional sweeps by Senate helijets. No one in the other estates would think of exposing themselves to a possible MalX risk. The Senate only checked on it to keep the Ferals out. As far as the Senate was concerned, Ferals should stay where they belonged – in the camps downriver and in the old city. The Ferals were the poorest people in Newperth, and ranked just above rodents on the Senate importance radar.

Pip had been a Feral when she'd first met him. At least he'd been pretending to be one, under orders from Helios. *Stop thinking about Pip!*

Rosie forced her mind back to the present and headed along a footpath that ran between the wall of the estates and the river. On her left the tops of the twelve-storey skyfarm towers rose beyond the estates, green against the pale sun-bleached sky.

After the cool of the shuttle, she was sweating heavily, and with each step she felt more ill. She pressed her hand against her stomach and choked down a sudden spurt of saliva. Finally, she reached the no-man's-land the Senate had bulldozed between the still-occupied estates and the quarantined one. One hundred metres of ground had been cleared. The new back wall of the habitable estate was topped with ship-class proton shielding to protect the citizens from MalX-carrying mozzies. Rosie could just see its blue shimmer rising several metres into the air.

She stopped at the corner of the wall and checked the sky for surveillance jets, then sprinted across the open ground. The houses were derelict, the streets deserted and easy to navigate. The estate was built in a grid, paved streets intersecting at right angles. Riley's house was deep inside, near the river, and was the same as all the others: a two-storey, thick-walled house with wide verandahs and a roof made of solar collectors. She went around to the back. Piles of leaves and dirt had accumulated against the back door and a broken statue of a naked woman was propped against one wall.

Riley was waiting for her in the large sitting room on the top floor, watching a bank of holo screens. He swivelled around in his chair as she ran up the stairs.

"Rosie—"

"Hang on!" Hand over her mouth, she dashed past him and into the bathroom. She almost didn't make it. The capsule came up in a rush of bitter stomach acid and the remnants of her meagre lunch. She hunched over the metal bin, shuddering. The smell of the spew made her retch even more. She closed her eyes, spat and tried to get hold of herself.

"I'll leave some water by the door." Riley put a glass down behind her then retreated. At least he didn't hover.

She took a deep breath, wiped her mouth and sat back on her heels, surveying the small pool of viscous liquid and specks of carrot in the bottom of the bin. Why was there always carrot? The message capsule was an oval tube, barely the size of her little fingernail. Rosie picked it out of the bin with a grimace and used a drop of water from her glass to wipe it off, drying it on her pants. The water was warm and tasted faintly of chemicals. Probably treated sea water. She took a few small sips then went to join Riley. He was waiting in the middle of the room, hands in his pockets.

"You okay?"

"Fine." She still felt shaky, but that would pass.

Riley's usually tidy light brown hair was sticking up slightly, as if he'd run his hand through it, but that was the only sign that he might have been worried. Other than that he was his usual calm but intense self. Blue collared shirt and dark pants, clean and unwrinkled. How he stayed so clean in this place was beyond her.

"Good work." He took the capsule and placed it in a slot in his desk. One word, *decrypting*, appeared on one of the lower holo screens.

"Don't drink too fast," he said, his back to Rosie. "You'll vomit again."

"Thanks, doctor. Any other helpful tips?" She collapsed into the only armchair. The red fabric was

23

ripped and dirty and the springs squeaked as she sat, but she was beyond caring.

"Tell me about the meet," he said.

He wasn't going to like this. Rosie rubbed a spot of sweat from her cheek. "The capsule's from Cassie."

He immediately tensed and turned to face her. "She's not supposed to contact me directly. Ever."

"I wouldn't say this is exactly direct, but Sharia was certain. Her source told her she was to be sure to pass on that this message comes from Cassie Shore."

"She used her name?"

Rosie nodded. She'd been as surprised as him. Cassie, Riley's nineteen-year-old sister, had been in hiding in Gondwana Nation – the Indige lands outside Senate control – for ten years, ever since their parents had been murdered by Helios. Riley hadn't seen her since then, as far as Rosie knew. He considered it too risky, what with him being on the top of Helios's hit list. For her to contact him, using their name, was unprecedented.

"It gets worse," Rosie said. "She thinks Helios is building a base up in Nation lands. The proof is supposed to be in that capsule."

Riley said nothing, but his face had gone hard and still.

"What do you think's on it?" she said.

"We'll know in exactly" – he checked the holo controls – "thirty-nine seconds." He looked pissed.

Riley was unremarkable in many ways: mid thirties,

clean-shaven, blandly good looking, not particularly muscular, but that was just his camouflage. Look closer and you saw a resolution of purpose that was relentless. He had survived horrific torture at the hands of Helios to keep his sister safe, and almost died bringing down their operation on Mars. Now Cassie had risked exposing herself with this message. Lucky for her she wasn't here to reap the consequence.

They waited in silence for the results. His tension infected her, a sick, taut feeling growing in her gut.

"That's not all the bad news. I got a call today," Riley said.

Rosie insides got even tighter. "Yeah?"

"You remember Chris and Jo from the Mars colony?"

"Are they okay?" Rosie immediately thought the worst. Chris and Jo had helped them on Mars after Rosie had crash-landed her aunt's spaceship when she and Riley were fleeing from Helios. They'd basically saved their lives.

"They're fine," Riley said. "But only because Helios is being extra careful now the Senate is hunting for them. I don't know how they found out Chris and Jo helped us – helped me – but they have. Essie's source said Helios threatened their child and Chris told them everything, especially about how he helped me get off Mars after I escaped when the Enclave blew up."

"So Helios knows you're not dead," she said softly. This was very bad news.

"Helios will leave them alone now. It's me they want. But you know what this means. If they know I'm alive, it means you and Essie aren't safe any more either." Riley gave her a significant look.

"Wait, hang on." She got to her feet. She knew where this was going. "I am not going into hiding," she said. "No way."

"Rosie—"

The decryption finished and a loud beeping interrupted him. It seemed to annoy him. Clearly this discussion wasn't over, but right now the capsule took precedence. He turned to the blurry image that emerged on the holo screen as a recorded voice rang out.

"Hey, bro, it's me, Cass," the voice said. "I know you'll be furious I've sent this myself, but I'm not there to yell at so suck it up." Rosie glanced at Riley and saw his jaw tighten. "What you're looking at is an aerial shot taken from one of our jumpers in Nation lands. I've included the coordinates where it was pinged. It looks like Helios has a base there, though we can't be sure until we get better intel. Don't worry about me; I'm fine. Your boy will be in touch. Stay safe." There was a sharp click and the voice ended.

Rosie couldn't stop staring at the picture. It was fuzzy but it seemed to be a huge base built in a valley of red rocks and clumpy grass. There were five domed structures and another massive building she couldn't quite make out, plus a few figures dressed in dark clothing. The domes were way too much like ones she'd seen on Mars.

"Is that really a Helios base?"

"It shouldn't be possible, but that's what it looks like." He pointed at the image. "Look at the style of the habitats. And I'd bet those people have the Helios crest on their shirts. Besides, Cass wouldn't have said it if she didn't have good reason."

A sick feeling grew inside Rosie. Gondwana Nation was the one place they had thought was safe. The councils that ruled it had helped Riley after Helios had killed his parents all those years ago. They were the first to condemn Helios when the news hit that they had caused the MalX, and their councils had pressured the United Earth Commission and the Senate to hunt down those responsible. They had powerful allies in the UEC and their borders hadn't been breached since the Climate Wars over three hundred years ago. That level of safety was the reason Cassie had been hiding up there for so many years. How had that been compromised?

Riley walked to the window, his expression brooding. Rosie wondered if he was thinking what she was: that it wasn't safe for his sister up there any more. But it wasn't safe here either.

"What do you think Helios is doing up there?" she said.

"Could be anything. I'd rather not speculate."

"But how can they be there without anyone in the councils knowing?"

"That's simple, they're not. Someone knows about it."

"Who? One of the councils?"

"Probably. But who isn't as important now as *what* they're doing there."

"Who's the boy Cassie mentioned? Can he find out?"

Riley went to his workstation. "She said he'll be in touch, so yes." He swiped a finger over the controls.

"So who is he? What's—"

"It doesn't matter. You just lie low. I'll find someone else to meet contacts and collect intel."

"But we need to get up there," Rosie said. "We have to find out what Helios is up to. I could go, I—"

"You start at the Academy on Monday, Rosie." He held up a hand as she tried to speak. "I've got some trails I can investigate in the city, but you won't be doing it. You've done your part for now."

"Are you serious? I just spewed my guts, literally, to get that message to you and you don't want me to do anything about it?"

"Rosie, Helios knows I'm alive. You can't do anything to make them suspect you're working with me."

"It's not like it's that hard to figure out," she said sourly.

Riley was unmoved. "So far you've only had a few operatives checking on you every now and then, but they're sure to step up the surveillance. You can't risk it."

"I would never lead them here," Rosie said. "I know how to avoid them."

"I'm not saying you would, but just do what I say, for now. All right?"

"No, it's not all right!" She couldn't believe he was doing this. "Riley, it's not like I'm some kind of amateur. I know what I'm doing. What about Aunt Essie? Are you going to cut her out too?"

He sighed. "Rosie, it's safer for both of you to back off at the moment."

"Back off?" She stared at him. "Are you seriously going to tell her that? Do you know Aunt Essie lost her pilot stripes because of Helios?"

"Yes, I do," he said stiffly.

"Did she tell you the whole story?"

His mouth thinned. "She hasn't talked about it much, no."

"Of course she won't," Rosie exploded. "Because she's too bloody proud." She lowered her voice, trying to get a handle on her anger. "Riley, Orbitcorp interrogated her like she was a criminal. They almost accused her of being part of Helios when she couldn't explain why she'd been on Mars when we brought the Enclave down. She had to make stuff up to protect us. They found her ship on Mars – which we crashed, by the way. Remember that?"

"Of course I do." He looked at her wearily, like she didn't understand.

"She never told them she was kidnapped by Helios," she said. "Or that they infected her with the MalX and she almost died. She hasn't told them how we got the

29

files out that exposed Helios, even though it could have exonerated her. She's kept our secrets. She told them she was on Mars alone and crashed her own ship. She said there wasn't any surveillance of her in the colony when we blew the Enclave because she was embarrassed she'd crashed. And she kept our release of the files about the MalX anonymous, so Helios's people in Orbitcorp couldn't find out about you, or me, or even Pip." She held his gaze, pleading. "You can't just cut her out after all that. You owe us. It was your parents' files that started all this, remember?"

"I remember," he said, but the look he gave her was set, inflexible.

"So what, that's just it? What you say goes?"

His face was grave, but also sad. "I'm sorry, but yes. And your aunt and I agree on this so don't go back to her with it. We have an understanding."

What did that mean? Rosie searched his face, but as usual he gave nothing away. Was he saying they were more than friends? It was possible; her aunt did get a little softer round the eyes when she mentioned him. Rosie kept staring, but it was clear he was immovable.

"Will you at least tell me who this boy is that Cassie was talking about?" she said. "You haven't mentioned him before."

"You know I don't tell you about any of the others who work with us; it's safer that way."

"Safer?" She almost snorted. "I can look after myself.

I saved your butt that many times on Mars–"

"Once," he said.

"Twice actually, but who's counting?" His calm was infuriating. "Riley, I can't just sit back knowing this. Let me go up to Gondwana. It won't take that long; the Academy can wait. Or at least let me do something!" She went to the desk and searched the stack of com parts and tech gear. She picked up a filament com that became invisible in hair. "I can wear this. I'll hang out places, try to pick up information. I'm sure I saw someone follow me from the apartment this morning. Don't worry, I lost him," she said quickly. "But I could track him to find out who he is."

"No." Riley reached for the com, but she flicked it out of his reach. "That's useless unless I activate it," he said.

"Then activate it."

He looked at her with the same patient but immovable expression she knew far too well.

She sighed and threw the com back on the desk. "How can you expect me to just do nothing?"

"Because that's what I need from you right now."

"Nothing?"

He nodded. "Yes, carry on like normal, Rosie. Go to class, be a schoolkid for a change."

A kid. What did that mean? She wasn't sure she knew how to do that any more.

"I need you to understand, Rosie," he said. "I can't

have you giving them any reason to pay you more attention. I don't want you or anyone in your family suffering again because of me. Essie has already told me in no uncertain terms that she expects me to limit your involvement and I'm not going to undermine her trust."

"Trust, sure," Rosie said, but her heart had gone out of the fight. She sighed. "Why do I always feel like you're not telling me everything? Do you know who runs Helios?"

"No one does."

"You know something, but you won't tell me."

"Knowledge is dangerous." He gave her that bland, almost apologetic look. "I tell you enough. Having my level of insight would mean certain death if they decided to take you in. You wouldn't hold out against their interrogation methods. Few can."

And Riley was one of the few. They had caught him not long after his parents were killed. They'd caged him, flayed him, put nanos in him that slowly shredded his organs, his muscles, just enough to almost kill him. The nanos were still there. He had to inject himself with a neutralising agent so they wouldn't reactivate. And that was just some of what he'd told her. It made her sick thinking about it.

"They won't have a reason to take me in," she said.

A barren smile curved his mouth. "They don't need a reason. Right now they've left you alone because they thought I was dead. That and because they are hoping you will lead them to Pip. If I had more people I could trust as well as I trust you and Essie, I wouldn't have even contacted you after I got back from Mars. I'd rather you weren't putting yourself in danger at all."

"I would have even if you hadn't come back," Rosie said. "I'd have found a way to get back at them."

"I know." He exhaled a laugh.

Rosie hesitated and leaned on the desk. "Riley, do you have any idea where Pip is?"

He didn't answer straightaway and that made her heart beat faster.

"Do you?" she repeated.

"I'm sorry, Rosie, but I wouldn't tell you if I did."

"So is that a yes?"

He sighed and said with finality, "Pip is alive. As far as I know." Her heart gave a leap, but then he said, "Now I think you should go."

She knew that tone. It meant this conversation was over. She straightened. "I guess Aunt Essie will start getting worried if I'm not back before dark."

"Before you go, take off the Bridget ident lenses. I've made another one for you."

Rosie removed the lenses and slid the new ones over her irises.

"And here." he handed her a disposable money card. "Your pay."

Rosie took it. It still felt weird taking money from Riley, but he shut her down every time she said anything.

And her pride wasn't so big that she'd refuse it. She'd been poor and hungry most of her life. Besides, she hated having to rely on her aunt for everything. "You'll tell me when you hear anything though, won't you?"

"I always do."

Rosie wasn't so sure about that, but she let it go. "You need anything? Food, MalX screeners?"

"Don't worry about me." He turned back to his screens. "Be careful on the way home. I'll send word."

Rosie left, but playing over and over in her mind was the expression on his face when she'd asked him about Pip. Riley knew something, she was certain. But the question was, what?

CHAPTER 3

Pip sat by the fire and stared into the flames. The night was warm and they didn't really need a fire, but it gave them something to gather around.

Cassie sat on the log beside him. Her blond hair glinted in the light as she gave him a lazy glance. "Thinking of tomorrow?"

He lifted one shoulder. "Lots to do."

She leaned closer. "Don't worry, Pippy, everything's planned. It won't be a problem."

His jaw tightened. "Don't call me that."

She laughed softly. "Why not, Pippy? You know, you worry too much."

"And you don't worry enough." He kept staring at the fire, hoping she'd go to bed, but she just sighed and rested against his shoulder. "It's a spying trip, Pippy, nothing more. I know what I'm doing."

He shrugged her off. "You only think you do. You should have stayed at Kev's."

"Are you worried about what my brother might do?" She drew back, mocking him. "What he doesn't know can't bother him, and he needs to find out what Helios is up to."

"And that's what I'm doing," Pip said. "Riley asked me to find out, not you."

"Two sets of eyes are better than one."

"We did have two sets of eyes – mine and Kev's."

She whispered in his ear, "But Kev's not as fun as me."

Their faces were only centimetres apart, close enough for him to see the satisfied gloat in her eyes. "Thanks, but I'm not interested."

She sucked in a breath. Her eyes gleamed with anger as she drew back, her smile brittle. "Don't be boring, Pippy. You think because you grew up in Helios you know more than I do."

"I do."

The smile dropped. "You know what? I've been stuck up here hiding from Helios, listening to what's been going on for years. Now that they've finally been outed for the bastards they are, it's my chance to take them down."

"You could end up dead," Pip said.

"Oh," she mocked him, "I didn't know you cared."

"Christ, Cassie!" He shot to his feet. "You should take this seriously."

"I am. I've been taking this seriously my whole life. Don't think you've got a patent on being the hero."

"I'm not trying to be a hero."

"Really?"

"Yeah, really."

Her eyes narrowed and her pretty, perfect face hardened. "So how much blood have you donated so far? 'Cos you're looking a bit pale."

Something inside him curled up tight. How did she know about that? He swallowed. "Maybe you should stop checking me out. I told you I'm not interested."

She smirked and looked him up and down. "Never say never, Pippy. But that's not the point, is it? I've seen you talking to Lakisha and the other doctors. I know you're trying to find a way to use that cure in your blood. You want to go the UEC as humanity's saviour or something. How's that working for you?"

"Shut up," Pip said through clenched teeth.

"That well?" Cassie arched an eyebrow. "If you need any help explaining anything—"

"I don't. And what I'm doing is none of your business."

"A cure for the MalX is everyone's business. Helios might be evil bastards, but they sure knew what they were doing when they bred you."

"They did not breed me."

"Oh, I'm sorry." She pretended to be concerned. "So are you saying your weren't born in the Enclave? I must be confused because I thought you used to be Helios's prize experiment. That must be another Pip. Wonder what your parents would think?"

"You shut up, right now." He was so angry, he was trembling. "Don't you talk about my parents."

"Gee, Pippy, did I hit a nerve?" She frowned. "You seem a bit unstable. Maybe you shouldn't be here risking yourself when what you've got running through your veins could save people."

"It's you who shouldn't be here," he said. "We don't need your help."

She gave him a speculative look. "Is this about your precious Rosie again?"

His insides somersaulted. "You leave her out of it."

"Why?" Cassie voice dripped with spite. "It seems like you can't. And nor can Riley. Both of you act as if she's the only one with a stake in all this. I was nine when I had to run up here. Alone. At least her dad is still alive. Helios killed both my parents."

"Yeah? Welcome to the club." Pip spun away from the fire, afraid if he stayed, he might hit her. And he didn't want to be that kind of guy.

"Walking away from me, Pip?" Cassie called. "This the same view Rosie got?"

He threw his hands up in a wide shrug. Let her think what she wanted. She'd be over it in the morning. That was the thing with Cassie: she didn't care enough to hold a grudge.

"You two fighting again?" Kev looked up from his sleeping roll as Pip crawled into the one next to him. His skin was so black Pip could barely see him in the dark.

"Like I give a crap." Pip lay down fully clothed.

"Proper attitude, bro. Don't let her mess with your head."

Pip didn't reply. After a moment Kev said, "Don't worry about it; she's just angry at her brother."

"Like that's an excuse." He hated that Cassie knew about his efforts to cure the MalX. He'd been trying to keep it quiet, under the radar. It was his business. Finally, he could control what happened to what was in his veins, not Helios or the Senate, and it cut him deep that it wasn't working. Not yet. It was the only good thing to come out of his previous life with Helios, and it wasn't working.

Well, almost the only good thing. Meeting Rosie had been a good thing.

The thermo waterproof mat was thin and he could feel the ground under his back. He shifted, trying to find a comfortable spot. Screw Cassie. Even if she was angry with Riley, did she have to bring up Rosie? He didn't like to think of Rosie too much, didn't like worrying about how she was doing. Her face came into his thoughts anyway: the cute freckles on her cheekbones, the way her smile made a dimple in her cheek, the way she'd looked at him the last time he saw her at the hospital. He rolled onto his back and stared up at the darkness, feeling hollow.

He'd done the right thing, he had to believe that. She was safer without him. Too many terrible things had happened up there on Mars, and Helios would never leave her alone if they knew he was around. He had to believe that.

They were all up before dawn the next day and, as expected, Cassie acted as if the argument hadn't happened. She was all smiles and enthusiasm as she zipped the food heaters up in her pack, talking about how they were only a few clicks from their target and should make it most of the way back before nightfall. It irritated Pip that she called kilometres clicks, as if she was in the Senate elite or something.

"Just like sunshine over a swamp of crocs," Kev said quietly as Cassie disappeared behind some bushes to relieve herself. He grinned and Pip snorted a laugh and shoved his blanket into his pack.

"What are you two grinning about?" Cassie came back and picked up her pack.

"Nothing." Pip shouldered his bag. "You ready, Kev?"

"I'm always ready." He took the lead, heading out of the small clearing to the open grasslands. Kev was twenty-five, with a stocky chest and thin ankles. He was the son of one of the Nation councillors and knew the land like the lines on his own palm. He could walk all day without complaint and never got lost. Not even when the land was as treacherous as it was now, in what Kev called the rump of the wet season. He was a contact of Riley's and had offered Pip a bed in his house.

"Careful, razor grass on the right." Kev indicated a thick tussock of chest-high grass.

Thankfully, it hadn't rained overnight, but Pip expected it might pour at any moment. The sky was dark blue with cloud, the first sun rays barely able to penetrate. The line of rocky escarpment ahead of them was nothing more than a dark shadow. Helios's suspected new base was over that ridge, and they were walking instead of taking a jumper in case the noise of it alerted anyone in the base.

They walked in silence, winding around boulders and palms. The air was still and no birds sang – a bad sign, Kev said. It was likely the rain would start soon.

Just as Pip thought it, he felt the first drops hit his head, and a few seconds later the downpour came. He pulled the hood of his jacket up. The rain sounded even louder, spattering against the waterproof material. He kept his head down and followed Kev's boots. The ground became muddy quickly, red sludge splashing up his jeans, and when they reached the bottom of the escarpment Kev had to shout to be heard.

"Leave the packs here." He pointed to a crack between some boulders.

Pip took his off, handing it over, then took Cassie's.

The escarpment was nearly twenty vertical metres of sharp-edged rock ledges. Narrow channels of water ran down it, following courses eroded over thousands of years and making it a bitch to climb.

Kev hoisted himself up on the first ledge. Pip stepped back for Cassie, giving her a boost up, then brought up the rear. Twice, he just missed getting booted in the head by Cassie as rock or dirt skidded out from under her feet, and by the time they made it to the top they were all breathing hard and their hands were covered in cuts.

The summit was a narrow stretch of gravel and scraggly grass that sloped away on either side to a deep drop before rising again to another hump. They lay side by side, their heads low, staring down at the Helios base.

"Holy shit," Kev said.

"More like holy jackpot," Cassie replied.

Pip didn't speak. He could hardly believe what they were seeing.

CHAPTER 4

Rosie squinted against the hard sunlight and wished it was winter, or at least below thirty-five degrees. Across the street, groups of returning students, Centrals mostly, were streaming through the gates of Orbitcorp Academy for the first day of school. She might have been turning seventeen this year, but she felt decades older than all of them.

She bet that few of those students gave much thought to what Helios had done. What was it about living in the richest part of the city that made them like that? Too much money? Few of them even glanced at the beggars clustered in ragged groups near the school gates hoping for handouts.

"Oi, Rosie, are you listening?" Aunt Essie said.

Rosie blinked. "What? Yeah, sure." She hadn't heard a word.

"I said, just be normal – you know, a kid."

"Yeah, normal, right."

"And keep your head down." Her aunt scanned the crowded streets with suspicion. She was wearing her Orbitcorp flight uniform, but the three white vertical stripes that used to be over one shoulder had been reduced to two. It hurt Rosie to see how Essie pretended she was okay with it. They'd had a huge row this morning about school. Essie had disagreed with Riley and hadn't wanted her to go anywhere at all now Helios knew he was alive. But Rosie had won. Just. She'd played the "Blacks don't back down" card and her aunt had grudgingly relented.

Aunt Essie nudged her. "Just keep your focus. Don't be nervous, all right? The security here is tight."

"Yeah, I remember saying that this morning." Rosie looked at her sideways and Essie frowned.

"Smart arse."

"Learned from the best." Rosie looked again at the rich Centrals strolling through the gates. "Now I just have to pretend like I care about what they care about."

"Hey, this is one place where money counts for squat. Nothing levels in the Academy like ability."

"Is that how you got through?"

"That and lying." Aunt Essie grinned. "Had people convinced I had a rich daddy in Sino city, but I don't recommend you try it. You're a bad liar."

"Right, good job on the pep talk." Essie was full of compliments today.

"You never know," Aunt Essie said, "maybe you'll make some friends."

Friends? She didn't have friends any more. Not since Helios had put a target on her back. The last friend she'd had had been Juli, and they'd killed her. She touched the twin pendants under her shirt. The green biostone circles were engraved with Helios's symbol: a horse and rider over a rising sun. One bore Riley's initials. He'd left it in their apartment to let them know he was alive when they escaped from Mars. The other had belonged to Riley's parents and contained the secret files that proved Helios had invented the MalX. She wore them to remember Juli and to remind herself what it had cost them all to defeat Helios.

This morning her eyes were aching with lack of sleep. Night after night she found herself hounded by nightmares. She was back in the Enclave, her dad and aunt lying there, dying from the MalX. Yuang threatening her. Pip holding the gun. The sound it had made when he'd fired, and Yuang fell. She was haunted by the look in Pip's eyes – and that last kiss before he'd disappeared.

She squeezed her hands hard so her nails stabbed into the flesh of her palms.

Stop thinking about Pip.

She glanced at her aunt. "You coming to visit Dad today?"

Aunt Essie's grin faded. "Don't know; there's a lot going on. Lots of fallout after that Oceanus fiasco."

Noncommittal again. Rosie was getting tired of visiting her father alone. Essie had been too busy last time as well. Her aunt could deal with people trying to kill her, but a brother that didn't recognise her was something else.

"Fine then. I'm going in; wish me luck."

"You don't need it. Your name's Black, remember?" Essie gave her a quick hug.

"So I keep hearing."

"Be careful. I'll see you tonight." Aunt Essie strode away and Rosie looked at the Academy gates. Time to go. She took a deep breath, then crossed the street and fell in behind a group of chattering girls whose white-blond hair shimmered with holo-shine glitter.

The Academy was spread over sixty hectares in Central South-West. There was a complex of buildings for each of the six educational departments, a main administration block, a solar farm to generate power, and a massive building called the Apollo Dome that housed the flight simulators. The Dome was also used by Orbitcorp's accredited pilots for trialling mission plans. Rosie had been there with Aunt Essie before her mother had died. The rest of the Academy she'd seen only when she'd visited on orientation day the week before. Now she was struggling to remember her way around as she followed the blond girls into the main building.

The lobby was dominated by a curving staircase bookended by two transporter elevators. Large hallways filled with students stretched away on either side and, in front of the staircase, a six-metre high bronze statue of the school's founder divided more streams of students heading for the lifts and stairs.

Rosie stopped in front of the statue. She couldn't remember where her house room was. She checked her com, loading the grounds map. Other students bumped and shuffled around her and she heard snickers as a group of girls wafted past in a miasma of perfume.

"Who let her in?" one of them said.

"I know. Look, she doesn't even have a temple patch for her com."

More giggles followed, which Rosie ignored. Patches were tiny circles you stuck on your temples. They relayed information from your com to your visual cortex so you could see it on a semi-transparent window in front of your eye. Most students had them, but Riley had killed the idea. Patches were far from secure.

She found where she was supposed to be and headed off. She was used to being the pariah in high school. Who said the Academy would be any different?

Perseus was her house and her first-year group had fifty students, almost all of whom had got there before her. Groups were sitting on backless lounges facing a raised lectern and an enormous holo screen. Rosie found an empty seat in the back row. A heavy-set man with a beard came in behind her and the door beeped shut.

"Greetings, Earthlings!" His voice boomed across the chatter. "Kindly shut up and listen to me or face the consequences."

Nervous giggling wafted through the room and the chatter slowly died away.

"Good, thank you. I am Commander Stryker." The teacher swept his gaze across the room. "And we shall–"

The beep of the door opening interrupted him and he turned to glare as a tall boy entered.

"Sorry I'm late." The boy smiled. "My driver is useless."

Commander Stryker's smile was thin as he checked his attendance com. "The last to arrive. I assume you are Mr Dalton Curtis."

"Correct." The boy grinned but Stryker wasn't impressed.

"So glad you've honoured us with your presence. I'll be sure to tell your father you deigned to join us."

"That would be so good of you." Dalton Curtis gave him a slight bow, sparking a giddy twittering from some of the girls, then he sauntered along the row of lounges looking for a seat.

"Over here," a dark-haired boy sitting on the lounge across from Rosie called out. Dalton made his way over to him.

He was so good looking he could have been a cosmetic enhancer's model. He had golden brown hair that curled against his neck, hazel eyes and the body of an athlete, and most of the girls in the room were pretending they weren't checking him out. He winked at a chubby brown-haired girl sitting near him and she turned bright red.

"Thank you, Mr Curtis." The commander's tone was dry. "If we could all calm down, we have a list of things to get through before your classes start, beginning with a run-through of how your first year will be structured and what Perseus can do to help you through it."

"Throw a party," someone shouted.

"Yeah, Dalton, when's the orgy?"

Laughter rang out.

"Quiet!" the commander bellowed. "As is tradition, Mr Curtis's father will hold a welcome party for first years this weekend, but an invitation is not going to ensure you pass, so eyes on me, if you please."

There was a general groaning and excited whispering. Rosie pulled her computer tablet from her bag and scrolled through, checking her schedule while the commander went over the list of house rules she'd read the day before.

"Hey, can you do me a favour?"

She looked up to see Dalton Curtis leaning across the aisle towards her.

"What?"

"Can you pass this to that guy?" He held out a disposable com and pointed to a boy on the lounge in front of her.

"Do I look like a messenger?"

He smiled. "No, I think you look like a girl, but you'd be doing me a favour. If I don't do it now, I'll forget and it's kind of important."

"Fine." Rosie took the com.

"Thanks." He smiled again. Rosie whacked the target of Dalton's message on the shoulder with the com. The boy wheeled around with an annoyed expression on his face.

"From Dalton," she said.

His face cleared. "Thanks."

Dalton gave her a thumbs up and she turned back to her tablet. Parties and messages. Centrals were all the same. It felt like she was back in high school again.

The rest of the morning passed quickly and it seemed every class Rosie had, Dalton Curtis had as well. He arrived late and always made charming but cheeky comments to the professors. She suspected he did it for the attention. Although from the whispers she'd been unable not to hear, it seemed he had enough attention already. Hover hockey champion, top of the class in his previous school's flight simulators and son of one of the Academy's wealthiest patrons, Dalton Curtis seemed to be the name on every girl's lips.

She'd almost forgotten him though by three as she made her way to the Apollo Dome. This was what all the study at the Academy was aimed at for those in the pilot-training stream. Only twenty per cent actually passed.

The course was tough and relentless, and many dropped out or switched to something else. Rosie was determined she wouldn't.

Rosie's reasons for wanting to become a pilot had changed. Before Mars it had been about her love of space, the thrill of it and wanting to get out of the Banks. Now it was about freedom and control. She'd had a chance to help fly a Helios ship, the *Cosmic Mariner*, on their escape from Mars, and she still remembered how it had felt when she'd panicked, staring at all the lights, not knowing what to do. She'd figured it out just in time, but that feeling, that terrifying gap of knowledge, wasn't something she wanted to feel again. When the pilot, Nerita, had shown her such respect and told her she might see Rosie in the skies again some day, it had opened a door. She wanted to be like Nerita. She wanted her own ship, and maybe one day she would have it.

There were five simulators in the Apollo Dome and five pre-flight lecture halls. She entered the third one. The seats were tiered around the lecturer's podium and screen, and each was fitted with a set of dummy flight controls and an immersion headset. The first term lessons would take place in the lecture hall using the dummy sets before they moved on to using the actual simulator.

Rosie had used the simulator a few times before her mum died, under Aunt Essie's supervision – and probably without Orbitcorp permission – so she felt confident that she might do better here than some of the other students. But that didn't quell her nerves as she took a seat. Amazingly, Dalton Curtis was already there and waiting in the second row. He saw her and smiled, causing a few girls to cast her suspicious looks.

Rosie ignored them and fixed her eyes on her control set.

Thankfully, the instructor arrived. "My name is Commander Mellar," he said. "Welcome to flight training. A few things you should know. One: I don't give second chances. Two: I won't suffer disruptions. Be here to learn, or use the door. And three: being a pilot means holding others' lives in your hands. If you can't take that seriously, you should leave now." He surveyed the now totally silent hall.

"Good, let's get started. Immersion sets on. As you've all had some basic training, we'll start with a cold run. I want to see what you've got. The set-up is a Class 2 ion drive, you have a crew of four and you've just lost your right-forward thrusters. Planetfall is imminent and death a real possibility. See what you can do."

Rosie slipped her headset on, the eye screens sliding down so she saw nothing but black for a second. Then she was thrust into a virtual ship, her hands at the controls.

The simulation was tough and Rosie was filled with disappointment when it finished. She hadn't landed the ship anywhere near as well as she'd hoped. The whole simulation caused her to be struck by a major flashback of crashing her aunt's ship on Mars that had thrown her, and made her performance less than stellar. She wondered how the rest of the class had done.

"Results." Commander Mellar touched his lectern and a display of numbers appeared behind him.

"As you can see, forty-one out of the forty-three of you crashed and killed everyone on board, including yourselves. Mr Curtis." He looked up at Dalton. "You're an exception. Although your ship was damaged beyond repair and you lost two of your crew." His gaze went across the class and settled on Rosie. "And Miss Black."

Forty-two pairs of eyes swivelled in her direction and Rosie swallowed, feeling her neck go warm. "Well done. You managed to land your ship with some unorthodox moves, which kept it mostly intact. However, your decision to order three of your crew to use their escape pods resulted in terrible injuries. One died. Pods should not be used so close to a planet's surface." His sharp, pale eyes felt like they were impaling her to her seat. Rosie looked away, only to catch Dalton Curtis watching her with speculation. He lifted an eyebrow and gave her a small salute. Rosie cut her eyes away and began packing up her headset. Great start at keeping a low profile. She got out of class as quickly as she could, checking the time on her com. This was the last class of the day and she had somewhere to be.

CHAPTER 5

Most of the first years went straight to the Academy bar at the end of the day to mix with the older students, but Rosie headed out the gates to the closest shuttle station. Central West B was half full and the cooling system had failed. Lines of hot and lethargic people queued at the stops, waiting to go home.

Rosie fanned herself with a flyer for a game parlour and was more than a little surprised to see Dalton Curtis sitting on a bench on her platform.

He nodded as she approached. "Hey, Pilot Girl, you not going to join the mass revelry at the bar either?"

Pilot Girl? Rosie stopped. There was no more room left on the bench.

"Don't you have a driver?" she said.

He smiled and got to his feet. "No, I just say that to entertain the professors. Besides, the shuttle's quicker. Do you want a seat?" His hazel eyes seemed golden in the light coming through the glass roof.

"Um, no, I'm fine thanks." Rosie felt awkward.

"So what's your first name, Miss Black? I can't keep calling you Pilot Girl."

"Rosie."

He held out his hand. "Dalton." There was a wry twist to his lips as she hesitated a moment before shaking.

"Not that you need an introduction," she said.

"Right, of course. I'm one of the famous Curtis men." His tone was light but he said it as if he didn't think much of the fact.

She checked the track and saw the gleam of the shuttle approaching.

"You're not from around here, are you, Rosie?" Dalton said.

"What makes you say that?"

He grinned. "Answering a question with a question – you hiding something?"

She frowned as the shuttle hissed to a halt and he beat her to the door, but then he stepped aside. "After you."

Rosie touched her token to the reader and was disconcerted when he sat next to her.

"Thought we could swap piloting tips," he said. "You know, the two top students."

"Don't you think you might be making that call a

bit early?"

Dalton shrugged and gave her a sideways smile. "We'll see."

He leaned her way to pull a thin com from his pants' pocket. The sleeve of his shirt brushed her arm and she caught a whiff of something expensive, like citrus and leather.

"So," he said, "how did you manage to land the ship in the simulator without totally trashing it? Been practising all alone or are you just naturally talented?"

"Maybe I'm just a natural," Rosie said.

Dalton chuckled. "No enhancements then – just what you were born with?" She knew exactly what he meant. Most Central girls had some kind of cosmetic enhancement by the time they were sixteen.

"All natural," she said in a cold tone. "Any other questions?"

"Whoa. I believe you. Besides, I'm not a big fan of all that stuff. I mean, what's the purpose of having sparkly flying birds on your face? Is it camouflage? Some secret girl language or the mark of a hypnotist cult?" He feigned confusion. "Can you explain it?"

"I really can't."

"Ah well." He sighed. "I am doomed to walk the Earth an ignorant arse then."

Rosie couldn't help smiling just a little.

"There, you see," he said. "I'm not as spoilt or obnoxious as you thought."

"I never said you were."

"No, but you thought it. He's just another spoilt rich boy, craving attention."

"That's not exactly what I thought."

"Yeah it is." Dalton laughed. "But it doesn't matter. I like making people think one thing then spinning their minds by being the opposite."

"What? You mean you're not rich?" Rosie said.

"Sorry, can't claim that. But it has its perks. You'd be amazed what people will do when you have money."

He didn't look amazed though; he looked disappointed. He caught her watching him and his expression smoothed. "But that's not your worry, Rosie Black. You don't seem the sort to do something just for money."

"That depends on what it is," she said. "Not everyone has your resources."

"True." He nodded and lounged back against the seat, tossing his com up and down. "So, if I gave you a hundred credits, would you tell me how you managed not to total your ship in the simulator?"

Rosie almost believed he was serious. "That's all my expertise is worth — the cost of a soy burger?"

"Okay, I'll throw in a drink as well, and hold your hand in class. It's a great deal: slake your thirst and rise to meteoric heights on the social scale at the same time. What do you say?" Dalton's smile held a teasing gleam.

"Tempting, but no. I think you can figure it out

yourself."

"A challenge, excellent!" He stood up. "Although I'm crushed my offer of classroom bliss holds so little value to you." He winked and walked backwards towards the door as the shuttle slowed to a stop at Central Park. "See you tomorrow, Rosie Black."

The doors swished open and he jumped out, giving her a salute as the shuttle pulled away. Rosie watched him go, the shuttle moving so fast she didn't have time to wave back. What had just happened? Had Dalton Curtis, prince of the Academy, been flirting with her? It seemed like it, but then also not. She didn't think of herself as ugly but she was hardly in his league, and in Central things like that mattered. A lot. Rosie twisted the strap of her bag between her hands. Weird.

* * *

Greenview Centre had its own shuttle stop and Rosie was so wrapped up in her thoughts about Dalton, she almost missed it. She scrambled out and the scent of eucalypts and dry, baked earth hit her like a virtual memory slap.

Juli had lived in these hills. But Juli was dead, killed by Helios. It got to her every time she came here. She had to make herself not think about it. She was here for her dad. She had to find her happy face for him – if he recognised her.

She was late for visiting hours, but the nurse on duty let her in. Her dad was in a room that overlooked a rocky valley of dry scrub and trees. Riley had insisted on taking over the payments for his care, so now he had a room of his own, instead of being in a ward.

The furnishing tried to emulate a home, with a large bed, and lounge chairs around a coffee table near the window, but nothing could disguise the medibot in the corner or the smell of antiseptic.

Rosie opened the door quietly. Her dad was sitting in one of the chairs, staring out of the window, a digi book on his lap. He looked so tired. His hair was brushed back to reveal his receding hairline, the black streaked with grey. He hadn't had any grey a year ago. Rosie's chest tightened. She still found it hard to see how frail he'd become. He was over two metres tall but looked smaller because he was always curled slightly in on himself. Lines radiated out from his eyes and there was a pallor in his cheeks that a man his age shouldn't have. He was only forty-two but looked like he was in his late fifties. The sound of clinking dishes came from the communal dining room and she shut the door to block it out. He didn't move.

"Dad?" Rosie tried to inject some lightness in her voice. She dropped her bag on the end of his bed. "Hey, you sleeping with your eyes open?" She put a hand on his shoulder and he exploded out of the chair with a shout, the digi book clattering to the floor.

She flinched back. "It's okay. It's me, Rosie."

His eyes were red-rimmed, wide with fear, and he held his hands up as if he was trying to fend her off, but then he seemed to focus and see her. He dropped his hands to his heaving chest. "Rosie, love, don't surprise me like that."

"Sorry." She tried to sound normal. "I thought you were asleep."

"Right, no, that's okay." His smile was tremulous. "Shouldn't you be in school?"

"It's finished for today." She picked up the book and put it on the table.

"It is?" He frowned. "It must be later than I thought."

"Probably. Sit down, Dad." Rosie sat in the chair near his and he slowly sank back down.

"How are you, love, and Essie?"

Rosie's paused for a moment before she answered. He was lucid today. "I'm good. So is Aunt Essie. I started at the Academy today."

"Good. That's good." A sad light came into his eyes. He looked out the window and she saw the glistening brightness of unshed tears. He was lucid enough to remember his wife was dead.

When Rosie spoke she was fighting not to cry herself. "I did really well in flight class."

"That's great." He turned back to her. "Maybe by the end of the year we can celebrate together. I'm sure I'll be out by then." He tried for a smile, but the fear behind his eyes was painful.

She nodded. "I'm sure you will; you're doing really well." It was a lie. This was the first time in weeks he'd known who she was. He kept slipping backwards, slipping away, and sometimes Rosie didn't know if she could keep coming to see him.

He let out a long breath. "Tell me about the Academy. Have you made any new friends?"

Rosie tried to tell him, making it sound as good as she could. She told him about the party planned for the end of the week by Dalton Curtis's father. It seemed to cheer him up. She invented friends she didn't have, and made no mention of Riley, or what she'd been doing for him. There was no way her dad was strong enough to cope with that. She stayed to eat with him, making jokes about that quality of the soy curry.

By the time she got home it was after dark. The strain of keeping up happy conversation had left her exhausted and she just wanted to sleep. There wasn't any sound coming from the apartment and no lights were on. Aunt Essie must still be out.

Rosie swiped the lock and pushed open the door. Something had been shoved underneath. The toe of her shoe hit it and sent it skittering across the floor. What was that? She kicked the door shut and turned on the light. A sliver of opaque plaspaper was on the floor. She picked it up, blowing off the dust. It was palm-sized and, as she looked at it, words materialised, generated by the electric charge of her hand.

Play me.

Rosie frowned. Play me? Play what, the thing she'd kicked a moment ago? She peered around, searching the living area with apprehension. Something metallic caught the light just under the leg of the sofa. She dropped her bag on the coffee table, got on her hands and knees and pulled it out. It was a small vision storer, disposable, barely the size of her thumb tip.

Who would shove this under the door? Her heart began to beat too fast. She went to the digi unit in the wall opposite the sofa and pushed the vision storer in. A holo screen sprang up. Her mouth dried. A 3-D image of her dad appeared. He was lying in a hospital, a medibot beside him and the red rash of the MalX spreading over his chest. Then she saw herself come into the room, and her chest contracted.

She knew what this was.

This was the hospital they'd fled to with her dad after they'd got back from Mars. She knew what was coming next.

She watched herself carry a bag of blood to her dad's side. Then she saw herself attaching that bag of blood to her dad's drip. It was Pip's blood. He'd come back to the hospital to give it to her and it had been the last time she'd seen him. It was Pip's blood that had cured her dad.

Rosie took a trembling step back. Her legs hit the couch and she slumped on it, her gaze fixed on the vision.

Whoever had sent this must know what it meant. They would know that if the Senate saw this they would ask her questions she couldn't answer. And worse, if Helios got hold of this, it would be bad, very bad. It was clear proof that Pip was around, that he was using his blood to cure and that Rosie might even know where he was.

The image wavered, then it blanked out to be replaced by words.

The Senate hasn't seen this.

Helios haven't seen this.

Yet.

Rosie hugged her arms around her chest, feeling cold. The words vanished and more appeared.

I'll be in touch.

The holo disappeared and Rosie sat staring at the space.

CHAPTER 6

"You'll need all of these, plus you'll have to put in an application for a zero-g suit. We don't loan them out any more, too much damage." The Academy assistant glanced briefly at Rosie as she handed her the stack of research download tags. "That will be five thousand and sixty-five. Are you charging or do you have an account?"

"Account," she said. The woman's expression didn't change as Rosie pressed her thumb to the pad. This was the second lot of research material she'd had to access this week and the continuing cost made Rosie queasy.

It was Thursday and the resource shop was crowded with students loading up on their course requirements. Since she'd received the vision, Rosie had been checking her com for the promised message every five seconds. But she'd heard nothing. Riley hadn't contacted her either. Apparently, he'd meant it when he said he didn't want her to do anything. She hadn't had a chance to tell her aunt about the anonymous threat. Aunt Essie hadn't come in until well after midnight on Monday night, and had been out late and gone by the time Rosie had woken up every day since. She'd been trying to stay awake for her each night, but exhaustion had taken over. What could Aunt Essie possibly be doing that kept her out such long hours? Fear and anxiety were starting to send Rosie crazy. She couldn't use her com to tell Aunt Essie; it was too risky, even with the fail-safes against tracking Riley put in it. The day before she'd left a note to say they had to talk, but her aunt had only pinged her com again to say she couldn't make it. Tonight, she was going to stay up all night if she had to.

She left the shop, already late for her next class. The building was one of a number spaced out around an open recreation area. There were benches, which were almost always filled with students socialising when they should have been studying. Rosie saw a group of girls hanging around one bench with Dalton and two other boys. The girls were wearing see-through dresses over skin-tight short suits. They were giggling and pouting. One of them was sitting on a boy's lap playing with his hat.

Rosie walked past them, annoyed that they were all so carefree and could play such stupid games.

"Hey, Rosie, wait!" Dalton called. His boots scuffed

the gravel behind her and she glanced back at him.

"So you remembered my name," she said as he caught up. He loped alongside her, a bag slung casually over one shoulder.

"Hey, I think Pilot Girl's a cute nickname, but if you don't like it—"

"I don't."

"Okay then."

He gave her a smile that could have lit a stadium and her anger faltered under the wattage.

"What are you so happy about?"

He leaned in close and lowered his tone. "I think I figured out how you landed the ship in flight class." He looked seriously pleased with himself.

"You did?"

"Sure. Genius move, by the way. How did you come up with it?"

"It's in the text." There was no way she was going to tell him she'd got the idea of switching the power relays from the time she'd crashed her aunt's pod on Mars.

"Oh, the text, yeah, of course." He nodded, sceptical. "Except it's not. But that's okay. You don't have to give away all your secrets. I mean, we've all got secrets, haven't we?"

A jolt of unease hit her, but before she could answer, he said, "So are you coming to my dad's famous welcome-to-the-rest-of-your-life party on Saturday? It'll be worth it. You'll never see anything like it, really."

"I haven't decided."

"Seriously?" He raised an eyebrow. "But where else can you be surrounded by overdressed, self-involved rich brats ingesting insane amounts of illegal substances and grinding against each other on the dance floor? It's a spectacle worth your free entry."

"It does sound amazing," Rosie said, "but I'll think I'll pass. I've got nothing to wear. It's really hard to find something that suits a grinding-rich-brat fest these days."

"I'll buy you something," Dalton said. "We can go shopping after class."

Rosie thought he might be serious. "Ah, no, that's okay, and a bit weird."

He chuckled. "I know, sorry. I have a Prince Charming complex. But seriously, why don't you come?" His gaze was warm. "It might make it bearable, raise the IQ level to above pond algae. What do you say?"

Rosie was flustered by the way he was looking at her so intently. He was way, way too pretty. "Um, well, I'll think about it."

"Okay, I guess that's better than a no."

He checked the time on his com and whistled. "I'm late for hover hockey training. Catch you tomorrow?"

"Yeah, sure." She watched him walk away.

Something felt off. Sure, he was a friendly guy, but why so friendly to her? And that crack about secrets. Now that Helios knew Riley was alive, they'd be stepping up surveillance. They could have an operative anywhere. Could it be Dalton?

It seemed far-fetched, but still ... She headed towards her next class. She needed to talk to someone and Aunt Essie was too hard to get hold of, so that left one option.

Riley might not have called her in, but too bad. She couldn't handle all this on her own. She was going to see him. Today.

———◦◦◦———

The afternoon dragged and she left the Academy at a run as soon as classes finished. It seemed to take forever to get through the painful process of switching shuttles and it was just before sunset when she reached Riley's. She pressed her thumb to the door scanner and ran up the stairs two at a time.

"Riley," she called out as she reached the top and burst through his operations room door. "Riley, I've got–" She stopped. Standing next to Riley was someone she was not prepared to see. Not prepared at all. All the breath left her body and she let the door bang back against the wall.

"Pip?" Her voice sounded strangled as she said his name.

They'd been looking at something on Riley's holo desk and they both turned swiftly around at her entrance. A weird mix of emotions crossed Pip's face and she thought for a second he was glad to see her, but then his expression closed up and Riley said, "Rosie, you shouldn't be here."

She took a step into the room. There was a pulse beating so hard in her neck it was painful. "What the hell's going on?" she said.

Riley put down the computer stylus he'd been holding. "Pip brought information about the base."

"He's the boy Cassie was talking about?"

Riley spoke quietly, like he was choosing his words carefully. "We thought it would be better if you didn't know."

We thought? The implication was clear. Riley had been in contact with Pip for some time and he hadn't told her. The betrayal hit her hard, right where she needed to breathe. She couldn't speak for a moment, totally blindsided. She turned on Pip.

"So Gondwana Nation, *that's* where you've been?" She was surprised her voice was steady. He looked the same, but different. His shoulders were broader, his skin darker. It was more coffee than caramel now. His hair, which had been shaved close to his skull, was longer, dark waves reaching to the nape of his neck. He pushed a few strands of it from his dark blue eyes but didn't answer right away. He looked nervous.

"Pip, is that where you've been?" she repeated.

"Ah, yeah," he said, guarded.

"For how long?"

"A little while." He glanced at Riley as if to confirm it was okay to tell her. It made her angry.

"Don't you think I can be trusted to know?" she said.

"It's not like that," Pip said. "We just thought it was safer this way."

"For who exactly?"

"For both of you." Riley stepped forwards. "Rosie, you know Helios are watching you, hoping you'll lead them to Pip."

"I wouldn't do that."

"Not on purpose, no."

"You could have told me he was working for you," she said.

Riley regarded her like she was being unreasonable. "You know I keep things separate for a reason. For safety."

She couldn't believe this. How could he keep this from her after she'd asked him? "So what did he bring you?" she said. "Or is that a secret as well?"

Riley gestured to his computer tablet. "I was just about to look – and show you at our next meeting," he added as she opened her mouth.

"It's pretty serious, Rosie," Pip said. "They're building something big."

"I'll put it up." Riley turned back to his desk. "Come have a look, since you're here."

Rosie paused. Pip, arms folded, had half-turned back to watch Riley. She crossed the room to stand behind Riley's other shoulder. She was acutely aware that Pip was barely an arm's length away. There was silence for a moment as Riley accessed the files. Rosie could feel Pip glancing at her and forced herself not to look.

"Here," Riley finally said, and her attention was taken by the images on the screens.

These pictures of the base were much more detailed than before. The five habitat domes and a few smaller ones were in closer focus, but it was the massive hangar-sized shed that was most interesting. Now they could see piping fitted down the side of it, and a spherical structure on the roof, but what really got her were the parts people were pushing into it on trolleys.

"What are they?" she said. The parts were odd. Massive circular tubes, gleaming silver shards, and a lot of canvas-covered boxes. Some of the people had gloves on, as if the parts they were handling were too delicate to get dirty. Like it was serious tech.

"Whatever it is they're making, it's big," Riley said. "I've got an idea, but ..." He leaned forwards, studying the images. "I'll have to look at these carefully to be sure. You said you had some thermal mapping as well?" he asked Pip.

"It's all on the drive. Energy readings and a few close-ups of some of the staff. We could only isolate a couple, but Cassie's pretty good at cleaning up the vision." It sounded like grudging praise, but there was also another note in his voice when he said Cassie's name that sent a jolt through Rosie. She glanced at him, but he was staring at the vision like he was deliberately avoiding her gaze.

"I'll need some more gear to analyse this." Riley pushed back his chair so they had to move. "I have to go downstairs to call Sun. Don't mess with it while I'm gone." He seemed oblivious to the tense air between the two of them. Pip walked a few steps towards the window.

Rosie had no idea what to say. The last time she'd seen him had been when he'd kissed her goodbye in a hospital corridor over three months ago. Unless you counted all those dreams. She held onto the back of Riley's chair, scratching at the fabric.

"So, you're going to the Academy?" he said after a while. He turned back to her, but was staring at the floor, his legs spread wide. He swayed from side to side, hands clamped over his biceps.

"I just started."

He nodded and looked up at the walls, the door, anywhere but at her. She couldn't decipher what he was thinking.

"So you're okay, after everything, I mean?" she said.

He shrugged and put his hands in his pockets, slouching. "You know me; I'm always five by five." He gave her a crooked smile and Rosie tried to ignore the sudden case of butterflies inside her.

"And you've been up in the Nation lands all this time – with Riley's sister?" Cassie was older, nineteen. Was she pretty? *Don't think about that.*

"Yeah, most the time, and I wouldn't say *with* her. I'm just staying at—" He paused, caution filling his expression. "Maybe I shouldn't say."

Seriously? Anger overtook her confusion. "No, of course not," she said. "I'm such a security risk. You shouldn't tell me in case I blab it all to Helios."

His shoulders tensed. "It's not like that."

"Oh, it's not?" She thrust the chair towards the desk so hard it banged against it. "What's it like then? Just how many times have you been back?"

He went very still. "A few."

"Would it have killed you to leave a note?"

"Riley didn't think it was a good idea."

"Well, lucky for him you're such an obedient little boy."

His jaw clenched, eyes glinting. "It was safer, okay? And I'm never here for longer than a few hours. I get in and get out."

"How?"

"It's safer—"

"If I don't know," Rosie interrupted. "Yeah, I got that. Thanks for being so thoughtful." She didn't think she could be more sarcastic if she tried.

"Oh, come on, Rosie. It's not like I don't—" He paused. "I mean, we're not trying to cut you out."

"Really? Then I guess all this secrecy was for another reason."

"Yeah, it was actually." Anger made his eyes bright

74

and he covered the distance between them in two long strides. "You remember Helios, you know, the ones who'd like to turn me into their own personal science project?"

"Like I could forget them," Rosie said. There was barely a hand's span between them, but she kept her gaze locked with his, daring him to drop his first. Her heart was racing, but she wasn't about to back down. "It's been three months, Pip. For all I knew they could have got you already."

"Riley would have told you if something happened."

"Would he? He didn't tell me you were here. And what have you been doing up there anyway? Hiding?"

A muscle in his jaw ticked. "Would you rather I gave myself up? I hear Helios are real sweet to traitors nowadays."

"Don't be stupid," Rosie said.

"Then what?" He shrugged and that just made her even madder.

"Why do you always have to be like this?"

"What, charming?" A half-amused smile curved his mouth.

"No." She wanted to smack him. "Pretending like you don't care."

"Maybe I don't."

She stared at him, heart pounding hard. A tiny cold spot was growing in her chest. Pip was looking at her like he was working hard to stay calm. What was he hiding? It made her angry and scared. It made things come out of her mouth that shouldn't. "You've still got the cure for the MalX in your blood, Pip," she said. "Have you stopped caring about that too?"

His eyes narrowed. "Do you seriously think I could?"

"People are still dying. Have you thought about trying to find a way to use it, to make a cure? Or are you just acting as Riley's messenger boy?" Even as the words came out, she wanted to take them back. *Good one, Rosie, hit him where it really hurts.* She knew having the MalX cure in his blood tortured him. His parents had died of the MalX. They stared at each other, the tension between them like a cord stretched to breaking.

"Rosie—"

"What?"

He opened his mouth as if he was going to say something. The pulse in her neck throbbed.

"What?" she said again.

His lips clamped into a line and all emotion fled his face like a switch had been flipped. He swallowed, his Adam's apple moving against the smooth brown skin of his neck. "Riley didn't tell you I was here because I asked him not to. It was my choice."

It was like he'd punched her in the stomach. Rosie blinked and for a second she couldn't speak. She was such an idiot. What had she thought – that he'd been up north with Riley's nineteen-year-old, probably gorgeous, sister, pining away for her? Clearly, he didn't want to see her. He was watching her like he was scared she was going to start bawling.

"God, Pip, don't look so worried," she said. "It's not like I'm going to take a swing at you." Her heart was thudding too fast and she tried not to let him see how upset she was.

"Rosie, it's not—"

"It doesn't matter. I've got to go." She turned towards the door.

"Wait." He grabbed her arm. "It's dark now, you should—"

"What? Wait for you or Riley to escort me?" The hurt was making her voice sharp. "That doesn't seem practical, does it? Besides, I can look after myself."

"I know." He let out a frustrated breath. "But look, Rosie, I ... It's not like I don't care." His voice was low, soft.

Something inside her broke. This was worse. His pity. She stared down at his hand on her arm. She wanted to wrench away, but he was stronger and she was scared she would just start crying and lose any dignity she had left by getting into a tug of war.

"Please let me go," she said quietly. He didn't. He moved closer so she could feel his breath on her hair.

"I'm sorry I couldn't contact you," he said. "I didn't want to risk it."

An angry ache lurched inside her. "I would never lead Helios to you. If that's what you're so worried about."

"No, that's not—"

She cut him off. "Let me go. I have to get home." He was frowning as if he couldn't work her out. Being so close to him after wanting him for so long, but knowing now he didn't want her, was more than she could take.

"Rosie—"

"Pip, I've got to go," she spoke sharply.

"Fine." He lifted his hand away and she bolted out the door.

CHAPTER 7

By the time she made it back to the apartment, it was after eight. Aunt Essie was actually home for a change. She was waiting, arms folded, her back against the kitchen bench as Rosie came in. Angry was an understatement.

"Where the hell have you been?" she said in a tight voice.

Rosie closed the door behind her. She was not up to this. She felt drained, exhausted, like she'd run a marathon in heavy gravity. "Funny, I could ask you the same thing," she said. "Isn't this a bit early for you to be home?"

"Excuse me?" Aunt Essie said curtly.

"You've hardly been home." Rosie dropped her bag

on the floor. "Now you want to burn me for being out late?"

"I've been working. You know, making the credit to pay for this place. Or are you going to pay the rent this week?"

Rosie closed her eyes and said softly, "Fine, whatever."

"Whatever?"

Rosie's eyes shot open. "I was at Riley's, okay?"

"What? You didn't have a meet scheduled. Did he contact you?"

"No, I–"

"You know you don't go unless it's necessary. It's too goddamn risky, Rosie."

"I know, I know!" Rosie leaned against the bench and stared at the counter. "Pip was there."

"Pipsqueak? He's turned up again, has he?"

Rosie straightened. "He was showing Riley some info on the Helios base, which he brought from Nation lands."

"So, that's where he's been. What did he have with him? Anything more we can use?"

Did she not understand the implication? "Aunt Essie, Riley was expecting him," she said. "He knew he was coming. He's been in contact with Pip for God knows how long and neither of them wanted me to know. It's like this conspiracy to keep me in the dark."

"Why?" Aunt Essie said calmly.

"I don't know! Maybe because Riley seems to think

I'm a security risk."

"Acting like you did today, you are."

Rosie was shocked into silence. She stared at her aunt, who watched her for a minute then sighed and unfolded her arms. "Rosie, I know this is tough for you. I know you don't have my training or Riley's experience and we sometimes ask more of you than we should, but you have to remember what the stakes are."

"I know what the stakes are. I know what Helios can do," Rosie retorted. "I just want you both to stop treating me like a child."

"Okay." Aunt Essie nodded, her voice knowing. "That's what this is about is it?" She cocked her head to one side. "When was the last time I treated you like a child? Hell. It's clear I have no idea how to be a parent." She threw up a hand. "If Riley doesn't tell you things, he has good reasons. Reasons that keep us all safe. This – how upset you are now – this is about Pip."

Rosie's heart lurched. She couldn't admit it, even to her aunt. It hurt too much.

"Pip didn't want you to know he was here, did he?" Aunt Essie said.

Rosie didn't reply. Her chest was starting to tighten up and she was afraid if she spoke, she'd start crying, and tears were no good. *There's no use crying, Rosie Black.*

Aunt Essie sighed. "Rosie, hon, I'm really sorry. Men, and boys, can be unfeeling bastards, but you can't take it to heart. We are at war here. There might not be any clear battlelines, but make no mistake about it."

"I'm not a soldier," Rosie whispered. "I'm not tough like you."

"Yes, you are." Her aunt grabbed her shoulders, forcing Rosie to look at her. "If it wasn't for you, none of us would be alive. None of us. You got us out of the Helios Enclave on Mars. You didn't give up and run when you could have. Don't think we've forgotten that."

Rosie's heart lifted a little to see the certainty in her aunt's gaze, but it didn't erase the pain.

"Listen," Essie said. "I know it hurts when people reject you, but you have to get your head in the game. You can't let your personal feelings get in the way. It can get you and those you care about killed. You understand?"

Rosie nodded with reluctance.

"Okay," Aunt Essie said. "There're noodles in the cooker if you're hungry." She moved towards her bedroom, then stopped. "You going to be okay, kid?"

"Yeah."

"Right then." She paused as if she wanted to say something else, but Rosie knew she had no clue what to say. There was a reason Essie had never had children. "Okay then; try to get some sleep. I'll see you in the morning. She turned away, already unzipping her flight suit.

It was only when Rosie was in her room that she remembered about the vision she'd been sent, but she was so bone-tired she didn't have the energy to talk about it. In the morning, she decided. First thing.

The next day Rosie struggled to drag herself out of bed. She'd not slept well, her dreams full of Pip.

She lay staring at the ceiling and swore silently at him, then forced herself out of bed and into the dry-blast shower. Why did he have to surprise her like that? Why did she have to feel this way about him? Why didn't he feel the same way?

Aunt Essie had already gone when she emerged in a towel. There was a note on the bench. *Don't forget to visit your dad.*

Obviously, she wasn't coming and she wasn't here, again, for Rosie to tell her about that vision. Great. Anxiety ghosted through her. She hadn't told Riley about it either, what with the Pip thing. Maybe she should just ping Essie. She reached for her com and dialled. Straight to stand-by. Frustrated, Rosie went in search of something to wear.

She threw on a pair of hand-me-down jeans of her aunt's and a red tank top, then rummaged through a pile of clothes on the floor for a heat-screening UV jacket. The only one she could find was dark purple. She glanced at herself in the mirror. It too had been Essie's but it actually looked all right, and it helped take the focus off the horrific dark circles under her eyes. She tried to brush her hair flat, but had little success. Giving up, she let it hang and was taking a self-heating noodle cup from the cupboard for breakfast when her com pinged.

About time, Aunt Essie. Rosie rushed to check it, but stopped dead as she saw the message, feeling like she'd swallowed a lump of ice.

Today's the day. The line of text blinked at her. There was no indication who it was from. Rosie leaned against the kitchen bench, her pulse racing, hands shaking. What to do?

She tried to contact her aunt again, but got nothing. Should she go to Riley? But what if Pip was there? She wasn't sure she was up to seeing him again, no matter how much she wanted to. And what if whoever had sent the message was watching her? She felt a brief moment of panic. Why hadn't she thought of that yesterday? She could have led them straight to Riley.

She'd wait and maybe by some miracle be able to get hold of Aunt Essie. And if not, she was just going to have to figure this out on her own.

＊＊＊

She was running late for class by the time she got to the Academy. She took a shortcut across the recreation area and saw Dalton lounging alone on one of the benches. He jumped up with a wave as he saw her crossing the gravel and jogged towards her.

He was wearing the Academy hover hockey uniform: a skin-tight dark blue singlet and matching loose pants. It made him look even more muscular than usual and nerves played along her insides. Was it possible he was Helios?

"Hey." He smiled as he reached her. "How're you doing today?"

"Okay. You late for astronomy as well?"

"Yes, yes, I am." He fell into step beside her. "Weird how we have so many classes together, isn't it?"

"Is it?"

Dalton peered at her with concern. "You all right today? You don't look so hot. Not that I'm saying you're not hot," he added quickly. "I think the pale worn look really works for you."

"Good save."

He grinned. "Well, I am a champion receiver."

Rosie shook her head. "I'm fine – just tired from studying, you know."

"You sure?"

"I'm sure."

"Okay, but if you need any help with anything, let me know. I don't have a study partner at the moment." His smile was relaxed and easy, but there was something about the way he was watching her that pricked at her. He was one of those people who really looked at you when you spoke, paid attention, like what you were saying was more interesting than anything else. It was unsettling.

"Um, thanks, but I'm all right."

"Offer's open."

They walked in silence for a while, until he said, "You still haven't said if you're coming tomorrow."

The party. She'd forgotten all about it. Rosie stopped. "Dalton, I'm sorry but I can't come."

"Got somewhere else to be?"

"No – I mean, yes." She stuttered and the corners of his eyes crinkled in amusement.

"Well, which is it?"

"It doesn't matter, I'm not coming."

"Is it some other guy or do you just not like me? Which seems weird because I am very likable." There was a light of mischief in his expression.

Her smile was weak. "If I change my mind, you'll be the first to know."

"Okay." He put his hands in his pockets. "But are you sure you're all right?"

"I'm fine, Doctor Curtis, thanks," Rosie said dryly.

"Hey, I'm just checking." Someone shouted to him and he waved at them over her head.

"I've got to go see my minions," he said. "But don't forget you can always change your mind. See you in class." His hand touched her shoulder lightly and then he strode off to join his friends.

Rosie watched him go. Why was he so persistent? She found it hard to believe Dalton was interested in her, in a dating kind of way. Could he really be a Helios agent?

Confused, she headed for the lecture room.

⸻ ◆ ⸻

By the last class of the day, navigational physics, Rosie felt sick with nerves, gnawing tension growing in her belly. She tried to reach her aunt repeatedly, but got nothing but her com on stand-by.

It seemed to take forever for the class to finish and by then she'd almost decided she wouldn't go to see her dad, but risk going to Riley – though caution won out. If she was being watched, going to Riley would be exactly what they wanted her to do. She should go see her dad, try to act normal.

The shuttle station was busier than last time and she had trouble finding a bench amid the after-school crush. Loud ads and announcements filled the air, along with the smell of hot metal, human sweat and fried onions.

The trip to Greenview didn't help ease her nerves and, by the time she got off the shuttle, her anxiety had moved into high gear.

Her com pinged as she walked up the path to the main entrance. She stopped and took it out, not really wanting to look at it.

Some information is better shared, the words said. *Let's see what happens.*

Her insides took a dive to her feet. She spun around,

staring at the trees, the building, the grounds, as if expecting someone to be standing there smirking at her. But there was no one. Her breath got short. What the hell was going on? She didn't know what to do, or what the message even meant. Had whoever sent the vision shared it with Helios? She tried her aunt again. Nothing.

She stared at the hospital entrance. She couldn't just stand here. *Go inside,* she told herself. *Act normal.*

Sure. Great, normal. Heart pounding like she was high on stims, she pocketed her com and headed for the door.

The hospital seemed quieter than usual. There was no one on the front desk or in the halls. That should have been a big clue right there, but she wasn't thinking straight. It wasn't until she got to her dad's floor and looked through the window into the doctor's office that she got it. The doctor was in there, but there were also two big men in Senate uniforms. They wore guns strapped to their hips, and both of them saw her.

Rosie froze. She stared at them, they stared at her and for a nanosecond nobody moved. Her only thoughts were: they know about the vision; they've come for me. Then instinct took over. She spun on her heels and bolted back down the hall.

"Stop!" one of the men called, but she didn't turn around. She skidded around a corner, knocking over a trolley of medical supplies, and kept running. Adrenaline pumped through her veins like cold fire, her back prickling with fear that at any moment she'd feel a shot.

The men pursued her, their boots thundering on the hard floor. Her dad's room was on the second floor and Rosie had no idea where the stairwell was. She'd always taken the lift. Terrified, she ran blindly around the next corner and past the bank of elevators. It had to be close. A door. Rosie saw a sign on it saying *No Admittance* before she ran through and slammed the door shut, locking it behind her. A heavy fist smashed on it, rattling it in its frame.

It was dim inside, hard to see. Opposite the door was a flight of stairs going down. Rosie took them two at a time, almost twisting her ankle as she rounded the platform at the bottom of the first flight.

Now that the Senate knew, how long would it be until one of Helios's moles saw the vision and spread the word?

Crashes came from above like someone was trying to kick the door in. The stairs ended at an outer door. She pushed it open. Directly opposite was a small car park with a few solar cars and a big hover delivery truck. Thick trees and scrub backed onto the far side of the car park. There were more buildings on the right and open lawn on the left. She ran towards the car park but caught a movement from the corner of her eye. A Senate guard was sprinting across the lawn. She ran as hard as she could for the car park, not really sure what she was going to do.

"Stop," the guard shouted, and she heard the whine of a weapon powering up.

Rosie ducked, but not quickly enough. A pulse shot swiped her shoulder. She screamed and staggered. It burned like a rod of fire scraping her skin. Tears filled her vision, but she kept going. The Senate guard was bigger, faster. She couldn't outrun him, but she'd be damned if she was going down without a fight. She reached the car park, but he was almost in grabbing distance now. Then there was the rumble of an engine and she looked up to see a bio bike racing down the centre of the car park. It swerved side-on and screeched to a stop next to her. The black-clad rider turned to her, the visor on his helmet reflecting her petrified face.

"Get on!" The voice seemed familiar and a gloved hand reached for her.

She grabbed it instinctively, the skin of her left shoulder burning, just as the guard closed in. The guard snatched at her, but the man on the bike yanked her onto the seat, out of the guard's reach, and took off.

"Son of a bitch!" Rosie heard the guard shout, and she hunched down as a shot of pulse fire whizzed past her head.

"Hold on!" the driver yelled. She clutched at his waist as he manoeuvred the bike out of the hospital car park and onto the road, cutting in front of a catering transport. Brakes squealed and Rosie thought they were done for as they headed straight for the side of another truck. The bike corrected at the last minute, leaning hard sideways to come up alongside the truck. Rosie could hardly breathe. Her shoulder down to her elbow felt like it was being peeled off in thin strips. Air streamed past, her hair whipping out behind her as the driver opened the bike up. The cars, trees and buildings around them became a blur of motion and she could do nothing but hold on.

Bio bikes were two-wheeled power monsters with camouflage shielding. The driver wove the bike effortlessly through the traffic as if all the other vehicles were standing still. They were soon over the bridge, bypassing the checkpoint as if they were invisible, roaring through the Rim.

Rosie clung on. For all she knew she could have just leaped into Helios's hands, but it was too late to rethink. She was sure she recognised the voice though. Male, but not Riley. She didn't try to ask for a name – the speed they were travelling at made it impossible to talk without helmet coms, and she was riding bare.

She hunched down behind him, using his body to cut the wind, and tried to pay attention to where they were going. It was getting dark, so she couldn't be sure. South maybe. They cut through busy streets. Rosie saw the brief flash of a reader light scan the bike ID, but no alarms halted them.

The pain in her shoulder had become a hot spreading throb and she could barely feel her left hand clutching at the driver's jacket. She began to feel strange, as if she was suspended in time. There was nothing but the rush of wind, the rolling thunder of the bike and the pain. The bright lights of the spaceport flashed past. She blinked. Where in the hell were they going? She knew she should be afraid, but the pain was taking over. Her vision was blurry and there was a funny roar in her ears.

She blinked and her eyes closed briefly – or not. She suddenly jerked up, heart pounding. The bike was wobbling, the driver gripping her arm. She'd been sliding off sideways. She sat up and the wind hit her full in the face, but not so fast. They were slowing down. The bike turned down a wide road flanked on either side by tall stone pillars.

They were in the Ocean Estates, playground of the rich, and about as far from the life of a Banker you could get. The pain in her shoulder asserted itself and Rosie swallowed a cry. She was suddenly wide awake. How had they got here? She must have passed out. The Estates were at least two hours south of the city.

They took a turn into a driveway, great steel gates opening before them. A sign above the gate was illuminated by soft lighting. *Newport*. The driveway ended at a sprawling mansion, the bike thrumming to rest in front of the door.

Rosie tried to slide off fast, make a break for it, but the driver was faster. The bike wasn't even switched off before he'd twisted around and caught her by the arm. Not that it made any difference. Her legs buckled and she yelped in pain. He'd grabbed her injured arm.

"Ow, let go!"

"Sorry." His grip loosened. "Relax, it's okay. Wait." That familiar muffled voice again. "It's me."

"Who's me?" Rosie sounded hoarse and weak. He was still hanging onto her arm, but now he seemed to be holding her up more than restraining her. She twisted out of his grip and stood unsteadily, swaying slightly, a weird feeling coming over her. She knew that voice.

He swung his leg over the bike, switching the engines off. It was suddenly very quiet. She heard sea washing against the shore and smelled damp salty air, but it barely registered as he took off his helmet and shook out his hair.

Golden highlights glinted in the soft lighting coming from the house.

He smiled. "Hey, Pilot Girl. Told you I had a Prince Charming complex."

She stared. "Dalton?"

CHAPTER 8

"Wait, wait!" He dropped the helmet, arms spread wide as she took three big steps back from him. "It's okay. I'm not Helios."

"What?" Rosie stopped.

"I work for Riley," he said. "Really. He sent me to help you."

Gravel crunched under her feet as she took another step back.

"Seriously." He came slowly towards her, arms still held out. "I brought you here for safety. This is my family's place." He was watching her very closely, measuring the distance between them in case she bolted. She wouldn't get two steps in her present condition. She was feeling light-headed and really, really thirsty.

"You work for Riley?"

"I'll prove it." Without taking his eyes off her, he unzipped a pocket on the thigh of the black bike suit. "I've got a com here. Riley's going to call any minute." The com made a low urgent beeping noise. "Speak of the devil." He held it out to her. "It's Riley. Ask him yourself."

Rosie hesitated. He seemed sincere. She edged forwards and plucked the com from his palm. He didn't move, but was watching her every step of the way.

"We should go inside," he said. "You don't look so good."

"You keep saying that." She hit the receiver and an image of Riley filled the screen. There was a deep crease between his brows and he looked mad and worried at the same time.

"Rosie?" he said. "Are you safe?"

"I think so." She glanced at Dalton.

"Dalton's there?" Riley said.

Her insides did a flip. So this was another thing Riley was hiding from her. "He says he works for you. Is that true?"

"If he didn't, you wouldn't be there, you'd be locked up." His tone was hard, but still Rosie wasn't sure about this.

"He's a Central," she said, keeping an eye on Dalton, who was watching her like he thought she was going to run. "And how did—"

Riley cut her off. "You know those rogue news waves you keep seeing, about Helios?"

Rosie hesitated, flicking her gaze between Riley on the com and Dalton. "Yeah."

"He makes them," Riley said. "We've been working on them together. It's okay; he's safe."

Rosie was speechless. Dalton looked pleased and sheepish at the same time.

"It's true," he said. "It's how Riley found me."

Rosie didn't know what to say, but it didn't matter because Riley was back to barking at her. "Okay now?"

She nodded.

"Good. Go inside. I'll call again on this com. Yours is compromised; don't use it." The screen went black.

Damn. Rosie stared down at it for a second then gave it back to Dalton.

"So," he said. "You—"

"Shut up." Rosie walked past him to the house. Her head was pounding and she felt sick.

Dalton picked up the helmet and opened the door, standing against it so she could enter. Three shallow steps down from the entrance was a large open room, floored with dark tile. A long white couch and a coffee table faced a fireplace set in a freestanding wall, and the back wall was an expanse of glass. It held a faint, wavering reflection of her, courtesy of the one lamp in the room that was turned on. Beyond the glass was the suggestion of a deck and the white roll of the sea. The house felt big and clean and empty.

"We should look at that pulse burn." Dalton moved past her, unzipping the bike suit. "Sit down." He threw the helmet on the couch and peeled the suit off his torso, tying the arms around his waist. Underneath he wore a black tank top.

Rosie followed. Her arm was throbbing like hell. Everything had happened so fast she felt spun off her axis. She'd been chased, shot and now she was here with Dalton. Who worked for Riley. Her ribs ached, but not as much as her arm. She lowered herself down slowly and couldn't stop a hiss of pain at the movement.

"You okay?" He moved to help, hazel eyes filled with concern, but she flinched back.

"Don't touch me."

"I need to have a look at the burn."

"Really, are you a doctor now?" The pain was making her snarky.

"I'll be back in a minute." He headed off around the fireplace and down a dark hallway.

Rosie tried to peel her jacket off and bit back a scream as agony flared right down to her fingertips. It felt like someone was scraping needles through her veins. The room went blurry for a moment and sweat beaded on her forehead. She stayed still, trying to breathe and willing the room to stop moving.

"What did you do?"

She jumped, startled. She hadn't even heard him

come back.

"Tried to get my jacket off." Rosie couldn't lift her gaze from the floor; she was certain she would throw up or pass out if she moved.

"You should have waited." She sensed movement, then his boots appeared in her field of vision as he sat on the coffee table in front of her. He leaned over and examined her shoulder.

"I'm going to take your jacket off." He didn't wait for her to respond but gently began easing it off. Rosie cried out as he got to her left arm and grabbed his forearm with her other hand, her nails digging into his skin.

"Sorry," he said, but kept going until it was off. He dropped it on the couch. The pulse fire had singed a big hole in the shoulder. "That was my favourite jacket," she said.

"Now it's religious." There was a faint smile on his lips.

She squinted at him.

"You know, holey," he said.

"Hilarious," she rasped.

"I'm going to put some stuff on the burn; try not to move."

He scooted forwards so his long legs were on either side of her knees. Sitting, he was still taller than her and she felt small and hemmed in. She wasn't sure she liked it, not after the day she'd had. And it was all too weird being here alone with Dalton Curtis. She watched half-dazed with pain, mesmerised by the way the muscles in his arms shifted when he moved.

"How does it look?" she said to his shoulder.

"Like you've been scraped by pulse-weapon fire." He took a tube out of the medikit and she felt something cold and soft touch her wound. A blessed sense of relief oozed along her shoulder, the pain receding as he spread whatever it was across her skin. She closed her eyes.

"Oh, God." The words came out involuntarily on a sigh.

He let out a short laugh. "Better?"

"Yes." Her voice cracked.

"Who said I'm not a doctor?" His touch was light, skating over her shoulder and down her arm. "You know, Pilot Girl, you should be more careful."

"Really? Thanks for the tip." Her muscles felt like they were turning into syrup. But as the hurt receded, a new awareness rose. His fingers on her skin. How close he was, his thigh pressed against her knee. Rosie opened her eyes and tried to shift back.

"Um, I think I'm good now. Thanks."

"Wait." He held her arm. "Nearly done." He smoothed the cream down her forearm, finishing at her hand. "Okay." He sat back, wiping the residue on the pants of his bike suit.

"Thanks." Rosie knew she sounded stiff and not thankful at all.

"Well, we are in this together, aren't we?"

"Together?" Rosie repeated.

"Yeah." He snapped shut the medikit and nudged her knees out of the way so he could stand up. "You know, both of us Riley's little helpers. Here, have some water." He picked up a glass from the coffee table and handed it to her.

Rosie drained it in three long gulps, watching him from the corner of her eye. Of course, it was delicious, pure water, not even a tang of recyc.

Dalton folded his arms loosely across his chest. "I didn't know about you working for Riley either, not at first anyway. In case you were wondering."

"Who says I was?" Rosie put down the glass.

He half-smiled. "I started to get suspicious when you beat me in the flight immersion test."

"It wasn't a test," Rosie answered automatically, and he grinned.

"Yes, it was. Of course, I knew about Mars – not names, but enough. I'm pretty good at putting clues together. Then when you show up at the Academy and blitz me, well, I got curious."

So that's what his attention had been about. She was disappointed, then annoyed with herself for feeling that way. "That's why you've been so friendly."

He gave her a look she couldn't quite decipher. "Want some more water?"

She held out her glass and he picked up a bottle from the floor that he must have brought in earlier.

"Is it only the news waves you make for Riley?"

"Mostly. It takes a bit of time to put them together. I cut them here, broadcast them from a portable uploader." A wry smile curved his lips. "Quality's a lot better since Riley tracked me down. He has some serious tech."

"Yeah, I know." Rosie's tone was still cool and his smile faded.

"What happened today?" he said. "How did you manage to end up on every Senate alert in the city?"

Rosie wasn't sure how much to tell him. She hadn't even told Riley about the message. "I made a mistake." She took another long swallow.

He lifted an eyebrow. "That's what you're going with?"

"For now. Is that how you found me?"

"Riley was tracking the Senate wires. He sent me a ping saying they were looking for you, said I should get on my bike and get my arse to the hospital to pick you up. I was the closest."

"And you knew it was me?"

A touch of self-satisfaction glinted in his eye. "Riley told me it was you, but like I said, I'd already guessed you were one of his, so I wasn't surprised. I'm actually smart – for a rich Central boy." He gave her a sideways look and she felt a blush creep up her neck. She had judged him pretty quickly when they'd first met.

He picked up her bag from the floor. "Come on. I'll show you your room. Then I've gotta get changed and go out for a bit, make an appearance at the party." He headed to a hallway that led from the lounge room. Rosie followed. She'd forgotten about the party. He'd been so keen on her going. Now he sounded bored with the whole idea.

"You're still going?" she said.

"Can't disappoint my fans, can I?" he said. "Down this wing is the bedrooms. Back there, past the fireplace, is the kitchen. Help yourself to anything you like."

"I'm not hungry." Being shot had a way of driving the appetite right out of you.

"You sure?" Dalton glanced over his shoulder. "You could stand to put some steak on."

"Gee, thanks. Any more compliments for me today?"

Dalton turned away with a shrug.

The hallway followed the long glass wall then made a right-angled turn and dog-legged back to another hall. Dalton stopped at the next door, opening it and dumping her bag on a large bed that took up a good portion of the spacious room. The bedhead served as a room divider and behind it was a walk-through wardrobe and the white tile of a bathroom.

"Hope it's okay. My room's a bit further along, if you need anything. You'll be on your own for a while till I come back. My dad basically never comes here and my mum, well – she's away at the moment, so ..." They stood looking at each awkwardly for a moment. "See you later then," he said.

"Yep." Rosie nodded. He left, closing the door behind him.

As soon as he'd gone, Rosie didn't know what to do. She was tired, but it felt too early to sleep. She went to the one big window. It looked out over a deck, but beyond was just darkness and the night sky, stars bright against the black. She glanced at the com Riley had said not to use, then sat on the bed and took off her shoes very slowly. Her shoulder was stiffening up and starting to throb again. But that wasn't what occupied her. She just couldn't believe she was in Dalton Curtis's house and that he worked for Riley.

———◆———

Rosie was woken by soft knocking on the door.

"You awake?"

She opened sleep-crusted eyes. She was fully clothed and it was still dark outside. She rubbed her eyes and blinked. She didn't remember lying down or turning out the light.

"Rosie?" Dalton was outside her door.

"Come in."

The door opened and she squinted in the sudden glare of light from the hall.

"Sorry." He was a dark silhouette in the doorway. "Riley's here to see you."

She struggled to sit up, her whole body aching. "Now?"

"Yeah, I know. He said it was safer to come now." He took a step into the room. Her eyes had adjusted and she could see he was wearing a pair of loose dark blue pyjama bottoms and a T-shirt. His hair curled against his face on one side and stuck up on the other.

"What time is it?"

"After three."

"In the morning?" Rosie stumbled as she got to her feet.

"He's in the lounge. You don't mind if I don't wait up, do you?" Dalton's last words were lost in a huge yawn. He covered his mouth and pushed hair away from his face.

"Sure, go back to bed. It's me he wants to tear into shreds anyway."

"All right, good luck." He turned away, and she watched his shadow grow on the wall as he went back to his room.

Riley was sitting on the white couch staring out through the floor-to-ceiling glass. The house had that weird hushed feeling all places get in the small hours of the night: an absence of life, a bated breath feeling of the world waiting for the light to return.

A pit of dread sat in the base of Rosie's stomach as she approached him.

"Dalton said you got hit by a pulse. How are you

feeling?" His tone was deepwater calm, his gaze cool and assessing.

From outside came the soft persistent roar of the sea on the beach. Thud and wash.

"Um, yeah, I'm fine. He put some stuff on it." She sat down.

"You've brought trouble to us, Rosie," he said quietly. "And at a time when we really do not need it."

"I know," she said. That quiet tone was worse, a million times worse, than getting shouted at. The disappointment in his eyes made her feel ill. "I've ..." She swallowed, her mouth suddenly too dry, then tried again. "I need to tell you something."

"About how the Senate has vision of you in the hospital?"

She felt a scared leap inside. "I got a message on my com." She pulled it from her pocket and held it out to him. "Two days ago."

He took it and silently scanned her messages. The lines of his face deepened, but his voice was weary when he spoke. "Why didn't you come to me?"

"I did," Rosie said, "that day Pip was there. I was going to tell you but everything got ... complicated." She exhaled. "Then I was scared to go back in case whoever it was followed me. I could have led them to you. I didn't know what to do. And Aunt Essie wasn't around." Anxiety and fear made her voice rise. What was she supposed to do? She knew she'd messed up. "She's been out a lot." Rosie clenched her hands into fists. "Has she been with you?"

"Sometimes." Riley rubbed the bridge of his nose. "It's not all your fault. I should have thought about the hospital surveillance long ago and got rid of it."

"We all should have," Rosie said.

He shook his head and they were both silent.

Rosie pulled her knees to her chest. "I shouldn't have gone to see Dad," she said softly.

"You couldn't have known."

Why wasn't he more angry with her? Rosie was too tired to figure that out. "I thought Dalton was Helios," she said. "I thought ..." She shook her head. "What are we going to do, Riley? Who do you think's behind this? Helios?"

He tapped a finger on her com. "I don't know. It doesn't make sense if it is. Why wouldn't they just take you?"

"But now the Senate know that there's someone who can cure the MalX," she said. "What will they do to me?"

"They'll have a lot of questions." He flicked the back off her com and began fiddling with the workings. "I'll need to adjust this, make sure it can't be tracked – again."

"But I can't hide from the Senate," Rosie said. "They've got eyes everywhere."

"No." He met her gaze. "Your aunt's coming tomorrow to get you. There's only one way to sort this situation and I've got some things I need to take care of."

Rosie swallowed hard. "What way?"

"We'll have to turn you in to Senate Prime."

She couldn't have heard him right. "What?" It felt like something cold had just squeezed all her guts out. Prime was Senate headquarters, where the agents worked – and where prisoners were interrogated. "But Helios has spies in the Senate."

"It's all right," he said. "I've got a contact inside; she'll take care of you. We'll find a way to get around the questions and get you out."

She felt stunned and very, very scared, not quite believing this was the only choice.

"Are you sure?"

"I'm sorry, Rosie. This way we have a shot at controlling things, and you'll be okay." His words were calm, but beneath them she sensed a strain that hadn't been there before and there was a shadow behind his eyes, like he wasn't telling her everything. Like always.

"I've brought something that will help." He reached into a brown messenger bag and pulled out a small injection tube filled with clear liquid.

"What's that?" Rosie regarded it.

"It's not what you think."

"I was thinking it's a needle."

His mouth twitched. "Suspended in the fluid are nanoplants programmed to construct a molecular implant behind your ear when injected."

"And what do I need that for?"

"Rosie, you know I wouldn't ask you to do this if it wasn't safe and necessary," Riley said. "The implant is virtually undetectable and it's biologically based. You won't even know it's there. But I will. At its base level it's a tracking device, so if anything does happen in Senate Prime—'

"At its base level?" Rosie said.

A strained yet patient expression crossed his face. "It also monitors your life signs."

"In case they stop."

Riley's mouth thinned. "Its purpose is to make sure I know where you are at all times, so if the worst case scenario does occur, I can find you."

Rosie didn't like the idea one bit. An implant in her skull.

Riley put the tube in his lap and that shadow came over his face again, making the fine lines harder, deeper. "Look, Rosie," he said. "I know you're not keen on this but I need you to do it. I would never do anything that harmed you, you know that. I only want to keep you as safe as possible."

There was sadness in his eyes behind that determination he always wore, but there was also something else. Worry. And that made her feel awkward and scared, because she counted on him not to be worried. Riley being worried reminded her he wasn't superhuman. She tilted her head, brushing her hair back from her neck.

"Okay, fine, fill me with nanos."

He got a sanitiser patch from his bag and swabbed her neck. "It won't hurt — just don't move." There was relief in his voice.

She felt the sharp touch of the needle against her skin and kept her eyes on the fireplace as he pumped the tube. It was painless: all she felt was a tiny surge of coolness then it was gone.

"Good girl." He wiped the spot and put the tube back in his bag then got up. "It will take a few hours for the nanos to construct the implant but it should be done by the time Essie comes."

Rosie touched the place on her neck where the needle had punctured the skin.

For a second he seemed to be considering telling her something, a slight frown between his brows. But then he turned away and Rosie got that scared feeling again. What wasn't he telling her?

"Riley?" He paused at the steps, his gaze calm. "Um, are you ..." She was going to say okay, but couldn't quite get the word out with the way he was looking at her, steady as always. "I'm sorry. I didn't mean for this to happen."

A small almost-smile touched his mouth. "I know. Get some sleep. You're going to need it."

CHAPTER 9

Despite thinking it was impossible, Rosie managed to go back to sleep and woke to bright sunlight. She squinted and wished she'd remembered to activate the window screens. Her shoulder was stiff and jabs of pain poked at her back and ribs. What time was it?

The floor-to-ceiling window revealed a wide pale brown deck and a waist-high railing, beyond which were low dunes, tufts of greyish grass, then ocean. There were no other buildings in sight and the sky was cloud-scuffed and glaring with heat already. She rubbed her face and sat up slowly. The burn from the pulse gun had left an exclamation-shaped streak down her left shoulder blade and the back of her arm, but at least it wasn't throbbing with pain any more. Dalton's cream had done the job.

Good thing she was right-handed.

She touched the spot on her neck where the needle had gone in. Besides a tiny bump, there was no indication she had nanobots circling up into her skull, busily building a microscopic implant. The thought of it made her skin feel paper-thin and supersensitive, as if she was aware of every cell in her blood moving. It wasn't a great feeling. She grimaced as she caught a whiff of her own armpit and got up to investigate the bathroom.

───◆───

Ten minutes later her hair was washed and her body was clean but she had to wait another five for her clothes, which she'd shoved in the cleaning unit. Wrapped in a towel she stared moodily through the window of the cleaner. Inside her tank top zipped by in flashes of red. Her insides were hollow with anxiety and too many thoughts crowded into her head. Everything felt like it was falling apart and she had a strong desire to run. But where would she go?

The cleaning unit beeped and she jumped. *Stop festering.*

The faint sound of a guitar being played was in the air when she emerged from her room and she followed it past the white lounge and fireplace to a very large kitchen. She slowed as she neared the door. The music was coming from in there. It was a soft strumming, rhythmic, and as she hesitated Dalton began to sing. His voice was husky, soulful, rising and falling with the strumming. It sounded private and Rosie stood in the doorway, unsure if she should go in. She turned to leave, but her shoes squeaked on the floor and the music faltered.

"Rosie?" Dalton called.

She paused, wondering for a second if she should pretend she wasn't there.

"I can hear you breathing," he said.

She stepped into the room, peering around the door. "Hi."

He was sitting at a long table, a beautiful golden-coloured guitar on his lap. Beyond him a transparent barrier that mimicked an expanse of glass separated the room from the deck outside. It shimmered, deflecting the heat of the morning. A screen projection on the wall near the door detailed the UV index and the latest news waves.

"You hungry? Thirsty?" he said. "We've got pineapple juice." He indicated a jug of something yellow on the table in front of him.

Rosie had never in her life had pineapple juice. "Starving," she said.

"Get what you like from the dispenser. Glasses are in the cupboard next to it." He went back to plucking at his guitar strings. "How's that burn this morning?"

Rosie shrugged, then immediately regretted it as

pain ran down her arm. "I'll cope." She chose a bowl of noodles with soy from the dispenser and carried it and an empty glass to the table, sitting opposite Dalton. He kept strumming the guitar, not looking at her.

"You're pretty good," she said.

He let out a short breathy laugh. "Thanks; flattery will get you everywhere."

Rosie twirled some noodles around her fork. "So do you play a lot then?"

"Not any more. Father doesn't approve. A waste of good study time, he calls it." There was a bitter edge to his tone. "Music is not an acceptable career path in the Curtis household."

Rosie hadn't met Dalton's dad but she suddenly had a mental picture of him. One of those sharp-jawed Central types, ruthless, probably old money. Never been in the Banks in his life. "How about your mum?" she said.

Dalton's fingers paused on the strings for a millisecond and there was the tiniest tightening of skin around his eyes. "She's away a lot. But enough about me. Did Riley tear you to shreds?"

"More or less." Rosie was curious about his reaction. It was the same one she had when people wanted to know about her mum, about her family. She poured some juice. "I have to go to Senate Prime today, hand myself in."

He stopped playing to stare at her. "Repeat that?"

"Senate Prime," Rosie said. "You know, big building in Central, home to all things Senate."

"I know what it is. But Riley sent me to get you away from them, didn't he?"

Rosie tried to swallow more juice around the tightening of her throat.

"How much do you know ... about me, I mean?"

He leaned back, cradling the guitar. "A bit. Your father was kidnapped by Helios, taken to Mars, you went after them with Riley, brought him back." He smiled lightly. "How am I doing so far?"

She didn't smile back. "Anything else?"

His gaze dropped briefly to her neck. "One of those pendants you're wearing has Riley's parents' files on it. You used it to expose Helios's part in creating the MalX and letting it loose on Earth. And you had some help from a guy named Pip – who used to be Helios and who I've met. Once."

Rosie's heart jumped. He'd met Pip? "Is that it?"

He shrugged. "Any blanks you want to fill in?"

She tapped her empty glass. If he didn't know about Pip's immunity to the MalX, it was probably best left that way. And besides, she really didn't want to get into it. She already felt too lightly tethered to the earth, weightless with anxiety about going to Senate Prime. And talking about Pip meant thinking about him. Too hard. "Maybe later," she said.

The amusement in his face faded and a slight hesitation came into his voice as he said, "I also know your dad almost died from the MalX – and that he's in

Greenview now. That's gotta be tough. I mean after your mum and everything–'

"He's fine; it's just temporary," Rosie said quickly.

"I didn't mean–"

"It's okay." She pushed the glass away, tried to pull in the desire to spill her guts. "We're fine." She cleared her throat. "So how long have you been working with Riley?"

Dalton looked at her for a second as if he was going to pursue it, but then seemed to change his mind. He started strumming again. "Since after he got back from Mars. He saw the news waves I'd started doing. Found me." He shrugged again.

"How come you do them?" Rosie said. "I mean, it's weird, for a Central."

Dalton tilted his head at her and she saw a shadow behind his eyes. "Who says all Centrals have to like the status quo? Maybe I hate the way the world is as much as you do. It made me angry, seeing what Helios has done to it."

"Right," Rosie said, but she got the feeling there was something else besides righteous anger. He strummed the guitar harder. "Then of course there's how much I hate what my dad does."

"What does he do?"

Dalton stopped playing. "Water, terraforming, planet colonisation. The big three." He said it with distaste, like his dad was involved in gangs or something worse.

"Our family company owns the largest share of the water mining on Titan and is part of the Gliese colony initiative. You know that ship, *Leviathan*, that broke up on the way back to Earth?" Rosie nodded. "It was full of Curtis and Co equipment. To say my father was pissed is an understatement." He shook his head, a bitter smile on his face. "He didn't give a toss about the people who died. He was angry none of them had thought to airlock the freight compartments before they inconveniently got sucked out into space. The whole fight over the wormhole project is mostly being led by his company and I wouldn't be surprised if he was the one who leaked the news." He plucked the guitar strings, tense with repressed anger. "Sometimes I wonder if he's not caught up somehow with Helios. He wasn't exactly shocked by the MalX revelations or the tests they were doing up on Mars. His response to the number of Ferals Helios kidnapped and killed was that they would have died here on Earth anyway, and at least they got to see Mars."

Rosie wasn't surprised. It wasn't exactly an unheard of reaction for a Central type. "Do you really think your dad could be involved with Helios?"

"I don't know."

"Have you ever, you know, looked through his stuff or anything?"

He stared down at his guitar. "Once, but that's not the–" He stopped and Rosie got the idea he was debating whether or not to tell her something.

"Have you told Riley?" she said.

"Nothing to tell – yet. But if I find something …"

"You'll have to do something about it," Rosie said.

Dalton held her gaze for a moment, then looked away. "Yeah, well, anyway." He began to pick at his guitar again and made an effort to lighten his tone. "So, why do the Senate want you?"

She cleared her throat. "Someone – I don't know who – sent them some information. The Senate think I might know something about how my dad recovered from the MalX."

"Do you?" he asked quietly.

Rosie couldn't answer.

She could feel the weight of his stare, but all he said was, "It's okay. Later, eh?"

She nodded, then scooped up the last of the noodles and spoke around them. "Riley says it's better if I turn myself in rather than trying to hide – or run away. Personally, I'd rather run – if I knew some way of disabling men twice my size."

"You mean like self-defence?"

"My aunt's been saying she's going to teach me, but she never has the time."

"I can show you, if you like."

"You?"

"Sure." He smiled. "You got something better to do? We've got a fully equipped gym here."

"Of course you do." She pushed her empty bowl away.

118

"But I've already got enough aches and pains, thanks."

"I promise to go easy on you."

Rosie sighed and thought about it for a minute. It was better than sitting around stewing. "Okay." She got to her feet.

Dalton's gym was a separate bungalow. It had every new piece of high-tech training gear, from AI running pods that made you feel you were running on a beach or in a forest, to hologramatic trainers and AI fighting programs, but what Dalton showed her was all simple, hand-to-hand defence.

After an hour of practising, Rosie was tired and sore and her shoulder was aching, but she didn't want to stop. Dalton was a good teacher. She had managed to throw him off his feet and was trying to pin him down, with one arm locked around his neck, when the security alarm suddenly chimed loudly. Startled, she tightened her grip and he wheezed.

"Sorry." She loosened her grip.

"It's the gate alarm," he said. "Your aunt must be here."

Rosie let him go, pushing against him to regain her feet. "How did I do?" she said. "Were you really disabled or only pretending?"

"Oh, I was disabled," he said and rubbed at his neck. "I think you're a natural. Your reflexes are pretty good." He headed out of the gym.

"Seriously?"

"Yeah. Christ, it's hot out here!" He squinted in the sun as they crossed the deck and went back to the house. The generated wall of glass dissolved as he waved a hand at the outside sensor and they went back into the kitchen. "Help yourself to a drink. I'll go let your aunt in." He spoke over his shoulder as he walked down the hall.

"She's going to be mad," Rosie called.

"I hope you're not expecting me to solve that problem. My Prince Charming act doesn't extend to rescuing you from relatives."

"Just let her in." Rosie laughed.

He disappeared down the hall with a parting shot. "If you hear cries for help, just run, save yourself."

Rosie chuckled and went to get some water. Her smile faded though when Aunt Essie came down the hall. She looked like she was scoping for someone to use as target practice. Dalton had disappeared. Wise move.

"Aunt Essie." She faced her. "I'm sorry."

"Goddamned right." Essie strode into the kitchen, hands on hips, dressed all in black. "You're lucky Riley has such good contacts and could get that boy to get you out of there."

"I know."

"Why didn't you tell me about that message?"

"When, exactly? You haven't been home. You're never home. And it's not like you could bring yourself to come with me to see Dad." Even as she said it she knew she sounded like a whiny brat.

Aunt Essie spoke through gritted teeth. "I was working. I told you that already."

"All night? I couldn't even contact you on the com. Riley said you were with him sometimes."

Her aunt exhaled hard, running her hands through her hair. "I'm allowed to keep some things to myself, aren't I? Just what do you want from me, Rosie? I'm doing the best I can. I'm not cut out for this. I'm not like your mum, or like Adam used to be." She was looking at her with a desperation that Rosie had never seen before. "I thought we were in this together."

"So did I," Rosie said. "But lately you're just never there."

Essie sighed and sat down heavily. "I know," she said quietly. "I'm sorry, kid. Sometimes I forget how young you are. You're just so capable."

An apologetic half-smile crossed her face and Rosie whispered, "Doesn't feel like it sometimes."

Aunt Essie's smile faded. "I know. And I know I should go see him, but ..." She shook her head. "I don't think that helps either of us. Him or me. Still, you should have told me about that message. I was home a bit, enough, wasn't I?"

Rosie could feel her heart shrinking to the size of an amoeba. She was scared but she didn't want to voice it. Silence settled over them, only interrupted by the distant rush of the ocean and the faint sound of Dalton playing his guitar again.

Her aunt touched her arm. "I understand that you're scared, but we've got to deal with what's happening now and I'm not going to let anyone get to you. Are you going to be a Black and sort this out?"

Rosie took in a long breath and straightened up. "Sure. Let's get it over with."

"Good." But she was still eyeing her like she wasn't quite sure she was ready. "Come on, I've got a car waiting."

"I'll get my bag." Rosie went to the room she'd slept in. When she came out Dalton was leaning against the wall.

"So," he said, "Senate Prime."

"Yep." Rosie slung the bag over her good shoulder.

"I'm guessing Riley has a plan."

"Hope so." Rosie's fingers felt cold where they clutched her bag. "Thanks for the fighting lessons and, um, everything. My aunt's waiting." Rosie walked past him.

"Hey, Pilot Girl," he called and she turned. "Watch your back. I don't want to have to rescue you again." He smiled, but it was a smile that didn't quite reach his eyes.

CHAPTER 10

Senate Prime was a thirty-storey building that took up one entire side of Aurora Plaza in Central. The plaza was a massive pedestrian space dotted with patches of fake greenery and numerous AI information booths. A tall, clear column in the centre of the square provided access to a suspended shuttle station, several transport tubes shooting up and down inside it.

Rosie's heart was beating way too fast when they stopped at the entrance. She took a few deep breaths, trying to calm down, and stared up at the edifice of curved metal and solar glass. The sky above was the washed-out blue of late summer and she could see a slight shimmer coming off the top four storeys of the building, as if it was surrounded by some kind of invisible field. Maybe it was.

"Ready?" Aunt Essie said.

"No." They'd spent the trip going over how things were supposed to play out, but it hadn't made her feel any better and she was sweating despite the cool interior of the car. There were too many variables for her to feel anything close to calm. A woman called Agent Sulawayo was supposed to be meeting them inside. She was Riley's contact and was going to make sure Rosie was okay.

"Don't panic, kid," Aunt Essie said.

Rosie picked up her bag. "What if it goes wrong?"

"Then I'll get you out. But let's hope I don't have to. Just keep your answers short and don't deviate from what we talked about." She opened the door of the transport and stepped out.

Right. Simple.

Heat came from the sun above and radiated up from the pavement. The pungent smell of rubber and burnt electricals filled the air, mixed with the sweet scents of a bakehouse in the plaza. Senate Prime was set a few metres back from the road, the entrance one enormous revolving door through which a stream people, most dressed in Senate uniforms, were passing in and out. They joined the crowd and entered the huge atrium. A transporter hub took up most of the back of the space, with ten elevator tubes whisking people up to other floors, and in front of it was a long low counter manned by three guards. On either side, scattered across the floor, were several AI ports.

Aunt Essie stopped at one and waved her ident over it.

"Welcome to Senate Prime, Miss Black," it said. "Please select your interaction level requirement."

"Same goddamned cheerful voice every time," Aunt Essie muttered.

"That won't be necessary, Miss Black. If you could both come with us."

Rosie jumped and turned to see a large guard flanked by two others standing behind them. The guard who'd spoken had his hand resting on a gun at his waist. His stare was flat and unfriendly.

"And you are?" Aunt Essie slowly put her ident back in her pocket.

"We're from Unit Twelve," he said as if they were supposed to know what that was. "We detected you approaching the building. Come this way." He turned towards the transporters and held out one muscular arm.

Aunt Essie took Rosie's arm. "Looks like henchmen one, two and three are our welcoming committee."

The guard's jaw tightened a fraction, but he didn't say anything, only stepped back to let them by. Then he fell alongside while the others came up behind and frogmarched them to the hub.

The ride in the elevator was silent and fast. They exited on the twenty-sixth floor and were ushered into a small room with one table, two chairs and a window that looked out over the city. It was cool in the Senate, but Rosie was still sweating with nerves as the guards left them alone, closing the door with a quiet snick.

Her aunt did laps around the room, tapping the backs of the chairs.

"The decor's as bad as it ever was." She stopped at the window, peering down at the street.

"Did you used to come here when you were with the Senate Elite?" Rosie asked. Essie had been in the Senate Elite – the force the Senate sent to work for the United Earth Commission's Peace Alliance – for two years before she joined Orbitcorp.

"Occasionally."

Rosie leaned on the back of one of the chairs and chewed on her lip.

"Don't look so worried." Aunt Essie waved towards the light fitting in the centre of the ceiling. "They don't need the entertainment."

Of course, someone was watching them. The door opened and a short pudgy man came in. He gave them a cold smile, revealing perfect white teeth. "Rosie Black and her aunt, Essie Black, I presume?"

Rosie didn't answer. Essie looked him up and down and said, "Where's Agent Sulawayo? I was told we would be seeing her."

"She's occupied." He put his hands in his pockets. "I'm Agent Whitely."

This was bad. Rosie looked quickly at her aunt as he sat opposite. Essie's expression bordered on hostile.

"Whitely? I've heard of you," she said. "You're

the agent who locked up six Banker kids last year for staying ten minutes past their allowed time in a Central Immerse. Looks like we need more chairs, 'cos I'm not leaving her alone with you."

"No." Whitely took a wafer-thin com from his pocket and frowned at it. "You will be waiting outside while I conduct this preliminary interview."

"I don't think so," Aunt Essie said. "Rosie is still only sixteen and I'm her guardian."

"For a preliminary interview we are allowed to insist you leave – regardless of her age." Agent Whitley's smile had gone as he turned in his chair to regard her. "Let's not make this unpleasant, Ms Black."

Aunt Essie looked like she was considering belting the man. Rosie quickly said, "I'll be okay," and shot her a look pleading for caution. They didn't need more trouble.

"Fine," her aunt said. "I'll wait outside. But you can't hold her, Whitely, she's still a minor."

"Of course. We wouldn't consider it." He smiled blandly.

Aunt Essie looked at Rosie. "I'll be right outside the door. Listening." She swivelled her gaze back to Agent Whitely for a moment, then strode from the room.

"Alone at last." Agent Whitely smiled as the door closed.

"Lucky me," Rosie said with sarcasm.

The agent's gaze became bright with speculation.

"Are we going to have a problem with you?" he said. Then he spoke into his com. "Activate."

A very bad feeling stirred in Rosie's gut. One of the previously blank walls of the room suddenly shimmered slightly in the centre and a door evolved from the greyness. Pitch vibration technology. Special paint that could distort light waves and change what you saw.

"What's going on?" She got to her feet, but Agent Whitely ignored her. He rose and placed his palm on the door. It slid open to reveal one of the guards from downstairs.

Rosie's internal alarm went off the scale. She spun around and leaped for the exit, but before she got there the guard had her. Time to test Dalton's lessons. She leaned back, grabbed his arm and twisted outwards, sweeping the closest foot out from underneath him with her leg.

He grunted and went down. Rosie lunged for the door, but he was on his feet in an instant and slammed her face first against the wall, pulling her arms up. Agony streaked down her injured shoulder. She screamed and tried to kick him but met only air.

"That's enough." Agent Whitely raised his voice.

The pressure on her arms eased, but he still held her against the wall. Scared and furious, Rosie drew in a quick breath. "Aunt Essie!" she shouted.

"It won't do any good; she can't hear you," Agent Whitely said from behind her. "The room is soundproofed.

Now, stop resisting and this will all be over soon."

"What will be over?" The wall smelled sour and the pulse burn throbbed with pain. "You said we were just going to talk. You can't do this. I haven't done anything!"

"That's debatable. Bring her." He spoke briskly, ordering the guard.

Rosie almost lost her footing as the guard shoved her in front of him. She tried desperately not to panic. This was suddenly feeling all too similar to when Helios got her on Mars.

They went along a narrow short corridor to a set of stairs and then another door. It was all painted grey, with flat luminescent lighting that reminded her of the Enclave. Agent Whitely paused at the last door and glanced back at her with an indecipherable look before opening it. Beyond was a long, high-ceilinged room without windows. On one side were eight beige doors. The facing wall was taken up by Grid terminals, AI pods, and a line of six stationary robotic drones.

"In here." Agent Whitely headed to the third door. It was a cell. The guard shoved her inside and Rosie was suddenly overtaken by a furious fear. She turned and tried to lunge back out again, but the guard only pushed her in.

"You can't do this!" she shouted, but the door slid shut. She pounded her fist against it and screamed, "Let me out!" She kicked it, hammered on it, but the door remained shut.

Finally, she gave up and backed up against the wall. Where the hell was that Sulawayo woman who was supposed to be here?

A lone bare tube lit the room, giving it a garish shadowed look. It was cold as well and she shivered, pulling her com from her pocket. She tried to ping her aunt, but it wouldn't even power up. The room must have some kind of shielding. She slid down against the wall and sat on the floor, hugging her knees to her chest fighting a rising terror. The Senate could do anything with her if they wanted to. Who was going to stop them? She'd defied them, hidden possible evidence of a cure for the MalX. Why would they be lenient? And if Whitely was a Helios mole, who knew what he'd do to her?

She didn't know how long she was there alone. Too long – probably to scare her. It was working. *Get it together, Black.* She put her head on her knees, closed her eyes and forced herself to focus on just breathing.

After what felt like hours the door opened and Agent Whitely came in, followed by the guard.

"Are you feeling more cooperative now, Ms Black?" he said.

Rosie got to her feet. "You haven't even asked me any questions. How can you say I wasn't cooperating?" She was trembling with cold and fear, and she hated how her voice sounded weak and small.

"You were being smart mouthed." He considered her. "And that is not a good idea considering what the Senate believes you may be concealing."

"I'm not hiding anything," Rosie said.

"No?" His eyebrows rose. "So you told us about that blood we saw you attach to your father's drip?" He frowned. "None of us can seem to remember that. And then, miraculously, he recovers from the MalX. Explanations?"

"I don't know what you're talking about," Rosie whispered. "I'm just glad he's alive."

If only she trusted the Senate more. If she really believed they could make a cure from Pip's blood and that a Helios mole wouldn't find out and Pip would be safe, she would gladly help them find a cure. But she didn't. If she told him, Helios would know. They wouldn't stop until they had Pip, and he would be back in the place he feared the most. And the things they would do to him made her scared. She couldn't betray him like that.

Whitely was watching the emotions cross her face with interest. "What is it, Miss Black?" He eyed her like a bird eyes a worm. "Where did the blood—"

"Agent Whitely." The door swung open and a tall thin woman took one step into the room. "What's going on here?"

The guard whipped around with the reflexes of a soldier. Whitely turned more slowly, but not before Rosie saw the look of annoyance quickly suppressed on his face.

"Agent Sulawayo," he said. "I am interviewing a person of interest."

"Here?" The woman's voice was cold, restrained. She stepped further into the room. Her skin was ebony, her face so perfect she could only be a natural beauty. But her eyes were a glacial-cold dark brown as she stared down at Agent Whitely. She reminded Rosie of Nerita – fierce, commanding, inscrutable.

"Please tell me you have a reason for being here, Whitely," she said quietly. "And tell me fast."

"Captain, we–" The guard started to talk but Agent Sulawayo silenced him with a look.

"You may go," she said. "We have no more need for you here."

Without a glance at Whitely, the guard left in haste. For a moment there was silence then Agent Whitely said, "I thought it best, given the circumstances of this case, that the girl be brought here for processing. The aunt was becoming a problem."

"Was she?" Sulawayo regarded him. "That was not my impression."

"You weren't there earlier." Whitely's shoulders tensed.

"No. I wasn't. Unfortunately. But I am now and I think this interview is over."

"Not until I say it is," Whitely said. "This girl defied the Senate."

"And where is your evidence?" Sulawayo glared at

him. "Some anonymously provided vision, which could be fake for all we know. I don't believe that warrants you restraining a *child*," she emphasised the word, "in a facility designed for hardened criminals."

"She ran from Senate officers," Whitely said.

"She was afraid, and I believe one of them shot at her," Sulawayo countered.

"She cannot be allowed to defy us and just walk away."

"She won't, but this treatment is out of order. I am relieving you, Agent Whitely. I have already informed your Officer in Charge of my actions." Sulawayo's expression defied him to argue.

"This isn't over," he said and stalked past her out of the room.

Sulawayo regarded Rosie. She seemed barely more friendly than when she'd been talking to Whitely. Rosie was too intimidated to say anything.

"Follow me," Sulawayo said and led her out.

Aunt Essie was waiting in the atrium when they came out of the transporter. She was angry and glowered at Agent Sulawayo as Rosie joined her.

"You took your time," she said. "It's been two hours. They had her in there with Agent Whitely, the Senate's favourite rabid attack dog."

"I know, it was unavoidable." Sulawayo was unruffled. "I got her out as quickly as possible."

"Any tracking devices on her?"

"Not that I am aware of. I can organise transport

home if you wish."

"No need," Aunt Essie said. "I think we're safer on the shuttle."

There was a moment's strained silence, both women looking at each other like there was a lot more to say, but there were too many people around.

"Rosie will be fined for evasion of the Senate guards," said Sulawayo. "I will do what I can to discredit the vision, but you can expect her father to be the subject of many Senate-directed tests now. A possible cure for the MalX will not go unresearched."

"I expect not." Aunt Essie's expression was grim. "Though I doubt they'll find anything. The doctors already put him through every test they could think of."

"Yes, well ..." Sulawayo hesitated as if she would add more, but only said, "You should go." And she turned abruptly and walked away.

"I don't like her," Aunt Essie said, watching her go. "Wonder how she got mixed up with this."

Rosie felt the same. But Riley must have some faith in the woman, and she had got her out of the cell.

"Come on." Essie took her arm. "Let's get out of here."

CHAPTER 11

"You need to go," Riley said. "All you do by being here is put yourself at risk."

"And what about *her* risk?" Pip said. "It shouldn't have happened. If I–"

"Rosie is fine." Riley's tone was final. "You have to go back."

Pip clenched his hands into fists. "Who's going to make me?"

"Don't turn this into a pissing contest, Pip. I don't have time for it. The vision of your blood being used is out there. You can't be here right now and I need you to keep an eye on Cassie."

"Kev's been looking after her for ten years. I hardly think I'm making much difference." Pip sat in a chair at Riley's desk. He leaned back and folded his arms. "I'm not leaving." He stared up at Riley. "So the Senate know there's some mystery blood donor who can cure the MalX. I don't care. I'm not scared of them, and I know how to hide from Helios."

Pip couldn't help feeling that he was missing something. Riley was agitated. He was never this keyed up and Pip was sure it wasn't over him still being here. What wasn't he telling him?

"So, what's the deal?"

Riley drew in a deep breath. Pip knew he was weighing up whether or not to confide in him. Finally he said, "I may have been compromised."

The chair creaked as Pip stood up. "Compromised? You mean–"

"Helios is closing in on where I am."

"Are you sure?"

"No, but I can't afford to assume they're not."

"Jesus, Riley, you've got to get of here. You can't stay."

"And neither can you."

"So what's the plan?"

"The plan is you go."

"And?"

"And nothing." Riley picked up Pip's bag from the floor and tossed it to him. "You get back up north and wait there. You'll know when I need you to do anything."

Pip caught the pack one-handed. "Are you serious?

That's not a plan. That's you ordering me around, *boss*."
He filled the word with sarcasm. "If I stay here, I can
help you."

"No, you can help me better up north. If you stay
here, you're just a hindrance."

Pip's chin came up. He couldn't help it, what with
that bloody calm tone Riley used. The expectation he'd
just do what Riley said. "And what about Rosie? She's
got a big target on her back now. You can't just expect
me to leave."

"Rosie already had a target on her back, and it will
be a lot bigger with you hanging around. If you want
to keep her safe, you need to get back up north and stay
there."

Just the idea made Pip furious. That and knowing
Riley was right. He squashed the urge to fling the bag
at Riley's head. "So what are you going to do?"

"I have contingencies."

"What the hell does that mean?"

"It means, you go north and I deal with things here."

Pip debated pressing him, but Riley had that
stubborn look that meant Pip was getting nothing more.
It was almost like being part of Helios again. Everything
was always on a need-to-know basis. Secrets were like a
disease. Contagious.

He flung the bag over one shoulder. "Right, then,
guess I'll be off."

"Good." Riley didn't even blink. "And don't try to

contact me when you get there. I'll contact you."

"Whatever." Pip kicked open the door. "I'll send your regards to your sister, shall I?" Riley had already gone back to his holos. Furious, Pip took the stairs two at time, not bothering to turn on the light. It was nearly seven and he still had his surveillance jammer. Maybe he'd make a visit before he went. If Riley wasn't going to tell him what was going on, at least he could give Rosie the heads-up. If she was still speaking to him.

———◆————

Rosie could barely eat. She sat at the small table in their apartment and pushed the chilli Aunt Essie had made around the plate. Across from her, Essie was sipping from a glass of straight vodka and staring into space. She hadn't eaten anything either. They had barely spoken since leaving Senate Prime. It was clear something had gone wrong, really wrong, for Riley's contact to be so late. Rosie kept wondering if Whitley had been Helios, and if he'd engineered something to delay Sulwayo. But it didn't make sense.

"We're going to see Riley tomorrow," Aunt Essie said. Rosie wasn't about to argue.

"Why not go now?"

"Too obvious. We've got two tails on us. Better to wait, go in the morning as if we're getting breakfast.

Give us more time to shake them."

"When did they turn up?" Rosie hadn't noticed the tails.

"They followed us pretty much from leaving Senate Prime," Aunt Essie said. "They're better than the others. We must have been promoted to a higher class of Helios operative. Lucky us, eh?"

Super lucky, Rosie thought sourly. The sound of the city rose up through the walls. Someone next door had digi-tel on so loud they could hear the screams and cheers from some game. It made Rosie feel like they were in a dead zone, a black hole.

She pushed her chair out. "I'm going to clean some clothes," she said. "You need anything done?"

"Yeah." Rosie waited but Essie didn't move or give any indication what she wanted.

"I'll get them then," she said. Her aunt grunted a reply.

She collected the basket of clothes from her room then went into her aunt's. Pants, underwear and a few shirts were stacked neatly in a clothes bin. Her aunt might be out of the Elite but she would never get rid of her soldier's habit of order.

Rosie threw the clothes on top of her own then took an elevator tube to the basement.

The laundry was a small windowless room. One wall was lined with half-a-dozen cleaning units and the air smelled of cleaning fluid. At least it was in the building though. When she'd lived in the Banks, if you wanted clean clothes you had to go to a clean'n'go autocaf.

There was no one else there. Rosie shoved the clothes into a unit then sat on the end of a line of chairs pushed up against the opposite wall. She stared at the clothes churning around and around. It was very quiet and the warmth of the air and the hum of the machine made her sleepy. She rubbed at her face and yawned, her eyelids drooping.

The snick of the door closing woke her. She sat up too fast and banged her ankle against the chair leg.

"Ow!" she hissed, then froze. Pip was standing with his back against the door. "Sorry, didn't mean to scare you," he said.

He had a grubby black pack slung over one shoulder and looked like he'd been running. His dark hair was messy, ruffled. A patch of sweat darkened the chest of his blue T-shirt, a darker blue than his eyes that watched her with a degree of wariness.

"What are you doing here?" she said. "Aren't you supposed to be back up north?" She wanted to stand up but that might make him think his presence bothered her, so she just sat, trying to appear casual while her heart went a million kilometres an hour. He slipped the pack off and came further into the room, dropping it on a chair.

"Is it clean?" he said. His gaze darted around the room, frowning, worried. She knew what he meant.

"There're no trackers or listeners," she said. "We check."

"Right." But he was still frowning. "I heard about what happened."

"So you came to see if I said anything about you?"

"What? No." He looked surprised. "I came because—"

Rosie cut him off. "It doesn't matter." She picked up the laundry basket and went to the clothes unit. It had finished some time when she was asleep, thank God, because it gave her something to do. "You can think what you like, but you shouldn't be here. We had two operatives follow us from Senate Prime. Good ones."

"Rosie, do you really think I'm worried you'd tell Helios about me?"

She shrugged and pulled a pair of jeans out of the unit. "How should I know?"

"Well, I'm not."

Rosie didn't answer. She drew out a handful of her knickers and shoved them quickly in the basket before he saw. She could feel him staring at her, agitated, waiting for her to say something. He was going to be waiting a long time.

"Right," he said after a while. "You're still mad at me then."

Rosie tried for a short laugh, but didn't succeed. "I think I've got bigger things to worry about, thanks very much."

"That's not what I meant."

"Doesn't Riley need you up north?" Rosie kept yanking out clothes and dropping them in the basket.

"Actually, that was kind of what I came to see you about."

"Going behind Riley's back now, are you?"

"No, this is about Riley." His voice was tight and angry.

"If you want advice about how to deal with him, I'm the last person to ask," she said.

"For Christ's sake, Rosie, something's going on. He thinks he's been compromised, that Helios might know where he's hiding."

Rosie stopped, a shirt clutched in one hand, and slowly turned to face him. "What?"

"He's not totally sure, but that doesn't matter. He said he's made plans – contingencies – but I can't get anything out of him about what that means."

Rosie swallowed a sudden flood of saliva. Was this her fault? Had she led them there that day when she'd burst in on him?

"What is it?" Pip came closer. "Do you know something? Has he told you?"

She shook her head. "No, but ..."

"But what?"

She dropped the shirt into the basket, not looking at him. "I don't know." She went back to pulling the last of the clothes from the machine.

"Rosie." He was behind her and his voice was hesitant,

hopeful. "He won't tell me, but he might tell you. If you ask him …"

He was so close, if she leaned back, she knew she'd feel his chest against her, his solid warmth. But he didn't want her, not like that, he'd made that pretty clear. A tight ball of pain formed inside her. He didn't want her, but he didn't mind asking her to do things for him. She threw a final bra into the basket and slammed the door closed then spun around. "This might come as a surprise to you, Pip, but he doesn't tell anyone much."

"I know, but this is different."

"And you expect me to find out? I'll just get right on that, shall I? But how will I tell you if I find anything, since I'm not in the Pip and Riley secret club?"

Pip went very still and a muscle twitched in his jaw. "I tried to tell you before, it's not like that."

"Really? You know what, it doesn't matter." She stepped around him to head for the door, but he was in front of her, blocking her way.

"Wait, will you? Can you just let me explain?"

"Fine, go ahead." He drew back, clearly not expecting her to say that. "I'm waiting," she said.

"It's not that easy." He swallowed and for the first time looked unsure.

"Good job." Rosie tried to push past, ramming him with the basket, but he grabbed it and held on.

"Let me finish, will you?"

"Can you?"

His face darkened. "The reason I asked Riley not to tell you I was in Newperth was to protect you. Helios will do almost anything to get at me. I didn't want you in the firing line. You're safer away from me."

"So, what are you doing here then? And by the way, I don't need protecting, thanks all the same. Dalton's been teaching me some great moves."

He blinked. Why had she said that? It had made it sound like, well … She felt heat spreading up her neck.

"Dalton?" Pip said.

"Yes, I think you've met." She tried to wrench the basket of clothes away but he wouldn't let go.

"You mean Dalton Curtis, Central pretty boy?"

She wasn't sure she liked the way he said that. "Yes, Dalton, and he said he knew you, by the way."

"We've met." He let go of the basket, his tone cool. "And he's been teaching you … moves?"

The way he said it made her neck even hotter. "Self-defence," she said. "In his gym."

Rosie saw a quick flash of what might have been hurt in his eyes, but it was quickly smoothed over and the cocky amused look he liked to wear came back. "He goes to the Academy too, I suppose." He smirked.

"He's doing the pilot course."

"Of course he is." He picked up his bag and slung it on his shoulder. "I just thought you should know what Riley said – you know, if you've got time between pretty boy and all your training to think about it."

"It's not like that." Rosie glared at him, but he just gave her a half-smile and turned to the door.

"Hey, I've got nothing against pretty boys – someone needs to buy the hair glitter. I've gotta go, got a corporation to bring down. Oh, and by the way ..." His smile turned glacial. "That stuff you said about me and the cure? I have been trying to make one. I haven't found a way yet, but I will. Just thought you'd like to know. Look out for the snipers."

Then he was gone and Rosie was left staring at the door swinging closed behind him.

CHAPTER 12

It was just after seven when Rosie and Aunt Essie left the apartment the next morning.

"You want to go to Fat Fareeks or The Bun Palace for breakfast?" Aunt Essie said.

"Wherever."

"Fine, Fareeks then. After, we'll go look for some new boots; mine are falling apart."

Rosie nodded. Essie was saying it for the benefit of any operatives, Senate or Helios, who were following them, because after breakfast they'd actually be heading to Riley's. By then they should have dumped the tails.

She shifted her bag strap from her shoulder to across her body, so the bag bounced against her hip, and shoved her com in her pocket. She'd told her aunt about Pip's visit and what he'd said about Riley, but they couldn't have left the apartment any earlier without raising suspicion. As a result, both of them were stupidly tense. Rosie was also confused and gutted that she'd accused Pip of not caring about a MalX cure when clearly he did. He'd told her that like he wanted to hurt her. Maybe he was jealous about Dalton. Could he be?

The thought tormented her as they spent two hours wending their way to Riley's via the bun place and seven shuttle changeovers plus a few detours. It was a route Aunt Essie had mapped out and it made good use of the confusing streets of the Rim and Sunday crowds.

Sunday was prime swap day and hordes of people were out towing carts of goods they could exchange with others for food, tech or – most highly prized – water. In front of practically every apartment rows of people hunkered down behind makeshift stalls, haggling loudly, getting into fights and blocking traffic. It was after nine when they finally got across the river on a boat that Aunt Essie occasionally used.

The day had turned blazing hot and sweat dripped off Rosie's nose as she followed her aunt up the cracked mud of the embankment. They'd been dropped in a shallow bay alongside the belt of scrub and trees that ran outside the wall of the estates. It was closer to Riley's and away from the surveillance, so they didn't need to use any idents. They ducked into the trees and reached the open swathe of ploughed ground fast, sprinting across it and into the estate.

Rosie couldn't shake off a growing feeling of unease as they crossed the deserted streets and was checking constantly over her shoulder.

They reached Riley's house and pushed through the weeds down the side. It looked the same, but something felt off. The broken statue was there, the back door, dust-covered as usual. "It feels empty," she said.

"Certainly does." Aunt Essie pulled a small pulse gun from a leg clutch under her pants and led the way.

They checked every room on the ground floor. Upstairs, Riley's operations room had been cleaned out. Pieces of holo deck were scattered across the floor along with disabled computer tablets. Shredded bits of paper that appeared singed were everywhere, and there was no sign of Riley.

Aunt Essie put her gun away and walked to the desk, parts crunching under her boots. "This is all too methodical."

"Riley did this." Rosie's throat tightened. "Aunt Essie—" Rosie stopped, pulled up short as a flashing light caught her attention. "What's that?" She stepped towards it. It was a tiny white light flashing under one of the ruined holo desks. Aunt Essie turned and followed her gaze.

"Get out!" Aunt Essie yelled.

Rosie flung herself back through the door and half-jumped, half-ran down the stairs, her aunt right behind her. They had almost reached the bottom when the bomb exploded. A massive force flung Rosie off her feet and into the doorframe. She screamed, but the sound of the explosion was so loud, she couldn't hear her voice. Objects fell on her, scraping, scratching, sharp short pains raining down on her back as she rolled, trying to protect her head with her arms. It lasted only a few seconds and she lay stunned, coughing from all the dust and smoke.

Aunt Essie grabbed her arm. Her face was streaked with blood and dust and she was shouting, but Rosie couldn't hear over the ringing in her ears. A lancing pain stabbed through the left side of her head. Essie pulled her to her feet, but something was dragging at her. Her bag was trapped under debris, the strap still on her shoulder. Rosie shook it off and they helped each other out of the house. The stink of burning was in the air and they almost fell down the back steps, turning to see the top storey on fire.

"The river," Aunt Essie rasped, and they ran to the scrub behind the house. All Rosie could think of was that if Riley had set that bomb, it meant he knew Helios was coming.

A hollow ringing still filled her ears, but now she caught the sound of heavy vehicles, then overhead the beat of blades. A helijet. They crashed through the shrubs and under the trees. Aunt Essie sagged against her, almost falling. Blood was dripping down one of her legs. Fear flooded Rosie and she stopped, but Aunt Essie shook her head, her face pinched with effort.

"Keep going." Aunt Essie pushed her forwards. Rosie held her up as best she could and shoved through the low prickly shrubs. The whump of the helijet was close. Her chest was tight with panic and she forced herself to focus. *Get to the river.* She could see it now, through the trees.

They staggered to the water's edge, the ache in Rosie's head intensifying with every step. A thick belt of reeds grew in the shallows and they crawled into them, their hands and knees sinking into the stinking muddy sand just as the helijet swooped over, its blades whirring, sending the reeds thrashing over their heads. Sharp pain cut through her skull and Rosie stifled a cry. She put her head in her hands, trying to press it out. The jet passed right over the top of them. She didn't dare look up. *Please don't let them be using any ground-scanning equipment.*

Ten seconds went past, but it felt more like a hundred as Rosie battled agonising pain. She couldn't remember anything hitting her that hard in the head. Dimly, she registered the sound of fire retardant being dumped on the house.

"Fire jet," Aunt Essie croaked. Rosie almost cried with relief. It was just an automated response jet. That didn't mean Helios wasn't around though. The pain in her skull subsided, dulling down to a throb, and she squinted at her aunt.

Essie lay curled up among the reeds. Her eyes were nearly closed, her breathing short. A piece of metal was embedded in one thigh. Rosie crawled over and inspected the wound.

"Leave the metal in," Aunt Essie said hoarsely. "Bleed like a bitch if you try to take it out."

"I'll try to stop the bleeding if I can." Rosie wiped her muddy, wet hands on her top, then stripped off her over shirt and tied it around her aunt's leg above the wound. The bleeding slowed but didn't totally stop.

"Don't panic," Aunt Essie said. "I've had worse."

The fear that was working its way up Rosie's throat was hard to swallow down. Her aunt might still be talking, but she was pale. They couldn't stay here.

"I'm going to have a look," she whispered. Rosie crouched, almost lying down, and began to slide back through the reeds towards the riverbank.

Her chin was just above the level of the water. It stunk of rotting weed, dirt and salt. Tiny insects buzzed around her face. She slithered between the reeds until she was close enough to see the estate through the stalks. She couldn't see the house but there was a thick drift of black smoke where it had been. There was no one on the immediate riverbank but there were people on the other side of the trees. Four. All in uniforms that looked like Senate. They had to be an estate security team here because of the fire. They weren't the only ones there though – three more people were melting

152

through the scrub line between the river and the house. The Senate guards were oblivious to them. They were all in black and she was one hundred per cent certain they were Helios. They looked like grunts, Pip's nickname for Helios's stimulant-enhanced, implant-weapon enabled, trained killers. Rosie very carefully retraced her steps. Her muscles were quivering by the time she made it back.

"Three," she whispered at her aunt's questioning look. She didn't bother to number the Senate guards.

"They'll have at least two more out front," Essie said. "We've got maybe five minutes. We need to move."

"I know." Hands shaking, Rosie pulled her com from her pocket. Aunt Essie made a noise and grabbed her hand in a surprisingly strong grip, her voice a harsh whisper.

"What're you doing? They'll find us!'

"It's okay. Riley fixed it so it can't be tracked."

She looked unconvinced. "You sure?"

"It's not like we've got many options." Rosie dialled up her com, hoping it hadn't run out of charge or been damaged. It hadn't and Dalton answered on the second tone.

"Pilot Girl." He grinned on the screen. "What—" His smile disappeared as he took in her mud- and blood-smeared face. "Are you okay?"

"No," Rosie whispered.

He looked alarmed. "Wait two seconds." A dizzying scene of blurring grass and trees whipped past the screen, then his face came back on. "Where are you?"

"In the river, in the reeds behind Riley's place." She took a breath. "Aunt Essie's hurt pretty bad. Riley's gone. He set a bomb for Helios. We got caught in it, and now we're stuck. There's a Senate fire crew and Helios operatives. Can you get a boat?"

"My dad has one. But Rosie, are you hurt?"

"Aunt Essie is. Can you bring a doctor, someone we can trust?"

He frowned. "I think so. But it's going to take me a while, and if there're operatives they'll see the boat."

"I know." Rosie glanced at her aunt. She was so damn pale. "I've got to find a way to get out without being seen."

"Can you walk about half a kilometre?"

"I hope so. Why?"

"You're near the edge of the old city," Dalton said. "There should be some ruins along the riverbank. You can use them for cover."

Of course. Rosie could have kicked herself for not remembering. The explosion must have really rattled her brain.

"I'll need about an hour," Dalton said. "The boat's called *Libertine*. It's white and has a five-pointed blue star in a circle on the prow. Do you know what a prow is?"

"I'm not a moron," Rosie said.

His smile was tight, worried. "Right. I'll be there as soon as I can. Hang on."

The screen went blank. Rosie looked at her aunt.

"I'm okay, kid," her aunt whispered. She held out a hand to her and Rosie took it. "Get my gun."

Rosie swallowed.

"I won't be able to use it and move. Get it out." She pushed Rosie's hand down towards her leg.

Rosie reached reluctantly into the shallow water and pulled the small pulse weapon out of its clutch. It was heavy. "It's all wet," she said.

"It'll still work. But we can't go out along the bank; we'll have to use the river." Aunt Essie gritted her teeth and hauled herself up to her good knee, then gestured for Rosie to go ahead. "Find a path through the reeds. I'll follow."

Rosie began to crawl towards the open water.

It was hard going. The reeds grew thickly, the roots tangling in the muddy bottom, threatening to trap hands and feet. The river got deeper quickly and soon they could no longer crawl and keep their heads above water. They staggered to their feet. Aunt Essie had started to shiver. She was swearing under her breath. Every second, Rosie expected to hear someone behind them, or feel the thud of a pulse in her back. The river stretched away to the opposite bank, wide and brown, sunlight glinting on the ripples. On the opposite bank the city was a humming mass of towers and shuttles, a beige-tinted haze hanging over it. There was about another thirty metres of reeds that would give them cover from the bank, but then it was open water until the old city. Aunt Essie had an arm around Rosie's shoulder and was on the river side while Rosie shuffled along, gun in her hand, against the reeds.

"Rosie," Essie whispered, "if I pass out, you leave me."

"Shut up." Rosie blinked. Her vision was wrong, blurry.

"Don't be so stubborn."

Rosie didn't answer. Why was her vision blurry? She heard a sudden high-pitched whine, like her eardrums had popped, and something flashed across her line of sight. Words. A map in glowing green. She stumbled and nearly pitched them both under the water.

Aunt Essie swore and Rosie struggled to regain her feet.

"I'm okay." Rosie shook her head and blinked.

"What happened?"

"I don't know. Nothing. Keep going." She tugged her aunt forwards. It was as if she'd been suddenly immersed in a virtual connection, but that was crazy. Must have been the bump on the head she didn't remember.

The water was deeper, the current swifter as they reached the end of the reeds. Rosie stashed the gun in her waistband and they clung together, letting the current wash them downriver. She kept an eye on the bank, terrified they'd be spotted. The scrub and trees were thicker the closer they got to the old city. Too many spots for a grunt to hide. The ache in her head returned, making her light-headed and nauseous.

Aunt Essie was shuddering by the time they got close to the first broken walls of the ruins, her breath coming in short forced bursts. Rosie estimated about half an hour had gone by since she'd spoken to Dalton. She had to get them out of the water. She began to drift closer to the bank. Spindly trees grew along the edge, casting spots of shadow across narrow bands of grey-sand beach edged by tufts of salt grass.

She was in the shallows, pulling Aunt Essie along behind her, when she saw him: a grunt, moving higher up against the tree line, his back to the water. He hadn't seen them. Yet. Rosie froze. Aunt Essie's saw him too and her hand clenched hard on Rosie's arm. Just a few metres further down the river was a narrow strip of sand with a broken wall that tumbled into the water. If they could get there, maybe they could hide against it. Rosie tilted her head towards it and her aunt nodded.

Slowly, slowly, they drifted further along, so low their noses were just above the water. The grunt was searching the scrub along the higher part of the bank, methodically moving along looking at the ground. *Please don't look up, please don't look up.* The words circled Rosie's brain. He didn't. They made it to the wall and crouched behind the crumbling brown bricks, hidden from the grunt on the bank. Relief washed over Rosie so hard, she was shaking. Beside her, Aunt Essie was hanging onto a protruding brick, her injured leg floating out straight, but she didn't look relieved. She was frowning and staring out across the river, towards the city. Rosie followed her gaze and saw the sleek white shape of a boat. A blue five-pointed circle was on the prow. At the same time she heard the thud of boots hitting sand and the snap of a twig. The grunt was on the beach on the other side of the wall. The spark of hope that had risen at the sight of the boat fled.

They heard the snick of a com and the grunt spoke. "Boat coming in. No sign of Shore, but Bree suspects the girl and her aunt were in the house. No sign of them either, but the boat looks suspicious. Orders?"

Terrified, Rosie looked at Aunt Essie. *How the hell?* Then she remembered. Her bag. She'd left it in the house.

A reply came clear through the grunt's com. "If the boat stops and they show, get rid of them. Kill the aunt, capture the girl. Bree is on her way. Out."

Rosie felt ill. She crouched in the water.

Gun, Aunt Essie mouthed. Rosie hesitated. *Gun*, her aunt mouthed again. She frowned and raised a hand towards her, then quickly jerked it back as she almost slipped underwater.

Rosie's hand shook as she pulled the weapon from her waistband, but her hand was steadier than her aunt's. There was no way Essie could fire the gun when she couldn't even keep upright. She set the pulse to stun. It should knock the grunt out.

Dalton's boat was close; he'd be here in minutes. Her insides felt light. Rosie drifted towards the lower part of the wall, keeping her back against it. Her heart hammered so fast she could barely breathe. She crouched in the water and curled both hands around the grip of the gun, listening. The thrum of the boat's motor came across the water. Insects buzzed in her face. And then she heard the sound of water sloshing against boots. He was so close. If she missed, it was all over. But it was like her legs were locked down. *Move, Rosie Black. If you don't do this, Essie and Dalton are dead.* Strangely, the voice in her head was Riley's.

She pinched her lips together, put a finger over the trigger, faced the wall and slowly rose up.

The grunt was three metres away, slightly turned from her, staring out across the water. But his peripheral vision was good and she was moving. He saw her and reached for his weapon.

He was ferociously quick, but Rosie already had her gun raised. She pulled the trigger and the pulse hit him square in the chest. He arched back, arms flung skywards. His weapon, still clutched in one hand, fired harmlessly at the sky. She stared, frozen, as he hit the sand, a deep gasp pushing out of him. His whole body spasmed, but he didn't stay down. He was rolling to his side, to his feet. Too late she remembered Helios grunts were armoured and jacked-up on enhancers. Rosie lunged over the rough wall and dived under the shallow water as a savage whump of pulse fire hit the wall where she'd been a moment before. Shards of brick rained down around her. Rosie launched to her feet and surfaced, spitting water, firing blindly. But he was behind her and grabbed her right arm, almost wrenching it from its socket. She screamed at the pain and dropped the gun as he flung her onto the beach. She hit the sand face first. A half-buried rotted branch spiked her cheek, drawing blood, but it barely registered as she rolled over in panic. He was already coming for her again and Rosie kicked out hard, getting him right in the groin.

He groaned and staggered. She kicked out again, aiming for his face, but he caught her boot and yanked her forwards, dragging her across the sand with a snarl before pinning her down. Fingers hard as steel curled around her throat.

"Calm down." He swatted aside her paltry attempts to pry him off with the butt of his gun. Pinpricks of light sparked in her vision and pain streaked through her skull. Rosie's eyes rolled. Choking, she saw past him along the beach to the water and registered a miracle: Aunt Essie on her knees, dragging herself from the river, picking up the gun Rosie had dropped. Time felt like it was slowing down. Rosie writhed, fighting for air as Aunt Essie raised herself unsteadily from the water, aimed and fired.

The pulse got the grunt in the back and conducted through him and into her like a million sparks scraping along her skin. His eyes widened and he jerked, arching back above her. He let her go, then collapsed onto his side, wheezing. Rosie tried to crawl away, but his hand lashed out and grabbed her foot, and he dragged her back. She could hear herself making weird whimpering noises as he pulled her against his chest and crossed his arms over her. His gun ended up near her face and she grabbed for it, panting, wrestling for control. But he was still much stronger.

"Stop struggling, little bitch," he said hoarsely in her ear. His breath was hot on her neck, stinking. Rosie bit down hard on his thumb. He yelled and lost his grip on his gun. Rosie grabbed it, turned the muzzle over her shoulder and pulled the trigger.

For a second the sound disorientated her. Her ears rang with a high-pitched squeal, his arms went slack and she lunged away, her breath coming in gasping sobs, her throat burning. She saw Aunt Essie lying on the sand, not moving, and crawled to her without looking back. The heavy gun was still in her hand; it dragged over the sand. Blood was dripping from Essie's leg, but when Rosie touched trembling fingers to her aunt's neck she felt her pulse, thready but there. She was still alive.

Then she looked back.

The grunt had stopped moving for good. There was a black singed hole where his eye had been and slivers of glistening white bone. She stared. He didn't look real.

The rumble of the boat engine was louder and she turned to see it close to shore. Dalton dropped over the side and ran towards her.

"Rosie—" He slowed as he saw the grunt.

She got to her feet. Something felt like it was trying to crawl out of her throat. She swallowed it back down. "There's another one coming," she said. "They know you're here. We have to go now."

He was looking at her weirdly. "Can you get to the boat?"

Why was he asking her stupid questions? "Just get Aunt Essie." She stepped into the river. An odd numbness was rolling over her and time wasn't quite moving right. She reached the boat and Dalton was suddenly back and lifting her aunt up to another man who was waiting on the narrow dive platform at the back. He carried Aunt Essie inside the cabin.

Dalton turned to her. "Give me the gun."

"No." She shoved it in the waistband of her pants and climbed aboard.

The other man had Essie laid out on a long couch in the cabin and was checking her wound. Rosie stood dripping and staring at the barely perceptible rise and fall of Essie's chest. Why wasn't she more worried? She didn't seem to feel much at all. She barely noticed Dalton go past her to the bridge. The boat's engines revved with a deep rumble and they were peeling away from the shore. She staggered with the motion, falling down on another couch. Through the tinted windows she saw the dark speck of the grunt's body on the beach. Sweat broke out on her forehead and her stomach heaved. Rosie lunged for the door. She shoved it open, rushed to the side and threw up. Shuddering, shaking so hard it seemed her bones would crack, she vomited again and again until it felt like there was nothing left inside.

CHAPTER 13

She woke the next morning back in Dalton's beach house. Her mouth was dry and tasted foul and she was wearing only her underpants. She vaguely remembered getting here, the doctor bringing her aunt inside and Dalton's worried gaze. She sat up slowly and squinted out the window. The sun was high outside. A dull throbbing pain pulsed in the back of her skull and everything ached. There was no sign of her clothes, but her com was on the table by the bed. She picked it up. Totally dead. Next to the com was the grunt's gun.

She went to the bathroom, throwing her underwear in the cleaner.

The shower stung the cuts on her back and arms and when she got out and looked in the mirror, she was shocked at what she saw. Her face was pale with dark circles under her eyes, the freckles scattered across her cheekbones standing out in sharp relief. Red fingerprint-shaped marks dotted her neck.

I killed a man. The thought was in her head before she could lock it out. All the saliva in her mouth dried up and she sat heavily on the closed lid of the toilet, battling the urge to vomit again. She wrapped a towel tightly around herself and stared at the dark tiled floor. *Don't think about it. Not yet. You couldn't help it.* She tried to focus on Aunt Essie, on Riley, on anything else. She listened to the drone of the cleaning unit working on her underwear. After a minute she was able to get up.

She hunted through the room for her clothes, but found nothing, so she went to the kitchen still wrapped in the towel.

Dalton was sitting alone at the table with a cup in front of him. He got up as she came in.

"Hey, how you feeling?"

"Naked. Have you got any pain blockers?"

"Um, yeah, somewhere." He moved quickly, pulling open drawers and rattling things around.

The rattling made her head throb and she sat down in the chair he'd vacated.

"You passed out on the way back," Dalton said. "Had to carry you in. You don't remember?"

Rosie shook her head. His cup was full of tea and she took a sip. It was still warm and heavily sugared.

Dalton returned with pills and water.

She swallowed two. "Where're my clothes?"

"I'll get them. The doctor took them off, not me, in case you were wondering. He wanted to make sure you were okay."

Rosie shrugged. After everything that had happened, Dalton seeing her without her clothes seemed insignificant. She didn't care one way or the other, which was a bit weird because normally she would. She took another swallow of his tea. "Can I have this?"

"Yeah, I made it for you when I heard the shower." He sat down across from her. "Doc left instructions that you'd need sugar. I said you were sweet enough, but ..." Rosie gave him a blank look. The faint smile he'd been attempting faded quickly. "Are you okay? You're all cut up and—"

"Where's Aunt Essie?"

"In the room next to yours. The doctor took the metal out and patched her up."

Rosie got up. "Can I have my clothes? I want to see her."

"She's on a knockout drip; she won't be awake."

"I don't care."

"Sure thing, Pilot Girl." He got to his feet.

"Stop calling me that." Rosie knew her tone was curt, but the nickname was suddenly grating.

"Hey, sorry." He looked wary. "I'll get your clothes. Just, um, go see your aunt." He went for the door and

Rosie felt terrible. He'd rescued her, even made her tea and here she was snapping at him.

"Wait–" She paused as he turned back. She felt tongue-tied and her head was killing her. "Um, thanks for coming to get us yesterday, and for bringing the doctor. For everything."

"Yeah, no problem." His smile was hesitant though. "So Riley's really gone?"

"Looks like."

He exhaled softly and tapped a fist on the doorframe. "Go see your aunt. I'll bring your clothes in. Then we've got to talk."

Aunt Essie was still asleep like Dalton said. She seemed very small and pale in the large bed. A drip was connected to her arm and a medibot in the corner beeped, tracking her heartbeat. Rosie eyed it suspiciously as she approached the bed. It scared her how close she'd come to losing Aunt Essie again. She put her hand in her aunt's. It was cool, limp.

Rosie felt lost. Riley was gone, her aunt injured. They weren't safe. Not any more. But she didn't know what to do. She couldn't just sit around waiting for Essie to wake up. Eventually, Helios would find them. God knew where Riley had gone. She couldn't believe he'd just skipped out on them without leaving any clues behind.

She put her aunt's cold hand to her forehead and took in a long unsteady breath. There was a knock on the door and Dalton poked his head in, holding her clothes.

"Here." He tossed them on the bed. "I'll be in the kitchen."

Rosie slipped into her now-clean clothes. Her tank top had tiny holes peppered across the back and one of her pants' side pockets was ripped down the seam.

When she went back to the kitchen, Dalton was stirring something in a large white bowl.

"I made you some soup with beef," he said. "Sit down. And don't argue – doctor's orders." She didn't think she could eat anything. But Dalton's stern expression made her swallow her protest and she sat.

He put the bowl in front of her and she was immediately assaulted by a rich meaty aroma. Her mouth watered and she took a hesitant spoonful. It stayed down. She was suddenly starving. She'd had real beef only once before, at an Orbitcorp party her aunt had been invited to, and the reaction of her body to high-quality protein was intense. She finished the bowl in a few minutes flat.

"Want some more?" Dalton said, one eyebrow raised.

Her stomach gurgled. "Better not. Do you get meat like that often?"

"Often enough." He seemed embarrassed.

Rosie rubbed the side of her head. It was still throbbing, despite the pain blockers.

"So what about that doctor," she said. "Is he … will he keep his mouth shut?"

"He's paid enough never to mention anything he does for us. Ever."

Rosie found it hard to believe there was enough money in the world to stop anyone talking to Helios if they came looking.

"Dalton?" She leaned towards him. "Are you sure he's safe? You said before you were worried about your dad being part of Helios."

Everything about his posture screamed a reluctance to answer. "My dad doesn't know about him." Dalton stared at the tabletop. "He's my mother's doctor. That's all he does – works for her. He would never say a word about any of it."

"Your mum?"

Dalton nodded. "He basically keeps her alive. She's addicted to …" He flicked open a palm, his mouth twisting. "Well, just about everything. Has been for the last eight years."

Rosie didn't know what to say but he didn't seem to expect anything. A terrible sadness was in his eyes as he glanced at her then away.

"Hey, are you okay?" Rosie felt a twinge of worry. She'd never seen him like this before.

He sighed. His voice was unsteady as he said, "I, um … I used to have an older brother. He died." He stopped, swallowed. "She …"

"She wanted to forget," Rosie said quietly.

"Something like that."

Rosie knew how that felt. "How did he die? If you want to tell me; you don't have to."

"No, I think you of all people would understand," he said bleakly. "It was the MalX."

"Oh," Rosie whispered. He was standing close enough that she could touch him and without thinking about it she took his hand. Pain tightened his features.

"It wasn't meant to happen," he said. "My father. He has this way he thinks his sons should be. Chris wouldn't fall in line. It wasn't even—" His mouth tightened. "They used to argue, all the time, about how the Bankers, the Rims, even the Ferals got to be where they are. Chris was all about the company doing things to help them and Dad, well—" He made a bitter noise. "I think you can guess what he thought."

"What happened?" Rosie said.

Dalton shrugged. "An argument got too heated, so Dad thought he'd teach Chris a lesson. He had his boys take Chris out to the old city, where the Ferals live, and left him there. Dumped him out of a boat without any protection. Nothing. Of course Dad says he didn't know the mozzies hadn't been sprayed there yet, but ..."

"You don't believe him?" Rosie said.

Dalton looked down at their hands. He brushed his index finger against hers. "I don't know," he said quietly. "I want to. Chris caught the MalX there. I can't believe

171

Dad would—" He stopped.

"I'm sorry," Rosie said.

"It's not your fault."

"I know, but—"

"It's his fault." His face hardened. "And if it turns out he really is in with Helios ... then he knew about the MalX, didn't he? He might have even been involved in making it."

Rosie understood now what drove him, why he was here, and it made her sad, because she knew how it felt to lose someone to that terrible disease.

When her mum had died—

Her train of thought was suddenly cut off as agonising pain slashed through her skull. She gasped, almost falling off her chair.

"Rosie!" Dalton grabbed her. He sounded panicked. Consumed by pain, Rosie clutched her head. Then suddenly she saw the words, again in green, a map, and more words, splicing the blackness of her closed lids. She froze, eyes tightly closed as she struggled to make sense of it.

Don't ... Rosie ... backup ... of ... disa ... rance ... Nation tech ... decod ... alive ... iley.

The pain blinked off like a light. There was a sharp, high-pitched whine then everything went black.

She came to on the floor. Her head was in Dalton's lap and he was calling her name, his hands cradling her face.

"Rosie!"

"Okay, okay, I'm awake." She blinked, trying to focus.

Dalton looked terrified. "Christ, you scared the crap out of me! You just dropped."

"Yeah, well, good catch." She pushed his hands away and tried to sit up, but a wave of dizziness made the room tilt and she pitched sideways.

"Whoa." Dalton caught her and lifted her back up and onto the chair. "You going to stay upright?"

"Yeah, I'm fine. Stop hovering."

He complied only as far as letting go of her. "What the hell happened?"

"I ..." Rosie wondered if she was going to sound crazy. "I saw words behind my eyelids."

"Words?" Dalton's eyebrows rose so high they almost met his fringe.

"I know it sounds nuts, but it was ..." She glanced around the kitchen. "Have you got something I can write on?"

He went to one of the kitchen drawers and came back with a tablet. Rosie powered it up. She was beginning to get an idea of what might have happened and she didn't like it. Not one bit. She typed up the line of disjointed text she'd seen and showed it to Dalton, watching as he read it over, his lips slightly parted and a frown between his eyes.

"Don't … Rosie … backup … of … disa … rance … Nation tech … decod … alive … iley. That last word looks like Riley," he said.

"Yeah, it does." She rubbed her eyes. They felt gritty and sore, like she'd been up all night playing virtual games. "He put an implant in me when he was here the other night. He *said* it was just a tracking device in case Helios took me from Senate Prime."

"You think it's something else, like a cortex implant?"

"It would explain why I see words when my eyes are closed." Rosie could hardly believe Riley would have done this without telling her. A cortex implant was serious tech. It was the most secure way to store information because it was stashed in the one place most people couldn't get at – inside your skull. The only way to access it was by knowing the activation code – which she didn't – or by using the kind of sophisticated tech only Helios or the Senate would have. Or Gondwana Nation.

"But if it is a cortex, it shouldn't produce garbled information," Dalton said.

"Maybe the explosion at Riley's did something to it. Besides, I don't know the activation code, so why am I seeing anything?"

Dalton thoughtfully slapped the tablet on his palm. "One of the words is backup and another one looks a hell of a lot like it could be disappearance. Could Riley have set it up to activate if he took off?"

It was the kind of thing he might do. Rosie put an elbow on the table and rested her forehead in her hand. Had Riley put a whole lot of stuff in her brain?

"Hey," Dalton said, "there's a basic scanner on the medibot in with your aunt."

Rosie raised her head. "Good idea." She got up so fast Dalton put his hands out to her in alarm.

"I'm fine." She grabbed his hand, tugging him after her to the hallway.

The medibot was still in the corner. Swallowing her nervousness, Rosie flipped open its lower storage unit, searching for the scan wand. She sat at the foot of her aunt's bed trying to stay as still as possible while Dalton ran it slowly over her skull. A bio map of her brain appeared on its screen.

"There it is," he said. Rosie tried to see it from the corner of her eye. There was a tiny dark spot floating near her visual cortex along the optic nerve.

"Switch on the nano detector. See if it picks up any residue."

The machine's pitch changed as Dalton worked the controls. Rosie could barely breathe as she waited. Finally, he said, "It's not picking up much, but the nanos are definitely not tracking builders. They're way too complex for that. And it's one complicated sucker, with big storage capacity."

"Okay, turn it off." Rosie pushed the wand away.

"How much do you want to guess that I'm Riley's new backup?"

Dalton was still holding the wand. He was a long way from happy. "You know the thing with those cortex implants, don't you?"

Rosie got off the bed. "Yeah, they're permanent. Till death do us part." She left the room before he could answer.

She went back to the kitchen and stood staring out through the generated glass at the ocean. Everything was falling apart and she kept getting the feeling it was up to her to fix it. Thoughts, bad, guilty thoughts circled through her brain. How had it all come to this?

Dalton followed her in. She watched him in the wavering reflection.

"We have to come up with a plan," she said.

"What do you suggest?" He didn't sound enthusiastic.

Rosie faced him. "I think Riley was going to make a trip north, to check out the base. Maybe that's where he's gone."

"You think we should go up there?"

"We can't stay here. If Helios found him, they'll definitely find me. And if he has gone there, we can find him, help him."

"Help him do what?"

"I don't know!" Rosie threw up her hands. "But he must have put this stuff in my head for a reason. And Nation could have machines that can read it, figure it out. He might have even left more instructions on it for me – for us."

"You do know you can't just walk into Gondwana Nation."

"I'm not just going to sit here and wait for them to find me." She went to the table and picked up the tablet. "It says Nation on here. I'd bet that he's telling me to get up there."

He didn't say anything.

She dropped the tablet on the table. "I'm going."

"Alone?"

"You can't stop me."

"The hell I can't."

Anger flickered in her now. She didn't really want to go on her own, but she was damned if he was going to tell her what to do.

"Dalton, the best place to hide from Helios or the Senate is the Nation lands. It's big and they have their own rules. No one messes with them."

"Then how is Helios up there in the first place?"

"I don't know. No one does, except maybe Riley. Hell, we don't even know who really runs Helios, but that's what we need to find out, and maybe going north will help."

Dalton was silent for a moment and Rosie began to wish Pip was here. He would have agreed to go north straightaway, probably would have suggested it first. But he wasn't here. And she had to admit he would never have made her tea.

"Come with me," Rosie pressed him. "You have resources I don't have."

"You mean money," he said flatly.

"No, not just money, and I have some of my own, thanks." She took a step towards him. "You know how to fight, if we run into trouble." *And I'm scared out of my wits.* But she couldn't say that — it sounded needy, weak and too close to the truth. Right now, Dalton was the only friend she had.

"And how do we find our way up there?" he said.

Thank God. Rosie let out the breath she'd been holding. "There's a girl I've met before, Sharia — she delivered the message from Cassie. If I can get hold of her, I can get her to meet us. Hopefully, she can contact whoever she gets her info from and tell them we need help getting into Gondwana." She thought for a moment. "The Game Pit would be a good place. It's this bar in the Rim that Pip used to go to. The last time I was there it had total surveillance protection."

"It's a start." He ran a hand through his hair, leaving it ruffled. Rosie realised for the first time just how tired he looked.

"Thanks," she said awkwardly.

"You didn't really think I'd let you go alone, did you?" He gave her a slow, warm smile. "What kind of a Prince Charming would I be if I let Cinderella face the evil empire by herself? Seriously, I'd lose all my prince points."

Something inside Rosie fluttered ever so slightly at that smile. She took a long breath and pretended not to notice. "So what're we going to do about Aunt Essie?"

CHAPTER 14

Something liquid was dripping unseen on the other side of the thin wall and there was only one window, but the room was clean, dust free and smelled faintly of lemon antiseptic.

"Bath water warm, just the way I like it," Aunt Essie said.

Rosie gave her a tight smile as a young guy named Hadi laid her carefully on the single bed. He was the son of one of Riley's contacts, a tech specialist named Sun. Dalton had worked with her once, getting some gear from the Asiatic States, and luckily she was open to receiving a generous commission to look after Aunt Essie until they got back. She'd picked them up that morning in a delivery transport. They'd taken only a day to organise everything and Rosie prayed they hadn't forgotten anything vital, but every extra hour they spent in Newperth gave Helios more time to find them.

Hadi's hair was dyed bright blue and orange and styled into a Mohawk. "She should be fine," he said. "The doctor will come by this afternoon."

Aunt Essie's smile was sardonic. "Yes, she will be fine, cockatoo boy, no thanks to your bedside manner."

"All part of the service." Hadi grinned.

"We better get going," Dalton said from the door.

Rosie took her aunt's hand. Thin tendrils of red traced a spider web of short lines up her thigh. Hiding in the swampy dirt at the edge of the river had caused a bad infection.

"Stop looking so worried." Aunt Essie tightened her grip on Rosie's hand. "I can still do some damage if anyone tries anything, and you know I've had worse."

Rosie tried for a smile but failed. "I hate leaving you here."

"Just keep your head down. Once I get on my feet, we'll figure out what to do."

Rosie nodded, too worried she'd betray herself if she spoke. They had agreed not to tell her aunt where they were going. Rosie knew Essie'd flip and try to stop her if she found out, and she didn't want her worrying. Instead, she told her Dalton was taking her to another safe house he owned. She kissed her aunt's hot cheek.

"We'll see you soon," she said. "Get better."

"I'm tougher than the bug." Aunt Essie squeezed her shoulder. "Now take off. Pretty boy looks anxious. He'll get wrinkles if you make him wait any longer. Be no use to anyone then."

Rosie tried not to look back as she left the room.

"How long till Sharia's at the Pit?" Dalton asked as they jogged down a narrow back staircase.

"Hopefully, ten minutes. She should beat us there."

"If she turns up," Dalton said.

Rosie had spent half the previous night trying to contact Sharia using Dalton's com. Sharia had been none too impressed to hear from her, but had agreed to meet them in the Game Pit. It was the only place Rosie could think of that was totally under the radar. She had resisted telling her too much, making a point of not mentioning Riley. It was guaranteed Helios had every detectable signal watching for a mention of him. She just told Sharia she had a job for her and gave her a time. It was usually Riley who set these things up so hopefully the girl wouldn't get cold feet and be a no-show.

She pushed open the door and headed out into the alley behind the apartment. The stink of the Banks rose like a familiar ghost: dried seaweed, dank, salty river water and the pervading aroma of too many people living too close together. After some heavy charm on Dalton's behalf – and a heap of credit – Sun had grudgingly sold them two bio bikes. They were parked against the wall and it was almost impossible to see them with the camouflage sensors fading them into the dirty brickwork.

Rosie pressed the remote in her pocket and the bikes shimmered into view.

They were sleek, powerful machines, covered by a bio-controlled "skin". The handlebars were set low behind a curved shield, the driver's body supported by a self-moulding hub that flowed into the double seat. When she swung her leg over the bike, the skin expanded to form a protective cover around her legs that would expand further if the bike tipped. The controls were very similar to a spaceship and Dalton only had to show her a few of them before she understood how it worked.

"Easy." She swiped her thumb over the ignition. The bike vibrated beneath her and Dalton handed her a helmet. The air immediately smelled better with the helmet on as the air-purifying system kicked in.

"Ready?" She glanced at him. He stowed the bag with the supplies under his seat. Pain blockers, UV and MalX-shielding spray, flat packs of self-heating meals and two bottles of water were all they had. Hopefully, Dalton's credit would buy them whatever else they needed.

"You lead; you know the way." His voice sounded very close through the helmet com.

Rosie released the stabilising brake and let the bike coast to the street.

She took the most random way she could think of. Off the main access roads, the Banks was a warren of narrow, winding streets, many not much more than connecting alleys between apartment blocks and the myriad of illegal shops and debt houses that littered the whole area. Hadi had scrambled Dalton's com so it couldn't be tracked, but she didn't want to take any chances. She'd already noticed two helijets buzzing overhead, high enough to guess they weren't looking for anything or anyone in particular, but she kept to the narrow alleys anyhow, since they gave them some cover.

She headed down a particularly decrepit alley. Flags hung above their heads on lines slung between the buildings' upper floors and straggly groups of people shuffled along either side of the road. This was refugee central. Faces in all hues, from pale dirty white to darkest of the dark stared down at them from doorways and windows.

She shifted and felt the grunt's pulse gun press against her ribs. It was verging on too big for her. Dalton had offered to swap her for the smaller weapon he carried, but she wouldn't let him for reasons she didn't want to explore. She forced her hands to relax on the handlebars and blinked hard, trying to get some moisture in her eyes.

She hadn't slept much. Dreams, nightmares. She'd got up around three and wandered around for a while in the dark. Bored and too afraid to go back to sleep, she'd been poking around and found a few threads of stimulants in a bathroom. They were the good ones, chewable sticks thin as wire. Probably belonged to Dalton's mother. Normally, she would never touch the stuff. Stims weren't illegal but they were for overachievers or gamers who wanted to stay up for days to win tournaments – and they were way beyond her price range. But now … She'd taken some this morning and had stowed the rest in her bra, just in case. They worked too: she felt alert. *Slippery slope, Rosie.* She could almost hear her aunt's voice in her head, but blocked it out. It wasn't like she was going to turn into an addict.

The alley ended and she swerved right, joining a wider road. There were more cars now, plus a lot of bikes. The road led to a main artery not far ahead. She glanced at her rear view in the control screen. Dalton was right behind her.

"The South-West Artery is coming up," she said. "Remember to block the link."

"No problem." He revved his bike up next to her. The Artery, like most major roads, had an AI control function. All vehicles, apart from official transports, were automatically set to link into the mainframe traffic control. The AI took over the driving, ensuring almost zero chance of a crash. The auto link on bio bikes could be bypassed if you had the tech to do it, which Dalton had. It was one of the main reasons he had insisted they get the bikes. Now Rosie flicked the switch he'd jimmied into the controls to block the AI as they sped up and joined the feeder lane. On the Artery, speeds could reach over

200 kilometres per hour. Other bikes and cars hummed past. The road widened, spreading to four lanes, then to ten. On either side of them the buildings became bigger as they left the Banks, morphing into super high-rise blocks. The bike seemed to fly above the road and Rosie pushed it faster, enjoying the sensation of speed.

It was a strange feeling. The air in her helmet was cool, recycled by the filters, but the rest of her was hot from the sun beating down on the jacket Dalton had found for her. Looking at the road through the helmet's screen made her feel as if she were flying a ship.

"Rosie," Dalton said. "Behind us."

Rosie took her eyes briefly off the back of a hover truck and glanced at the view screen.

"What?" All she saw was traffic.

"Not on the road."

Rosie looked again and her insides did a three-sixty. A helijet, big and black, was keeping pace with the traffic about a half a kilometre behind them.

"It could be a random patrol," she said.

"I can't see any Senate markings."

"Our exit isn't far." Rosie tried to keep calm. If there weren't Senate markings, it could be Helios. But how would they have found them? "Let's get to the outer lane."

"Easier said," Dalton replied. There were four very busy lanes between them and that lane.

"Call up the road grid and chart a program for the exit," she said.

Rosie flicked another glance at the jet. Its position hadn't changed. Maybe it was just some rich suit. She hit the control on her screen, directing the bike to the exit. The sensor that judged safe distances between the vehicles around her came up with red lines all over it. No safe distances. She swore. The exit command wouldn't take.

Dalton was having the same problem. "Won't do it." He revved up alongside her.

"We'll have to go manual. You ready?"

She couldn't read his reaction through the reflective helmet, but she heard a grin in his voice when he answered. "Anything you say, Pilot Girl."

They would just have to go for it. A line of screaming bikes revved past on her right like enormous mozzies, followed by a huge transport that shuddered her bike's frame as the stabilisers fought the velocity of its slipstream. A minute space opened up between two transports in the next lane.

"Now!" she said and angled into the gap.

She wasn't sure if Dalton had followed her or not, but she didn't have time to check as the brakes of the transport behind screamed. She was too close. Her bike's screen went black and the auto collision kicked in, ripping the control from her and swerving the bike into the next lane. Goddamn it! Rosie switched it off.

"Careful!" Dalton shouted, but all her attention was focused on the traffic. The ripping whine of wheels and thunder of thermal engines surrounded her. The other vehicles on the road were a blur of shimmering metal. She lay even lower over the handlebars, swaying with the bike as she gunned the motor. The speed bars spiked to 240 kilometres an hour and she swerved across the next two lanes, scraping between a six-wheeled private car and a group of five bikes.

Her heart was pounding, adrenaline making everything clear-cut and diamond-edged. She glimpsed a pale face staring at her through the window of the car as she passed it. It was as if she could see the girl's pores. One lane to go. It was an easy swerve into it. High walls rose up on the city side of the outer lane, blocking her view of all but the taller buildings. She cruised along behind a line of transports and Dalton came up beside her.

"Helijet." His voice burst through her com again.

"Where is it?"

"Look up." It was a black silhouette against the sky, high up above them now. "Exit's ahead."

The outer lane was congested and they were locked in between transports in front and a line of solar cars behind. A huge sign in the air ahead of them announced the exit to the West Rim in five hundred metres. Rosie and Dalton rode closer together as the traffic merged into three exit lanes and they flowed off the Artery in a river of engines and wheels, slowing down as they joined the main road that ran through the Rim.

The western side of the Rim, like the east side where Rosie lived, was home to those who had just enough credit to escape the MalX-infected river areas. It was also the home of the gangs and, as they cruised down the wide boulevard, the signs of them were everywhere. Logos rendered in holo revolved above the more affluent-looking buildings and lines of the combat-style bikes the gangs favoured were parked in front.

The sidewalks were crowded with vendors and customers, and solar bike messengers weaved in and out of the mass. The stink of the Rim's bio oil generators was so strong it infiltrated Rosie's helmet, a mixture of rancid cooking oil and frying meat. It made her nauseous.

"Next right." She turned down a side street, almost running over a pedestrian who decided to cross in front of her at the last moment. The bike's brakes gushed air and the man screamed obscenities at her back, but she kept going. It was a bad idea to stop here. The Game Pit was south of the Artery, towards the river. The roads became narrower and dimmer, the sunlight blocked by the high-rises, and they seemed to have lost the jet.

They turned down another even narrower street that was deserted apart from a man carrying a gun the size of a small child. He watched them ride past with the disinterested stare of someone contemplating if it was worth his time killing them for their bikes.

"How far?" Dalton's voice had a hard edge. He was riding one-handed, the other resting on his thigh in grasping distance of the gun under his jacket.

"A few blocks," she replied. "Don't let anyone see the gun," she added quietly.

"Don't worry about me."

She angled left out of the creepy street, glad to leave it. A few minutes more and the Game Pit was in sight. Still dirty, still almost hidden behind a jutting wall, it looked the same as ever. They parked their bikes up against the wall. It was very quiet and the door was firmly closed. There were also four round metal discs, like hatches, set in the front wall that hadn't been there before. Rosie pulled off her helmet and glanced at Dalton. He was just as uneasy as her.

"Let's–" She didn't get to finish as the black helijet suddenly swooped over the high-rises.

"This is the Senate guard. Stay where you are." A voice boomed from the jet, bouncing off the walls. Three cables snaked down and figures dressed in black began descending to the street.

Rosie dropped her helmet and ran for the door. Dalton reached it first, but before he could open it, it was flung wide and they almost collided with a huge black man carrying a rocket launcher.

"Down!" he shouted. Rosie and Dalton dropped as a stream of blue shot from it with the sound of thunder. The pulse grenade hit the jet's shield with enough concussive force to shake the ground. Shouts to take cover came from the men who'd dropped from the jet and Rosie scrambled to her knees and crawled to the open door. A stream of bullets peppered the wall above her head. Dust and plaster shards spat down and she heard Dalton swearing. The man from the Pit fired another burst of energy, then he grabbed her by the waistband and threw her through the doorway. She cannoned into the stair rail head first. Dalton leaped in after, followed by the man with the gun, who slammed the steel door shut behind him and bolted it. The thud of pressure bullets hitting the outside rang against the metal.

"Are you okay?" Dalton helped her up.

Dizzy, head aching, she dabbed at blood trickling from a cut above her eye.

"Rosie!"

She knew that voice. Pip was staring at her, halfway up the short flight of stairs that led to the Pit's main bar. He looked furious. She didn't have time to be surprised. The man with the gun shoved her and Dalton towards Pip.

"Your goddamn girl brought the Senate to my door," he shouted.

"They're not Senate." Pip caught her as she stumbled into him. Her nose cracked painfully against his shoulder but she barely had time to find her feet before another spurt of fire hit the Pit door.

"Move," Dalton shouted. Pip half-carried her down the stairs while the man with the gun leaped over the low balustrade. The door buckled under the assault, but held.

In a brief glance Rosie saw the Pit had changed since

she'd last been here. The grungy old game pods were still there, but gang colours now hung over the bar, the gold and purple emblem of the Principality. They practically owned the Banks.

Half-a-dozen hard-looking men and women were pulling out weapons and the man with the gun was shouting out for backup and reaching over the bar to pull out another long-handled gun. Five more men came running from a back hallway, all carrying huge guns, Principality emblems tattooed on their bare arms. Pip, Rosie and Dalton were forced to retreat among the tables as they ran past.

"Come on!" Pip pushed her towards the bar.

"What are you doing here?" Rosie said as the men began shooting through the hatches.

"How do you know they're not Senate?" Dalton shouted over the top of the gunfire.

"Didn't you see their weapons?" Pip grabbed Rosie's hand and pulled her down behind the wide bar.

"We didn't exactly have time."

"Helios issue." Pip peered over the top of the bar. "They're just using the Senate name for cover. Oh, and by the way–" He flicked open Rosie's jacket to expose the gun holster. "Where did you get that?"

"Don't." Her insides lurched and she pulled her jacket closed.

He raised an eyebrow at her. "Touchy."

"What the hell are you doing here?" Dalton said.

"Curtis, right? Good to see you too." Pip didn't look fazed. "Sharia called me. Who do you think she gets her info from?"

"Where is she?" Rosie said.

"She never showed." He frowned then, looking more closely at her, or more particularly at her neck. "What happened? What are those marks?" He reached forwards as if to touch them but she caught his fingers before he could.

"It's nothing. Don't worry about it now." She pushed his hand back and flicked her hair over her collar to hide the marks.

He gazed at her as if he was going to pursue it, but only said, "How the hell did Helios find you, anyway?"

Rosie exchanged a worried glance with Dalton. "I–" Gunfire thudded against the building and they all flinched.

"It doesn't matter." Pip glanced over the bar again. "We've gotta get out of here."

"Do you know another way out?" she said.

He grinned. "Who do you think you're talking to? Follow me." He grabbed her hand and ran towards a back hallway.

CHAPTER 15

He led them to a small dusty room filled with broken furniture and computer parts. From behind them came gunshots and there was a heavy pounding that sounded like someone trying to batter down the back door at the end of the hall.

"There's a hatch somewhere in the floor," Pip said. He pushed aside bits of broken table, flinging them against the wall. Dalton joined him and Rosie scanned the floor. There was a thin sheet of metal to the right of the door.

"Pip!" She grabbed at the edge of it, scraping the skin off her fingers, and dragged it aside. Underneath was a neat square cut in the floor. She ran her fingers over it, looking for some kind of mechanism.

"On the side." Pip fell to his knees beside her and pressed a faint indent. There was a scraping sound, then the square dropped a few centimetres and slid away with a hydraulic hiss to reveal a metal ladder.

"I'll go first," Dalton said.

It was pitch-black in the hole and Rosie's heart was racing as she watched Dalton descending. He was only a few steps down when a massive boom shook the building. The floor shuddered and a pile of stacked furniture crashed over. But worse was the sound of something hard and metallic skidding along the floor of the hall. The back door.

"Give me your gun." Pip flicked open her jacket and snatched it from her holster before she could react, then pushed her down. "Go!" He stood guard as she braced her feet on the ladder's sides and slid down. The skin on her palms burned and rough edges ripped cuts in her fingers. After about three metres she hit the ground, splashing into a puddle. She moved out of the way fast as Pip came sliding down after her, pulling the hatch shut behind him.

It was completely dark. Rosie felt the familiar suffocating fear leap up in her breast and she instinctively shrank backwards, bumping into Pip's chest. Suddenly, a flat white light came on.

"Always carry a torch," Dalton said.

"I know someone else who should," Pip said near Rosie's ear.

Her stomach flipped, but she ignored him. "Which way?"

The tunnel ran off for about twenty metres both in front and behind them, ending at junctions.

Pip shook his head. "I just knew this was here, not how to navigate it."

Dalton's face was bathed in a soft green light as he activated a nav system on his wrist. "The river's that direction." He pointed right.

"Good as any." Pip took off.

Rosie had no idea what else this tunnel had been used for, but the stench was a cross between sewerage and decaying rodents, and some kind of greenish sludge was oozing from between the crete wall slabs.

They ran as quietly as they could, straining to hear any sounds of pursuit. Their footsteps sounded way too loud, echoing in the damp tunnel.

"Wait." Dalton stopped. "Listen."

They stood close together, trying to breathe as quietly as possible. Then they heard it: a faint splashing sound, like boots hitting a puddle. More than one pair. A beam of blue light hit the corner they'd just come around.

"Trackers," Pip whispered.

They fled as fast as they could, the light from the torch bouncing off the walls as they ran. There was no point in trying to be quiet; it was so dark the operatives would have seen their torchlight the moment they got in the tunnel. A second later a voice shouted, "Stop or we fire."

Dalton snapped off his torch. Darkness swallowed them. Fear and adrenaline pumped through Rosie. Dalton was just in front, Pip behind. All of them panting. Water splashed up her legs, wetting her to the knees. Where did the tunnel end?

"Halt!" The shout came from behind again, much closer. There was the escalating hum of a pulse weapon and a white light filled the tunnel. The roof above their heads exploded, raining chips of crete down on them. They all ducked, gagging from the fall of dust. Pip fired a shot behind him without aiming. More crete scattered as his shot hit the wall, but in the brief flash of light Rosie had seen the tunnel end up ahead at a short ladder.

"Exit," she said as they reached it. But it was going to take time to climb it. Rosie had an idea. "Pip, fire at the roof."

"Brilliant, the dust." Pip spun around and fired in short bursts at the roof between them and the fast-approaching operatives.

Crete shards and dust exploded in all directions. It was shockingly loud and Rosie's hands shook as she grabbed for the ladder. Dalton copied Pip, the pulse energy releasing into the rock in boom after boom. Rosie had no idea what the grunts were doing; she couldn't see anything but a cloud of dust. Shards of crete flew all around her, pelting her face and hands, drawing blood as she grabbed at the rungs, hauling herself up. Dalton was right behind her, climbing one-handed, still firing.

"Pip!" Rosie shouted. Where was he?

Heart pounding and her ears full of gunfire, Rosie climbed swiftly, the boys close behind her. Four rungs from the top, rock exploded near her hip. Dalton cried out and slipped, almost falling on Pip. Rosie reached the top, heaved the cover off, and dragged herself out of the hole and into the street.

"Gun," she shouted at Dalton, holding a hand out. He slapped it into her hand and she lay flat on her stomach and fired blindly into the tunnel as he hauled himself out. Pip was shoving him up from behind. Then all of them were out and Pip grabbed the manhole cover and heaved it over the exit.

"You all right?" Rosie looked worriedly at Dalton. One side of his jacket was ripped and blood was spattered on the fabric.

"I'm okay. It's just a scratch."

"Come on." Pip led the way out to the street. They were somewhere in the Western Rim, in the residential sector. Box-shaped twenty-storey buildings rose up on either side of them. The sounds of music and arguments drifted down. Random groups of people lurked, but none of them paid them much attention.

"Which way to the river?" Rosie asked Dalton.

"This way." He headed towards a dark alley. Metal scraped behind them as the grunts flung off the manhole cover.

The alley was narrow and filled with refuse, but Helios were closing in.

"We won't make it," Dalton said.

"Here." Pip swerved towards an overflowing dumpster. Next to it, behind a two-metre stack of broken crates, was a narrow door leading into a building. It had no handle. Pip stuck the gun in the back of his pants and wrenched at the edge of the steel, uttering a groan.

"A hand, Curtis."

Dalton grabbed a plank from one of the broken crates and together they levered the door open enough to get through.

Pip slid sideways through the gap. Rosie and Dalton followed and they pushed it shut just as the sound of heavy boots rang in the alley.

The three of them froze, staring at each other. Outside, the thud of boots stopped. Rosie met Pip's wide-eyed gaze. He'd lifted the gun again. She copied him, both of them holding their guns ready. Rosie's leg muscles trembled, aching to run, but she forced herself to stay still. Then, miraculously, there was a short sharp command and the operatives moved off, running away up the alley.

For a heartbeat, no one moved. Then Rosie exhaled. "Close." She handed the gun to Dalton. The thought of shooting someone again made her unsteady. He took it without comment, but Pip frowned.

"Rosie—"

She cut him off. "They could come back. We should find another way out." It was very dim in the dirty, dank room and she couldn't see much.

"There's a door over there." Dalton gestured to the back.

"Let's go then," Pip said tensely. He kept his gun out and led the way.

CHAPTER 16

The door opened into a much larger room that smelled like a colony of dogs had been living in it. Big holes in the ceiling let in enough light to see another door that seemed like an exit. They crossed the dirty floor in tense silence.

"Pip," Rosie said. "Stop. We need to talk."

He halted so suddenly she had to pull up sharply. "We sure do." His bright blue gaze settled on her. "What's going on? What are you doing with him?" He flicked a glance at Dalton. He still held the gun in his right hand, pointed down, and his stare wasn't exactly friendly.

"Riley's gone," she said.

"Helios got him?" Tension filled every line of Pip's body.

"No, I don't think so. He just disappeared."

Pip swore softly and shook his head. "I knew it. His goddamned contingencies. What happened?"

"Aunt Essie and I got caught by a small bomb he left for Helios." Pip frowned. "But it's all right," she said, before he could speak. "We saw it in time and got out. Aunt Essie was hurt, but she's okay. Some grunts turned up, but we got away. I called Dalton and he picked us up in his boat."

"Man of the hour, eh, Curtis?" said Pip.

"Something like that." Dalton was still looking at Rosie. In his eyes was the knowledge of all she'd left out, what had really happened on the riverbank. But she couldn't tell Pip about that, not now.

"There's more." She looked at Pip, avoiding Dalton's eye. "Riley put an implant in me earlier. He said it was to track me, but—"

"Wait, he did what?"

"I think there's information on it," she said. "I keep getting flashes." She told him what she'd seen in Dalton's kitchen, the string of disjointed words.

"So you think Riley left a message on the implant for you to go north and that he's gone there as well?"

"Possibly," Dalton said.

"If he has, I think I would have heard," said Pip. "Still, it's a start." He was examining Rosie, as if he knew she hadn't told him everything. It was making her nervous. She didn't want to tell him how the implant hurt her, didn't want him thinking she was weak. Anyway, maybe it would stop.

Dalton moved a step closer as if picking up on her anxiety and put a hand on her shoulder. "So what's the plan?" he said to Pip.

"We go north," Pip said. "I'll get us out. Same way as I always come in."

"And how's that?" Dalton asked. Pip didn't answer.

Rosie's insides flipped as Pip's eyes shifted with cool speculation from Dalton's hand to her face. "The bullet train."

"But aren't all tickets for that ident controlled?" Dalton said.

"Who said I ever bought a ticket?" Pip's smile was condescending. "Money doesn't buy everything – but I guess you've never had to find that out."

Dalton folded his arms. "If that's supposed to insult me, you'll have to try harder. I've heard that one about a thousand times. Tell me, Pip, what's your problem with me? Or do you want me to guess? Because I think I have a pretty good idea."

Pip's gaze hardened. He took a step towards him and Rosie's nerves snapped.

"Stop it." She pushed between them. "We've just got out of being shot and now you want to have a go at each other? In case all that testosterone has fried your brains, we've got a real enemy on our tail. Helios – remember them?" They both stared at her in surprise. "We have

205

to get out of here. Fast. If you can manage to get over yourselves, that is." She turned to Pip. "How do we get on the bullet train without tickets?"

His eyes were still bright with anger, but he said, "I usually sneak on in one of the freight cartons."

"Aren't they sealed?" Dalton spoke stiffly. "How do you breathe?"

"Breathers."

"Have you got one?" Rosie said.

He hesitated. "Yeah. One."

Rosie resisted the urge to swear at him. "So how exactly do Dalton and I breathe?"

"Two people can share one," he said quietly. "I wasn't planning on there being three."

"Thanks," Dalton said.

"We're not leaving him behind," Rosie said to Pip. "Don't even argue about it." She rubbed a hand across her forehead. A dull ache was starting and she was trying her best to ignore it. The bullet train was their best way of getting north. It ran straight up the coast to Capricornia, the border town between Senate lands and Gondwana Nation.

"Helios might expect us to head north," Dalton said. "There's sure to be grunts looking out for us."

"All the more reason to take the train," Pip said. "They'll think we won't risk it."

"Yeah, but how?" Rosie said.

"There is one way," Pip said slowly. "There's always

a Senate car on the train, for any officials who want to travel – and officials never pay. All they need is a key stylus to get on. It bypasses everything."

"A stylus?" Rosie asked.

"I've seen them," Dalton said. "High-end tech. Unhackable."

Pip snorted. "So they say. But if we can get one of those, we'll be home free. Sort of."

"So we just need to mug a Senate official," Rosie said.

A smile played at the corners of Pip's mouth. "Easy. There's always one hanging around the bullet station."

Rosie sighed, but it was all they had. "What time does the train leave?"

"Nine thirty every night."

It was around midday now, so they had hours to wait – and hide.

"My boat," Dalton said as if he was reading her mind. "It's easier to hide on the water than anywhere in the city. The bullet station's on the north coast side of the river anyway. If we get a com, I can contact the AI on board, program it to go to a dock. Helios shouldn't pick it up, the boat's registered to a false name." At Pip's raised eyebrows, he said, "My dad calls it creative accounting."

"Banks docks would be the best," Pip said.

"Okay then." Rosie winced as the ache in her skull increased. "So we should get– Ow!" She dropped her head in her hands as a streak of pain from the implant came, followed by a blurred sequence of numbers.

"Rosie?" Dalton reached for her but she swatted his hand away.

"I'm okay."

The pain spiked and a recurring stream of numbers and words spiralled behind her eyelids, making her dizzy. Her knees buckled and Pip caught her.

"What's going on?" He sounded angry and panicked.

"It's the implant," she heard Dalton say. "It's been malfunctioning."

"That son of a bitch. Rosie?"

Both Pip's arms were around her now, her head lolling back against his shoulder. She tried to speak, but felt like she was going to throw up. An unending stream of numbers kept repeating behind her eyes. Then there was that high-pitched whine and the pain vanished with the words and numbers. It had lasted maybe fifteen seconds, but it left her shaking.

She opened her eyes. Dalton was staring at her with deep concern and she could feel Pip's heart beating fast against her shoulder blades.

"What the hell did he do to you?" Pip sounded scared.

"I'm fine," Rosie said. Now the pain was gone she was left annoyed and embarrassed at her collapse. And very aware Pip was still holding her. It felt good and confusing, and also weird with Dalton watching. "You can let go." She pushed out of his arms, stepping away. He released her, but it felt reluctant.

"What did you see this time?" Dalton asked.

Rosie took in a breath. "I'm not sure." She stopped to wipe her forehead. Gross, she was sweating. "Numbers, lots of numbers."

"Can you repeat them?"

"Um, yeah." She recited the numbers she'd seen and Pip made a surprised sound.

"That's the GPS coordinates for the Helios base."

"There were also a few words." Rosie struggled to remember them. "Panthea, or panther? I'm not sure. And Equinox Gate."

Pip frowned like he was trying remember something.

"What is it?" she asked, but he only shook his head.

"Don't know. Let me think about it."

"He must have dumped all his research in you." Dalton touched her shoulder. "How's your head; is the pain worse?"

It was, but Rosie didn't want to admit it. She thought about the stims stashed in her bra, but didn't want to take any with the boys there. "It's the same," she said. Pip was watching her with that look he got when he thought she was lying.

"Once we get to Gondwana we can get the tech to fix it, right?" she said. "I'll be fine."

Pip's lips were set in a thin line and his blue eyes looked midnight dark. "There's a good medic facility at Worla Range, where I stay. Should have the tech, but Rosie, those implants—"

"Yeah, I know. They're permanent." She turned away,

tired and fed up with everything. "Come on, we can't hang around here."

⎯⎯•⊙•⎯⎯

They emerged from the shed into a narrow side street and made it to the Banks docks without any trouble.

The riverfront was teeming with people. The long busy road that ran alongside the docks was crowded with bars, gaming parlours and shops. Rosie led them to an eatery wedged between a noisy bar and beauty palace. It had an open front where they could watch the street. They found a table in the corner.

"I'll get a disposable com," Pip said and disappeared into the crowd outside.

The faux-wood tabletop was sticky under her hands and Rosie's insides were knotted so hard, she felt ill. Dalton's shirt was ripped along one side and dried blood decorated the hem.

"Are you sure you're okay?" she said to him.

"It's nothing." He fingered the fabric. "Guess I better clean up though." Other people were glancing at him. He went to the bathroom and Rosie watched the line of screens above the food counter showing continuous news waves. The sound was muted so as not to interfere with the booming rain of chino funk coming from the walls – which did nothing to help her head. Silent vision of the Oceanus mission failing ran on one channel and the steadily increasing MalX death count ticked in the corner of another. A particularly animated wave reader was gesticulating wildly while behind her a team of suited disease control agents stormed a shuttle stop.

"So, about Pip," Dalton said, sitting back down. "Riley mentioned he used to be Helios."

Rosie knew where this was going. "Yes, but you don't need to worry, he'd be the last one to betray us."

Dalton didn't look appeased. He was about to say something else when a waitress appeared at their table. Her age was impossible to tell and a calculating spark of interest entered her eyes when she spotted Dalton. She swayed towards him. "Can I get you two anything?"

"Thanks, but we're not ready," Rosie said before he could open his mouth.

The waitress's expression soured. "This isn't a rest stop."

"We'll ping you when we decide." Rosie splayed a hand over the interactive menu on the tabletop.

"Five minutes," the waitress practically spat at her, then walked away.

"I could have charmed something out of her for free, you know," Dalton said.

"I'm not hungry. Besides, the food here is toxic." Actually, it wasn't that bad, but the thought of eating so soon after the implant incident made Rosie feel sick.

Dalton was quiet again for a minute. Then he said,

"So why do Helios want Pip back so badly? Riley never said, but it seems like he put a lot of effort into keeping Pip out of Helios's hands."

Rosie glanced around. The surveillance inside was broken and no one was paying them any attention. She studied Dalton. He looked tired, on edge, his golden hair dusty and mussed, but his clear steady gaze made her feel safe, like she could trust him with anything. And he'd put himself in jeopardy to save her. He deserved the truth. "He's immune to the MalX," she said, barely above a whisper. "A result of their project." Dalton raised his eyebrows and she hurried on. "If they get him, they'll turn him into a lab rat. A vaccine would be worth—"

"A planetload of money and power," Dalton finished.

"Exactly," Rosie said. "And it gets more complicated." She told him about how the immunity was in Pip's blood, and how he'd saved her family and her with it on Mars, and about the message she'd got and the vision from the hospital.

"That explains why the Senate was after you," he said. "You know you could have told me before." He waved his hand as she opened her mouth to explain. "It doesn't matter. But still—" He leaned forwards. "If he's immune, don't you think he should try to do something with it?"

Rosie bit her lip. "He is. He's been trying to find a way to make a vaccine up in Gondwana, but it's not working yet." She looked at her hands, remembering how angry Pip had been when he'd told her that – and how she'd accused him of not caring. "Anyway," she said, "he has to do it that way. Helios has moles in the Senate and if he goes to them, Helios will just take him and–" She stopped, unable to voice what she knew they might do to Pip if they could. "I mean, do you know anyone who has the kind of tech to make a vaccine? Who also might give it to the people who really need it the most and not use it as a way to control everyone?"

Dalton didn't answer.

"God," she said softly. "I'm so sick of them. Helios and all their crap. I keep fighting but they just keep coming back."

Dalton took her hand. "Yeah, but you're not doing it alone. I'm with you all the way, Pilot Girl." He smiled and brushed his thumb over hers.

She felt an unexpected spark of warmth. "I, ah–" she stuttered, then saw Pip come in the door. Her heart leaped and she snatched her hand away.

Dalton followed her gaze. His hand drew slowly back and he looked back at her with a question in his eyes she didn't know how to answer.

Rosie put both her hands in her lap. "You get it?" she said as Pip sat down.

"Yep." He handed the com to Dalton. "Do your thing. Dock 43."

Dalton took it as if nothing was going on and held it under the table so he could dial up his boat without being seen.

"Something wrong?" Pip looked at Rosie.

"Only the obvious," she said.

"We were talking about the MalX," Dalton said quietly. "And the cure."

Pip turned to Rosie with barely concealed anger. "He knows?"

Rosie wished she'd kept her mouth shut. "Pip—"

"It's not her fault," Dalton said quickly. "I asked — well, guessed. You can't blame her. And I would have found out eventually, what with where we're going. Besides, what's the problem? It's a good thing you're trying to find a way to use that cure, right?"

Dalton's voice was calm, but it didn't do much to blunt Pip's anger.

"Maybe it's my business," Pip said.

"I would have thought a cure for the MalX was everyone's business, but then that's just my opinion," said Dalton

"Maybe you can keep it to yourself."

Rosie cut in before they went any further. "Why don't you both keep things to yourself? You're giving me a headache." That shut them up.

The boat arrived eight minutes later, just as the waitress was starting to look daggers at Rosie. They left the eatery and weaved their way down the street, keeping close together and trying to blend with the crowd. Dock 43 was one of the busiest jetties and Dalton's sleek white boat was idling at the end of a line of dingy vessels.

They crowded into the cabin, Dalton going straight to the controls. Rosie hadn't taken in what the boat looked like before, but now she saw the cabin was a spacious curved capsule with a bank of white upholstered couches on either side. To the right of the controls a narrow passageway led below to what she assumed must be sleeping quarters and hopefully a bathroom. A teardrop-shaped table was bolted to the floor in front of one set of couches and a cool unit and bar was built into the opposite wall, near the door.

She sank down on one of the couches as Dalton drove away from the dock. Pip remained standing, watching their progress through the pilot window over Dalton's shoulder.

Despite its size, the cabin felt crowded with the two boys and they were all quiet, tension filling the space between them. It was nearly two pm according to the clock among the sleek displays in the plas screen of the pilot window. The East Side docks were forty kilometres east of the North Coast Bridge. It wouldn't take them long to get there, so they would have to anchor somewhere until nine.

"Where are we going to stop?" Rosie asked.

"There's a bay." Dalton peered at the river nav system. "It's just up from the docks. I don't think anyone will bother us. And if they do, we'll just pretend we're partying. Senate river patrol won't care."

Of course. Central party kids weren't exactly high on their target lists.

"Is there a bathroom?" she said.

"Below deck, door at the end."

Rosie glanced at Pip as she went past him. He had on his indecipherable face and said nothing.

Down the stairs was a short corridor and three doors, one on either side and the third at the end. The door on her right was open and Rosie saw a wide double bed with super soft pillows. She was so tired and the urge to go in and curl up on it was strong, but her bladder had other ideas. She went into the bathroom and locked the door. It was narrow, with plush towels and a mirror on the back of the door. It smelled like green apples. Rosie used the toilet then washed her face with recyc. The steady thrum of the boat engines was louder below deck, a comforting hum. She could hear the faint swish of water against the hull and the boys talking above. She couldn't make out what they were saying. At least they didn't sound aggressive.

She pulled a thread of stimulant from her bra. It was going to be a long night and she was so tired already. Tired and confused. Would two stims in one day be okay? She ran it through her fingers. To hell with it. It wasn't like she was going to sleep, and the stim had helped the headaches earlier.

It tasted like nothing much, just sweet, and it dissolved fast. She felt lighter. Her headache faded and energy flooded back into her limbs. Enjoying the mild buzz, Rosie brushed her hair and tied it back in a ponytail.

When she looked in the mirror, she appeared more alive in a slightly off way: cheeks faintly flushed, eyes brighter, lips redder, but that would wear off quickly.

She went back upstairs. The boys had found some food and drinks while she was gone. They were sitting on opposite sides of the cabin with a plate of soy subs between them. Both had plascans of drink in their hands.

"Want one?" Dalton said as she came up. At her nod, he flipped open the cool unit next to him and tossed her a can. Rosie hesitated, not sure where to sit, but then decided on the couch near Pip because it was closest to the food.

She picked up a sub and they all ate in silence. The sub was good, the soy creamy, pickles salty sweet. A low beeping sounded from the controls and Dalton leaped up, jamming the end of a sub in his mouth and going over to it.

"Almost at the inlet," he said around the food.

Rosie kept eating, but she could feel Pip's eyes on her. It was annoying.

"What?" She looked at him over her can.

He was sitting back against the cushions, one leg hooked up on the seat between them. His eyes half-closed, like a dozing cat.

"What are you on?" he said quietly.

For a second Rosie froze. Then she lowered the can, wiped her mouth and picked up another sub. "I'm on the couch. You know, furniture."

"Cute." The cushions squeaked as he lowered his leg and shifted closer, leaning in so Dalton couldn't hear. "You look different."

"I washed my face. You should try it." Rosie went to bite into the sub but he snatched it out of her hand. "Give that back." She reached for it but he held it out of her reach.

"Not until you quit lying. I know what a stimulant hit looks like. It's in the eyes." He grabbed her chin with his free hand, pulling her face closer. "How much did you take?"

Rosie reared back out of his grasp. "Stop it!" she hissed, praying Dalton wouldn't turn around. "It's none of your business."

His gaze was intense. "What really happened on the river?" he whispered. "That gun – it's a Helios issue weapon. How did you get it?"

Rosie couldn't respond. All the saliva had suddenly dried from her mouth and her heart was racing so fast it felt like it might explode from her chest. It was enough to confirm what he thought. A range of emotion crossed Pip's face: anger, frustration, torment.

"Christ, Rosie. The grunt?" He was staring at her neck. "Is that where the marks came from?" He tried to brush back her hair, but she jerked away.

"It doesn't matter – leave it," she whispered, and his eyes widened with understanding.

"I *knew* you'd left stuff out." He rocked forwards, his

218

knees touching hers, his whisper harsh with emotion. "I should have been there. I was there, earlier that day. Christ, Rosie, I'm sorry. Is he dead, the grunt, is he—" He tried to take her hands, but something, some fear, was working its way up her throat.

"Shut up," she whispered. "Just shut up." She stood up, bashing her shin against the table.

"Wait." He reached for her, but she pushed him away and fled back down the stairs and into the bedroom. Heart pounding, she slammed the door and locked it, then stood with her back against it. She was shaking, sweat covering her forehead.

A minute later there was a soft knock on the door.

"Rosie, are you okay?" It was Dalton.

She didn't answer. Instead, she collapsed on the bed, curled up and stayed there hugging a pillow and staring at the wall.

CHAPTER 17

The afternoon light faded to dusk, then full dark. Soft lights came on over the bed but Rosie didn't move. Neither of the boys came down again, but she could still hear them, their voices low. Were they talking about her? Possibly. She didn't care. The sub sat heavy in her stomach and there was an ache behind her eyes that had nothing to do with the implant.

What was she doing here? Everything that had happened since that day at Greenview circled through her brain. Riley, the implant, the grunt on the riverbank, Pip, Dalton. It was all too much. She had to get some focus.

She forced herself to sit up. *Pull it together, Black.* Riley had chosen to put the implant in her, out of everyone, because he trusted her. He believed she could figure it out, so this was no time to fall apart. She put her hands on her cheeks and tried to slow her pulse. She had to get to Gondwana, find Riley, if he was there. If not, then it was up to her to find out what was going on at that base and do something about it – then try to figure out with Pip what to do about the MalX cure in his veins. And none of that could happen by hiding down here. No matter how much she wanted to. She pushed back her hair, took a long breath then got up and unlocked the door.

Dalton was still at the controls and Pip was on the couch. He got slowly to his feet as she came up the steps and her heart did a little flip at the look in his eye.

"What's the time?" she asked Dalton.

"Close to eight thirty." He glanced at her. "I was going to send down the search party, but Pip said you'd probably kill the messenger. You all right?"

"Better." She stood behind his shoulder peering through the pilot window. They were approaching the East Side docks. It was brightly lit and crowded with supply carriers for the mega marts. Behind the jetties was a line of warehouses teeming with workers and robotic transports moving crates of goods, and beyond that was the station stop for the bullet.

"So what's our plan?" she said. "Get on the train and ride it to the last stop on the line?"

"Pretty much," Dalton said.

"Capricornia." Pip moved to stand beside her. "Nice town if you don't mind the rampant muggings and murder. Once we're there I'll find a secure link and get my contacts to shoot us through Nation controls." He cast her a concerned, searching look, but Rosie quickly turned away.

"It's busy," she said.

"Prime delivery time for shuttles from the farms," Pip said. He was still staring at her. It made her even more nervous.

She exhaled and said to him under her breath, "I'm fine, stop it."

"Stop what?" He raised an eyebrow, feigning innocence. Rosie shook her head and turned away, but not before she saw his slight smile.

"Keep an eye out for a docking spot," Dalton said as he guided the boat towards the long fingers of jetties.

"How about the other side of that Amart carrier?" Pip pointed ahead.

"That'll do." Dalton drove the boat down a narrow passage between larger boats to the dock.

"How do we check if there's a Senate official at the bullet station?" Rosie said.

"There's always one there," Pip answered.

A message blinked on the bridge com screen. "Vessel identification requested." A robotic female voice chimed through the cabin. Dalton tapped a series of numbers in and they all waited tensely as it was processed.

"Identification approved," the voice said. "Docking time forty-five minutes. Please collect your cargo safely."

"I'll set the AI to take the boat back." Dalton looked at Pip. "Got the supplies?"

Pip picked up a small bag and Rosie reached for it. "I'll carry it, in case you have to use the gun." He handed it over.

Dalton switched off the engine and opened the door to the deck and they all peered out. They were at the end of a line of identical floating jetties that stretched out like pine needles on a branch from a main dock. Their jetty was empty and lit intermittently by overhead lights which threw shadows along each side. A long line of boats was tethered opposite. It was far from quiet. Men and women shouted to each other over the grind of the machinery bringing in crates of goods.

"Come on." Rosie led the way. They ran at a slight crouch towards the end, keeping to the shadows. Rosie paused next to a cruiser, the boys behind her. The main dock was wide enough for the robotic movers to trawl up and down loading the boats. They looked like four-armed metal spiders on wheels, the long loading arms lifting crates from the trailers up to where men waited on the carriers. The movers crawled up and down the main dock to the yards and bullet station. A high fence separated the dockyards from the station, and there appeared to be only one way in and out – past six heavily armed guards.

Dalton let loose a string of whispered swear words and

224

glared at Pip. "You didn't say anything about guards."

"They weren't there before."

"This is not something we can sneak past."

"What do you want me to do about it?"

"Shut up, both of you," Rosie said. "Let's hitch a ride in one of them." She pointed at the robotic movers.

They stared at the shining spider robots trundling up and down with their egg-shaped bodies. "The cabins aren't for driving," Pip said. "You might fit, midget, but not us normal-sized people."

"It's big enough," Rosie said. "We'll be squashed, but it's not far to the station and no one is watching. Look at that one there." She indicated one a metre away, beside a super carrier. "It's being loaded with cargo, not unloaded. It's got to be heading to the bullet."

Dalton said, "It could work."

Pip exhaled, shaking his head. "Let's get cosy then."

They watched as the crew of the carrier swung a final crate to the mover below and lowered it to its trailer. As soon as the men at the rail turned around, they sprinted forwards. Pip reached it first. He jerked open the cabin door and leaped inside. Dalton boosted Rosie in then jumped in after her. The tiny cabin had no windows and for a moment they were a tangle of elbows, knees and whispered swearing until Pip managed to press himself against the far wall, half-lying with Rosie squashed up against him, her back to his chest, the pack clutched against her and her face centimetres away from the operator's station. Dalton scrunched up on the other side, his knees pressed against the cabin door.

The floor vibrated as the mover began to turn. Then there was a lurch as it pulled the trailer with it. Rosie's head hit Pip in the chin and Dalton gripped the door shut as it threatened to open under his weight. Rosie wriggled, pushing back against Pip as she struggled to get away from something digging into her ribs.

Pip gripped her hip hard. "Stop moving," he whispered with a hint of strain. His lips were so close to her neck she felt his breath on her skin.

"Sorry."

He didn't reply, just released another breath against her neck that sent a shiver right through her. He took his hand off her hip and braced it against the ceiling over her head. The mover stopped turning and picked up speed. Rosie could feel every breath Pip took. The air in the mover was soon thick with the scent of their sweat and tension.

Sounds of other machinery and raised voices were audible after a while and Rosie guessed they were in the dockyards. The voices sounded close. The mover paused and they all stopped breathing. After a second there came the sound of something beeping, a scrape against the mover's hull and they were off again.

They all exhaled. They must have got through the checkpoint. After another few minutes of uncomfortable swaying, the mover stopped.

Dalton twisted awkwardly to look at them out of one eye.

"Do it," Rosie whispered.

He opened the door a crack and peered out. "Clear," he said.

They crawled out. They were in amongst a group of movers at the back end of the station that were waiting to load cargo into the bullet train. The glare of spotlights turned night into day and it was as busy as the docks. Robotic movers were everywhere, loading crates and shifting goods. The low whine of bio-fuelled transporters filled the air as men and women manoeuvred them into position to be unloaded onto the train's freight cars. The bullet was a sleek shiny silver and eight hundred metres long. Only the first few cars were for passengers; the rest were freight cars.

They were surrounded by ten stationary movers waiting to load goods on the train. Beyond was a wide expanse of busy platform, also brightly lit. Rows of shipping containers lined the back edge of the platform against the fence and next to them was a small administration building with a tinted glass front. Rosie could see the shadows of people inside.

"Any Senate official is going to be in there," Pip said.

"So, we wait until one comes out?" Rosie said.

"No, I go in. The toilets are our best bet. A man's got a take a leak sometime. I can steal one in there."

"And what if there aren't any, or it's a woman?"

"There's always one," Pip said. "And if it's a chick, I'll just charm it off her. I've got all kinds of talents." He smiled, eyes gleaming with suggestion.

"Just get it done," Dalton said with irritation. "Rosie, we can wait there." He pointed at the line of containers against the fence.

The mover they'd been crouching against suddenly whirred into life along with the others that had been dormant around them, lifting up on hydraulic spider legs.

"Now or never," Pip said. He walked casually out from the movers as if he was supposed to be there and strode towards the administration building without looking around. Rosie and Dalton hung back a moment longer, then walked out as well, keeping their heads down. They had to stop abruptly to wait for a line of trucks to trundle past them and Rosie felt exposed under the bright lights. She kept expecting an alarm or shouts, but nothing came and they made it to the containers seemingly unnoticed.

The boxes were stacked three high and several rows wide. Rosie and Dalton hovered in the shadows between them for what felt like hours, but was probably only five or ten minutes. Rosie was just beginning to think the worst, when Dalton whispered, "He's coming back."

Tense with relief, she saw Pip tilt his head slightly towards the front passenger section of the train. "He's got it," she said.

They stepped out of the shadows and walked swiftly up the platform. Few people gave them a second glance. Pip appeared more than pleased with himself.

"You got it?" Rosie whispered as they fell into step.

"Easy. Guy was weedier than Curtis."

"Funny," Dalton said quietly, quickly glancing behind.

Pip shrugged. "That Helios training comes in handy sometimes."

"Shut up," Rosie hissed, but he only smiled and a put a hand lightly on her upper back.

"This one," he said and pushed her in front of him to a door in one of the train carriages.

There was no attendant on duty, but an automated electro barrier prevented entry until a ticket was swiped. Pip handed her the key stylus, a slim black cylinder the length and width of his index finger. Rosie pressed the tip to the reader. The device made a bass humming noise and the barrier disappeared. The three of them crowded on.

The bullet passenger cars were divided into seating and sleeping booths with a single narrow corridor running along one side. To their right was a glass door, inlaid with a beautiful pattern of coloured holo lights and a sign on it that said "Premium Diner". Beyond that was the official Senate carriage. Through the glass, Rosie could see places already laid for an early breakfast. She caught a glimpse of herself in the windows. She looked as anxious as she felt.

"You got that surveillance jammer, Curtis?" Pip said.

Dalton pulled a device from his pocket. "Had one on the boat," he said.

"Could be another Senate official already on board. We'll be better off in the normal carriages." Pip turned away from the dining car and activated a door to a corridor. Dalton pointed the jammer at any surveillance points as they made their way along the carriage, and Pip and Rosie peered at the occupation indicators on the booth doors until they found an empty one.

Inside were six seats, three on each side facing each other. The wide window's glass was darkened into night mode so they couldn't see out.

Rosie sat near the window, dropping the pack on the floor while Dalton and Pip sat opposite, a seat apart. None of them spoke, waiting for the train to move.

It felt like the longest five minutes of Rosie's life, but finally a chime sounded and the whirring of the engines started. The train lifted to hover above its guide track and they were finally in motion, the bullet shooting smoothly away from the platform and heading north.

CHAPTER 18

It was six hours to Capricornia. The lights in the cabin faded to an ambient glow and they sat listening to the hum of the train. The ride was so smooth it was hard to believe they were even moving.

"What are the odds we got away without being spotted?" Dalton said.

"We're still alive," Pip replied.

"There could be operatives already here," Rosie said.

"Maybe," Pip said. "But they'd be on us if there were. We've just got to hope we didn't get clocked on any of the surveillance."

"We need a plan B." The stimulants were wearing off and Rosie felt the headache returning. The last thing she needed was for the damn implant to go off. She tried to surreptitiously rub her forehead, but Dalton saw her.

"You okay?" he said.

"Fine." She looked at Pip. "You know this train. What're our options if it gets boarded?"

"The freight cars are where I usually travel, and I've still got a breather. One." He held up a finger. "But forget that for a minute. Tell me again what you saw on the implant earlier."

"Now?" Rosie exhaled with annoyance. "Pip we've got to—"

"Just tell me."

"It was Panthea or something, and Equinox Gate," Dalton said. "Why?"

"Jackpot." Pip grinned. "Panthea has got to be Pantheon."

"What's that?" Rosie said.

"The Pantheon is what Helios calls the ruling five. The ones who run the whole thing. I couldn't place it right away. Even when I was a kid, the Pantheon was rarely talked about. No one knows who they are – at least, no one I've ever met. Maybe Riley found out."

"What about Equinox Gate?" Dalton said, but Pip sat back, shaking his head.

"Never heard of it."

"It sounds plausible," Rosie said.

"If Riley found out those names and put them in your head, that's power," Pip said. "We've got something no one has." He leaned across the space towards her, eyes shining. "Rosie, this is good," he said. "We could stop Helios."

"Yeah, maybe. If that's what's in there." Her head was aching hard. She felt like she was either going to spew or pass out again and she didn't want to do either in front of the boys. "I gotta find a bathroom." She pushed open the door and was out before either one of them could say anything.

The ladies was at the end of the carriage. She locked herself in and sat on the closed lid of the toilet until the urge to vomit passed. The implant didn't open but she felt like it was waiting to and every nerve in her scalp was supersensitive. She broke a tiny bit off a thread of stim and chewed on it. It cleared her mind so she could think. Knowing who really ran Helios could be good – but how would they use it? And would they escape Helios long enough to be able to? They'd got on the train, but Helios could still be tracking them. What exactly would they do when they got to Capricornia? Pip had said he'd contact someone when they got there, but what if that was too late? She left the bathroom and went back to the compartment, thinking, and saw the object of her thoughts leaning against the wall in the corridor.

"You okay?" Pip straightened as she neared him.

"Um, yeah, sure."

"The implant again?" He was looking at her closely, like he cared, making her insides all fluttery.

No one else was around. The corridor was dim, the

world beyond the windows black. Rosie cleared her throat nervously.

"I've been thinking … you still got that disposable com?" she said.

"Yeah." He pulled it out of his pocket, puzzled. "Why?"

"Can you use it to get a message to Cassie, or someone?"

He frowned. "Probably, but it's likely the signal would get hit. I was going to wait until we got to Capricornia, find a safe line."

"I don't think we've got that kind of time. Is there anyone in Capricornia to help us?" she asked.

"No, they're several hours out."

"So, if we make it there without getting caught, we'll have to wait a while for help. And if something goes wrong …"

He pursed his lips in thought. "So what's your idea? There're security protocols I can follow, but any call I make will eventually be noticed."

"But calling now might buy us some time. And if we do get caught, at least someone can be there when we arrive. Our chances would be better." Rosie watched him considering it.

"Okay," he finally said. "I guess. I'll send a message. It's safer than voice." He flipped on the com and began to punch in a complicated set of numbers. "It's going through." His blue eyes were intent on the com, a slight frown drawing his dark brows together. He had a crescent-shaped scar just under his hairline and Rosie got a funny ache near her heart just looking at it. He'd got that on Mars in the Enclave when they'd been running from the guards.

"What did you say?" she said. "You didn't mention Riley, did you?"

"Course not." He spoke absently, still watching the screen. "I used a code for 'coming in hot'. The trouble switch." He smiled at some private joke. "And I told them there're three of us." He looked back at her and his smile faded, his gaze flickering over her face suddenly filled with a naked vulnerability that made her breath stop "Rosie, I–" He was interrupted by a soft beep from the com. "That was quick." He turned the com so they could both see it. He was so close, she could barely concentrate. The message was simple. *8 Free. Special mob today.* That was it, but Pip seemed to understand and the tension he'd been holding released.

"Kev, you legend." He grinned.

"What is it?"

"It means we've got backup. They'll meet us at eight at the Freezone Hotel."

"But that's hours after we get there," Rosie said.

"I know somewhere we can hole up, and Kev's sending some of the Yalgu Warriors."

The Yalgu was the Nation's answer to the Senate Elite, but they didn't live in the towns, as far as Rosie

235

knew, and they were talked about as if they were more legend than real.

"I guess that's good then," she said, but she didn't feel confident. They still had to get through the night. Her head chose that moment to send a spear of pain through her, despite the stim. She pressed a hand to her forehead, closing her eyes. It was over in a few seconds though, no numbers.

"That implant again, huh?" There was tenderness in Pip's eyes, and he lifted a hand towards her face but stopped halfway, uncertain, as if he wasn't sure he was allowed to touch her. "Any numbers or ...?"

"No, nothing."

Pip slipped the com in his pocket and rubbed the back of his neck with one hand. "Um, Rosie, I'm sorry about how I acted before on the boat."

His eyes glinted at her from under his dark hair and he drew in an unsteady breath. "I shouldn't have gone off at you about the stims. I mean, it's not like I'm perfect." His mouth quirked down. "And I didn't mean to pressure you about ... what happened. I was just, I don't know ..." He stopped and Rosie couldn't help him. Really couldn't. Her insides were knotted up tight at the thought of voicing what had happened on the riverbank. She waited but he seemed to be struggling to finish, his mouth working like he couldn't form the words.

"I was just angry that you got hurt," he finally said. "That it happened, that's all."

Rosie nodded. "I'm okay." Except she wasn't, not even close. And she knew that Pip wasn't buying it. "Um, Dalton's probably wondering what's going on." She went to walk past him, but he pushed off the window, blocking her way.

"Wait." His hand landed on her waist.

The word was soft, nothing, but there was an intimacy about his tone that made Rosie's heart leap suddenly into her throat. She met his gaze and for a split second she thought he was going to kiss her. He swayed minutely towards her, his hand tightening on her waist. Her breath stopped somewhere in her chest. She was suddenly aware of every centimetre of skin beneath his fingers, but then a door slammed somewhere. They both jumped.

"Come on," Rosie said. "We should talk to Dalton, figure out what to do."

"Yeah." Pip's smile faded and he took a step away. Then he turned back to her, an odd determination in his eyes. "Actually, no, there's just one thing."

He was so quick, she didn't have time to be surprised. One arm went around her waist, the other behind her neck, and he pulled her to him and kissed her.

Rosie stiffened, her eyes closing involuntarily. His lips were soft, open and then his tongue grazed her mouth. A ripple of heat shot through her and long-repressed need erased everything else. She put a hand around his neck and pulled him closer, pressing against him. He tasted like pickles and sugar, salt and sweet, so good. His fingers crept under her shirt, traced her ribcage and desire exploded inside her. She hooked a leg around his thigh, desperate to bring him closer and he staggered, overbalancing. They fell hard against the window, Rosie knocking her head against the glass, and they broke apart.

"Ow," Rosie whispered, although it hadn't really hurt.

"Sorry, you okay?" He was breathless, trembling. They both were. He rubbed her head where it had hit.

"Yeah." She was embarrassed. They looked at each other for a second, then he let her go with a pleased but sheepish smile.

"Come on." He tugged on one of her hands and stepped back. His T-shirt stretched between them. Rosie was still clutching a handful of it. His smile broadened. She let go and felt her face get hot.

"Shut up."

"I didn't say anything."

"Just don't–" She stopped. Don't what? Do that again? Even though she had really, really not wanted to stop. She was suddenly angry at him and furious at herself. And her lips were still tingling from his kiss. She just hoped it wasn't written all over her face.

———◆———

Dalton had shifted to lean his back up against the window so he could put his legs up on the bench seat, and had the gun sitting in his lap. "Where have you been?" His gaze moved between her and Pip, a question in his eyes.

"I had an idea." Rosie told him about Pip contacting his friends.

"The Freezone." Dalton swung his legs to the floor. "Okay, but we still need an exit strategy for the train. I want to check out the freight car access." He nodded at Pip. "You coming?"

"Fine by me." Pip shrugged.

"I'll stay here," Rosie said. She needed a moment to process what had just happened. Her pulse was still rapid and every time Pip caught her eye it spiked.

"You want the gun?" Pip said.

"No. Just be careful."

"We'll be back before you know it," Dalton said. "Lock the door, and don't let anyone in except us."

Rosie rolled her eyes. "Yes, Dad." He grinned and shoved his gun in the back of his waistband.

Pip winked at her as he closed the door. "See you soon."

Rosie went through the backpack, rearranging the food and water as thoughts went round and round her head. Pip must care. You didn't kiss someone like that if you didn't. Just thinking of it made her face warm – and how she'd wanted him closer, against her skin. She'd had fumbles with other boys, kisses in corners, but not like that. *Stop it, Rosie, get focused!*

She tapped her feet, paced. They were taking too long. She was thinking about going after them when the train suddenly lurched and she was thrown back on the seat. A high whistle sounded.

She leaped back up and turned off the window darkeners. Lights. Pinpoints out in the dark getting closer, bigger. Glimpses of spindly shrub, wedges of rock flashed into view. The train was slowing to a stop. It could only mean one thing.

Helios had found them.

CHAPTER 19

Rosie slung on the pack, fighting panic, and opened the door. There was no sign of Pip and Dalton. She paused in an agony of indecision. People were starting to move around in other compartments; she could hear outer doors opening and raised voices. She couldn't stay here.

She ran down the narrow passage towards the freight cars, hoping Pip and Dalton were on their way back. A woman stepped out in her path, all sleepy-eyed, then leaped back with a squawk as she rushed past. Rosie glanced out the windows on her left. Darkness. Helios could be getting on anywhere. She dodged a man who took a hasty step back into his compartment and shouted at her, but she didn't turn around.

She reached the end of the carriage and punched the

door release. Nothing happened. She punched it again. Damn it! Everything must be in lockdown. She stared through the pane of plasglass in the door and her heart leaped in shock as she saw Pip at the opposite door in the next carriage, staring at her across the metre-wide space that separated them. He was saying something but she couldn't hear a thing.

The stylus! She'd forgotten she had it.

Rosie shoved it in the lock but again nothing happened. She wanted to scream with frustration. She stared at Pip. His eyes were wide and he was gesturing at her. She shook her head. What? She held up her hands. What was he saying? Dalton leaned over Pip's shoulder.

"Run!" he mouthed very clearly. Then he said something urgently to Pip and tried to pull him back.

Lights flickered outside the carriage the boys were in. Shadows moving. Fear leaped up and lodged in her throat.

"Run!" Pip's words were easy to understand this time, with his frantic gesturing.

With one last frightened look, she turned and ran back down the passageway, ramming people out of the way, ignoring their protests. The Senate car was her only option now.

The door to the premium diner wasn't locked, the tables empty. Rosie pounded past, her steps rattling the cutlery, and headed down a short corridor bisecting a kitchen. She halted at the door that led to the Senate car and shoved the stylus into the lock. The light turned green. The Senate car was empty, but Rosie had a bad feeling her luck wasn't going to hold.

The car was the same size as the other carriages but had one lounge area and four larger compartments, two on each side of a short corridor. She listened at the first door on the left, then carefully opened it. It was a bedroom with a tiny bathroom, empty, but with nowhere to hide. The next was the same. Muffled noises were coming from the first cabin on the right and the thud of boots came from the next carriage, along with shouts of protest. Desperate, Rosie pushed through the exit door at the end of the carriage.

She was outside on a narrow metal ledge less than half a metre wide. A waist-high rail separated her from the gap between the carriage and the back of the engine car. It was still idling and a piercing beam of light extended from its nose into the night. The air stank of biofuel and dust. Nowhere to hide.

Then she saw it. At the back of the engine car, low down, was a square dark crawl space. She ducked under the rail and dropped down to the shimmering propulsion discs that connected the train and engine. They overlapped like cards in a deck and were still active. Heat burned up through the soles of her boots and she stifled a cry as she skipped across and leaped for the opening of the crawl space. She caught the top of it and swung herself inside, scraping skin, her bag banging the sides just as the exit door opened.

A man's voice rang out. "Search the area around for footprints."

There was a crunch of dirt and stones as someone jumped to the ground.

Another voice came, a woman this time, and she sounded irritated. "Where are your Senate orders, captain? I demand to see them. This is most irregular. I will not be happy if I am late for my appointment."

"Your appointments are irrelevant." The man's tone was threatening. "Go back to bed and stay out of my way." He called to his man on the ground. "Four minutes, then come back in. They're more likely in the freight. Let me know." The grunt answered in the affirmative and the door slammed shut.

Rosie didn't move. The crawl space was a narrow dark tunnel, lined with dust-crusted mesh and stinking of fumes. She huddled against the side, barely breathing.

She guessed they must be somewhere in the no-man's-land between Newperth and the coastal hub of Oak City. There was nothing out here but dust and the remains of cities that once were, now long abandoned to the encroaching desert. There was nowhere to run to, no choice but to hide. Her heart was thudding so hard, she could almost hear it echoing in the small space.

Her legs were crunched up underneath her and a pulse behind her knee began to throb. She heard the grunt coming back. There was a creak as he swung himself up onto the platform, then the carriage door opened and closed.

Rosie listened for another long moment then, satisfied he wasn't coming back, shrugged the pack off and tried to get more comfortable. It wasn't exactly possible. Her knees were jackknifed up and her feet pressed against the opposite side of the space. What was she going to do? She had no idea if Pip or Dalton were okay and no way of contacting them. Her head was aching again, dangerously aching, and that wasn't the only part that hurt. Her entire body was a travelling circus of pain from the past few days.

She pressed her fingers against the underside of her breast and felt the thread of stimulant in her bra. Should she take some more? She had to be alert. She was trying to decide when she heard the sound of pulse fire.

———•◦•———

Pip ran, his boots thundering on the hard carriage floor, Dalton on his heels. People peeking out from their cabins reared back in alarm as they saw them.

The boarding door was just ahead and already sliding open. The first grunt came through as Pip reached it and he ducked low and ploughed into the man's chest. They went down, his neck jarring as the grunt hit the floor. Pip pummelled his fists into the man's ribs and got in a good punch to the gut before the grunt threw him off into the wall. Plas panelling splintered under the impact and Pip landed on his back, staring at the ceiling. He rolled and was halfway up when Dalton shouted, "Down!" He ducked and a shot of pulse fire split the air over his head. The grunt, who'd just flipped himself back upright, smashed back down to the floor. The stench of singed fabric and skin filled the corridor. Dalton yanked Pip upright one-handed, like he weighed nothing. Dalton's face was pinched tight, but he was in control, not panicking. Maybe Pip had misjudged the Central.

Dalton had locked the door but it wasn't going to hold long. Two more grunts outside were firing at it, and both boys ducked instinctively as pulse fire whumped against the windows, which rattled in their frames. They didn't break, but they wouldn't last.

"Come on." Pip jumped over the body of the grunt and led the way up the corridor towards the exit. Blood ran down his arm from a cut he didn't recall getting.

"The Helios captain went to the next carriage," Dalton said. Pip knew what he left unsaid. Rosie was in there. He ran faster. The men outside were keeping pace with them, firing shots at the windows. The sound was like fists smashing on an aquarium, and they were the fish about to get netted.

They reached the end of the carriage, but the door was on lockdown. Change of plan. "Open it!" Pip shouted through the slit window of the last compartment. The terrified elderly couple inside just stared at him, huddling together.

"Look out." Dalton pressed the muzzle of the gun against the lock and fired. His arms shuddered at the kickback, but it worked.

Pip shoved open the door. He elbowed the couple aside and pulled out the grunt's gun Rosie had given him. Muzzle pressed close to the plasglass, he pumped the trigger. The old woman screamed, but it was barely audible over the whine and thump of the gun. Dalton joined him and five shots later the window splintered. Two more kicks and it gave way, disintegrating to powder. They dived through, hitting the sandy soil hard.

"This way." Pip ran back towards the other carriage to find Rosie, but before he'd gone more than a few steps, two grunts leaped out from between the carriages.

"Hold it!" one yelled.

Pip whirled, almost colliding with Dalton and they raced back the other way. Shots spat dust up around their feet. He fired back as he ran, hitting nothing. They ran wildly, ducking and weaving so the grunts couldn't get a lock on them.

On the other side of the train, they could hear booted footsteps, and men calling to each other. Without having to discuss it, they both sprinted for the freight carriages. The only light came from inside the train and the glow of torches from the grunts. Fear and fury in equal portions were crawling up Pip's insides.

More grunts were behind them now. He almost

stumbled over some rocks. Shrubs scraped his jeans, a low branch whipped Dalton in the face, and the pulse shots kept coming. Something hot and hard streaked across his hip. Pulse graze. He staggered, but kept going. Dalton grunted a cry as he got hit as well and almost went down. Pip hauled him up without quite knowing how. Then he saw it. Lucky break.

He hooked a hand into Dalton's shirt, the fabric ripping as he brought him up short at the carriage.

"Climb!" He shoved him towards the ladder to the roof.

Dalton leaped for it as Pip fired a volley of shots at the pursuing grunts, forcing them to take cover. Then he followed, climbing like a monkey possessed. Pulse shot sang on the metal, missing him by millimetres as he rolled onto the flat roof. Dalton was combat crawling on his belly to an access hatch. He had it open in seconds, the flap smacking back, and he somersaulted headfirst inside. Pip followed, flipping into the dark space. He landed feet first, and cocked his gun so the muzzle glowed faintly blue, giving them some light. Dalton was panting, waiting for him, squinting in the sudden glow.

"What ..." His words died as he saw what Pip had known was inside: a row of shiny new bio bikes.

"See if any are fuelled up," Pip said. He went from one to the other. Empty. Empty. Panic was rising in his throat. He could hear the thud of hands and boots on the side of the carriage.

"Here." Dalton dragged one from the row. He was already powering it up, the sound a sweet low rumble Pip felt through his shoes. "It might not get through the side." In the glow of light from the bike, Dalton's face was deathly pale, his pupils dilated with fear, but his voice was steady.

"Then I guess we're dead men talking," Pip said. *And no help to Rosie at all.* His guts twisted with fear for her. "I'll drive."

"No." Dalton swung the bike at the wall. "Just cover me if we get out."

No time to argue, men were on the roof. Pip took the back seat and Dalton flicked the controls to turbo, but kept the brakes locked. For three seconds the bike's engine wound up, pitching higher to its top speed. Pip glimpsed the legs of a grunt coming through the roof, but then Dalton let off the lock and it was all he could do to stay on as the bike accelerated.

There was a wrench and the side exploded off the container as they hit. The bike's crash field expanded out, pushing the metal away, and they came through the gap like they'd been spit from a cannon. Two grunts that'd been standing outside were crushed and Dalton almost lost control as the bike hit the dirt. The back wheel slid out and they clipped a small tree, narrowly avoiding falling off. Dalton righted the bike and Pip hung on with one hand and fired a few parting shots at the remaining grunts as Dalton headed the bike flat out into the desert.

CHAPTER 20

Rosie sat hard up against the Senate car exit door, legs dangling off the edge of the narrow platform, and wished for the thousandth time she knew what had happened to the boys. She'd had to listen to the shots, the sound of men shouting and then, worst of all, the wrenching, explosive screech of metal.

Pip and Dalton could be dead for all she knew. She stared at the track and ground, nothing more than a blur beneath her. Rushing hot air sucked stray curls of hair from her ponytail and swatted her in the face.

After the train had started again, the crawl space had become very hot, very quickly. She'd risked crossing the propulsion discs again to the narrow platform at the back of the Senate car. The tread of her boots was partially melted now. In all the panic after the shots, she thought maybe she'd heard a bio bike. If Pip and Dalton had got away on it, their chances of getting to Capricornia were not great. There was nothing out there, literally. If they ran out of fuel, they were dead. She pulled the pack onto her lap. Every muscle in her body was aching and there were still hours to go until they got to the end of the line. There was nothing but the rushing sound of the engine, the dark sky and an ache behind her eyes that felt like it was branching all the way down to her heart.

She woke with a start, her heart leaping like it had been snagged by a hook, and almost flicked the pack off the train. It dangled over the edge, the strap caught around her wrist. She pulled it back, hugging it against her. The sky was lighter. She could see the shapes of trees, rocks and narrow pyramid ants' nests. A line of orange glowed on the horizon to the east, and in the north another kind of glow marked the sky. The kind that was man-made. Capricornia.

Rosie shifted, trying to get some feeling in her backside. She reached for a thread of stimulant and chewed down two. The stim coursed through her bloodstream, dampening her weariness and dulling the ache.

She badly needed to pee. She got to her knees to peer through the exit door window. A soft light was coming from inside and she could see part of one of the sofas in the sitting area. Someone's leg and foot were just visible.

Maybe she'd get lucky and the woman would go get breakfast.

It seemed like she was actually going to get her break. A little while later the woman got up and left. Rosie waited a few minutes then slipped inside and rushed into the closest bathroom. When she came out the sun was about to break the horizon and she could see the shadow of Capricornia, dead ahead. It rose from a barren landscape of low scrub and desert. Its skyline was punctuated by a series of spiked towers and the black specks of transports hovered above it like flies over a carcass.

Rosie slung the pack over her shoulders and dropped down again onto the discs, mouth pinched as she traversed the burning-hot surface. She levered herself into the crawl space and shuffled back into the shadows to wait. She had half a bottle of water, three packs of dry food and a few threads of stim. No credit, because Dalton had been carrying it, and no com, but she knew something. *Freezone, eight am.* If she could find her way there, maybe she could find some help. She tried not to think about what might have happened to Pip or Dalton, or to wonder where Riley was. She had to focus, get a clear head and stay out of Helios's hands so she could get them all back.

The bullet pulled into Capricornia station half an hour later. It was terrifically noisy. Engine sounds, people sounds and she was sure she could detect the whirring of hover cars and helijets outside the station. The train braked to a stop and Rosie peeked out. A curved glass roof soared at least fifteen storeys above and the platform was a few metres higher than her head. She couldn't see much, but she spotted hover transports taking off and the roofs of several city shuttles.

She slid out of the space and jumped across the discs to the platform. She checked around the corner, staring back down the length of the train, looking for anyone on the platform who might belong to Helios. All she could see was a crowd of movers and people converging on the freight cars. Now or never. She ducked under the metal rail and leaped across to the platform, hitting her knee hard. She sprang up and walked away, keeping her head low and trying to orient herself at the same time. Despite the early hour, people were swarming everywhere like ants out of a nest, rushing in all directions and Rosie merged with the crush. An old-fashioned overpass arched up and across the bullet track and crossed to the other side.

The crowd formed a bottleneck towards the exit. There were four large doors but only one was open. Rosie could barely move as she was shuffled along amid the suffocating scent of other people's sweat.

She was pushed out onto a four-lane street clogged

with bio bikes and hover trans all honking and swerving around each other. It was hot and barely light, the sky scudded with clouds that kept in the heat like a blanket. Across the road were shops and a string of apartment blocks topped with huge signs promoting energy drinks and robotics. The mosquito-like whine of helijets zipped overhead as three buzzed the station.

Rosie fought her way to the wall left of the door and paused, wondering which way to go. She had to figure out where the Freezone was, and this city was big; any move in the wrong direction could be disastrous. She stared at the people in confusion. She had no point of reference, nowhere to start and no one to help her. Her mum used to say you never felt so alone as when you were surrounded by strangers in a strange place. And that was just how she was feeling now. If she couldn't find the Freezone in time, she had no clue what to do.

Maybe she should find a way to contact Aunt Essie. But that would only worry her, and what could she do anyway? *Get it together, Black!* She forced herself to think. Then her breath caught in her throat. Was that a familiar figure coming out of the station?

She dodged around, spying through the crowd. It was definitely Agent Sulawayo. The tall, dark woman wore a snug-fitting sleeveless black coverall and half her face was obscured by oversize UV glasses, but Rosie was sure it was her. And she appeared to be alone.

What was she doing here?

She watched as Sulawayo stood on the edge of the road. The Senate agent looked around as if checking if anyone was watching, then moved swiftly down the street. After a moment's hesitation, Rosie followed, trying to stay behind her in the crowd.

Sulawayo crossed the street and headed down a pedestrian mall. It was a major thoroughfare, lined by shops and eateries, many of them just opening. Staff were setting up tables and chairs and there were a few decrepit-looking public comnets clustered at one end.

Sulawayo turned down a pathway between some buildings. It was narrow and curved between the high walls of the shops on either side and was paved with faux cobblestones. It was also quieter; even the buzzing whine of the helis above sounded duller. Rosie reached a sharp bend and stopped to peer around the corner. Ahead was a tiny cafe with one table set out the front of it and sitting there was Agent Sulawayo. Rosie's heart vaulted and she pulled back sharply.

"Rosie," Sulawayo called. "I know you're there."

Rosie's skin prickled hot and cold.

"We haven't got all day." Sulawayo sounded calm, but annoyed.

Rosie went around the corner. She wasn't really sure why she was so afraid. "You knew I was following you?"

The agent took her glasses off and put them in her breast pocket. "I was counting on it. I saw you at the station. I have to say, I was surprised. After Riley's disappearance I thought your aunt would be making you lie low."

"Things kind of went pear-shaped," Rosie said. "Why are you here?"

"I got a strange message from Riley just before he left, telling me to get up here. I was slightly delayed." She glanced over Rosie's head at the mall and stood up. "We should go somewhere more secure. There's a place I know. Come on."

"Wait." Rosie drew back a step. "I've got to be somewhere, at eight."

"Where?"

When Rosie didn't answer, Sulawayo became impatient. "You can trust me, Miss Black. Where do you need to be?"

Rosie didn't want to say, but she needed help and if Riley trusted Sulawayo ... "It's called the Freezone. I'm meeting some people."

"I know it," Sulawayo said. "It's not far from where we're going. Who are you meeting?"

"I don't know."

"Well." Her mouth thinned. "We'll find out. There're still a few hours till then and we can't stay out in the open. Come on."

———•◆•———

Sulawayo's hotel was a half-hour shuttle ride from the mall. It was a narrow ten-storey building squashed in between a row of identical dilapidated hovels. The pallid woman manning the reception desk barely glanced at them as Sulawayo paid for a room.

It was on the sixth floor and faced out onto a long dried-up riverbed. There were two capsule beds in one wall, a tiny bathroom, a table bolted to the floor, one chair and two broken data ports. It smelled of mildew and blocked drains.

Rosie went immediately to the window but it was sealed shut.

"Don't bother." Sulawayo turned on the air filter and a low-pitched stuttering hum started. It didn't do much except move the stinking warm air about.

Rosie dumped her pack on the floor between her feet and sat on the lower capsule bed. All the stim was leaving her system in a rush.

"Here." Sulawayo shoved a bottle of water at her. "Do you have any food?"

"Yeah." Rosie pulled the packs of dry noodles from her bag and offered one to her.

"Not for me, for you."

Rosie wasn't hungry, but after a moment she decided she should eat something anyway. She ripped open the pack and poked at the noodles with the disposable fork.

"So where is the Freezone?"

"Four blocks." Agent Sulawayo was at the window.

She turned. "So tell me what happened. Why are you here?"

Rosie swallowed. "Started after the bomb at Riley's." She went through it all, from her aunt's injury to the Game Pit, the grunts on the bullet and how she'd ended up here alone. She told her almost everything, except for a few small items. She didn't tell her about the implant, or go into detail about Pip, and she left out the man she'd killed. There were some things she couldn't admit, even to herself.

"You don't know what happened to Dalton and Pip?"

"No."

"And you've come up here to see if you can get some answers about the base from Riley's contacts?"

"Something like that."

Sulawayo sat on the chair and watched Rosie with a quiet, thoughtful expression, her perfectly proportioned face difficult to read.

Rosie was about to ask her exactly what Riley had said to her to send her up here when the implant chose to reassert itself. A bolt of pure pain reverberated from her ear to her eyeballs. She screamed short and sharp and pressed her hands to her eyes. Her teeth ground together, every muscle in her face fighting it as numbers and words spiralled around her vision. *Gate, Leviathan, trust, exotic, Pantheon* and more that were merely fragments. It felt like something was clawing open her brain, tiny talons clutching at her mind. She felt her knees hit the floor and heard Agent Sulawayo's voice calling her name, not harsh and scared, but controlled.

It stopped abruptly with a sensation like a flower curling tight back into a bud inside her skull. Rosie opened her eyes, panting for breath, shaking.

"Are you all right?" Sulawayo had her by the shoulders, her thumbs pushing in hard against the bone.

Rosie stared at the thin brown floor covering. It was stained and scattered with specks of dirt. "I'm fine. Really, I'm good." She straightened, shrugging out of Sulawayo's grip, and pushed herself back up onto the bed.

"Are you going to tell me what that was about?"

Rosie licked her lips and looked for the water bottle. She'd knocked it over. She picked it up and drank the remainder. All the while Sulawayo watched her, calm, cool, as though Rosie hadn't just collapsed.

"Riley put a tracker implant in me, before he left. I think it's malfunctioning."

Sulawayo cupped an elbow in one hand and tapped the fingers of the other on her chin. She seemed puzzled, even faintly concerned. "A tracker would dissolve into your bloodstream if it malfunctioned," she said. "Are you sure that's what it is?" One hand touched Rosie's chin, tilting her face up. "That was not good, Miss Black."

Rosie pulled away. She felt shaky. Even her eyelashes ached, and she either needed to lie down and sleep for a week or take some more stim. It was the drug fading that seemed to trigger the implant. She looked at Sulawayo, hoping it was okay to tell her. "It's not a tracking implant," she said. "It's a cortex implant. Riley put information on it as a backup before he left. It triggered when his house blew up."

"And it hasn't been working right," Sulawayo said. A look of intense interest came into her eyes.

"Yeah, I guess." Rosie wasn't sure quite what that expression meant.

Sulawayo sat down on the chair. "Have you been seeing any of the information?"

"Just fragments. They don't make sense. I'm hoping Nation tech might be able to fix it, make it stop hurting me."

Sulawayo nodded, watching her thoughtfully. "Yes, good idea." She tilted her head to one side like she was considering something carefully.

"What?" Rosie said. She was making her uncomfortable.

Sulawayo frowned. "I wasn't planning on telling you this now, but if what you're saying is true, it certainly changes things. Makes matters more pressing, if you like." She inhaled. "That vision of you in the hospital – I sent it to you and released it to the Senate."

Rosie stopped breathing. Gobsmacked didn't cover it. "You ..." Words failed her.

"You're surprised?" Sulawayo seemed disappointed.

"But why would you do that?"

"Because I needed you to think about what your

options really were, to realise the best choice, the only choice when it comes to creating a cure for the MalX, is to join me."

Rosie blinked. What the hell was this? Her tenuous feeling of safety disappeared. She began to rise.

"Don't." Sulawayo's tone was quiet but laced with cold threat.

Rosie sat back down, heart racing. "Who are you really? What do you want?" she said hoarsely.

"You can't guess?" Sulawayo eyed her. "I am Helios, or at least a part of them."

Rosie swallowed hard. "I don't understand. If you knew where Riley was—"

"I am not one of those who believes Riley Shore should be neutralised. He is far more valuable alive. I made sure he was aware they were closing in so he could get out. There is a fracture in the organisation, a parting of ways if you like, since your escapade on Mars. Not all of us knew exactly what was going on up there – the killing, the tests. We were lied to. It made us question what else might not be as we thought."

"Such as?"

She smiled coldly. "Let's just say some of us think there are other ways of doing things." She paused. "You've heard of the Pantheon, haven't you?"

Rosie nodded. "The ruling five."

"Very good. One of them – and I don't know who, so don't bother asking – is leading us."

"Leading you to what?"

"A rebellion."

Rosie's mind raced, wondering what this meant. "The base," she said, "is that—"

"It doesn't belong to my faction," Sulawayo said. "But it will."

"What are Helios building there?"

"That is not your concern."

"Then what do you want with me? Why did you show the Senate and have them chase me all over the city? And what choice am I supposed to make about the MalX?" Her anger was beginning to outweigh her fear now. "And don't tell me Helios is the best choice for making a cure after what happened on Mars. You killed people in the name of science."

"Not me." Sulawayo's eye glittered. "Them. The rest of them. We don't want that. We want to create a cure that will save this planet, without killing the one who can provide it. Can anyone else offer that? We know the Senate and the UEC don't have the capability to do it. And Gondwana? They may have high hopes but as good as their tech is, it doesn't match ours. How much success has Pip had up there so far?"

Rosie glared at her. How did she know about what Pip was doing?

"I've been listening in on you at times." Sulawayo tapped her sleeve. "Your aunt was far too trusting. She should have checked your clothes."

Rosie's insides plummeted. She must have planted a listener on her at Senate Prime. "Why should I believe anything you say?" she said. "Besides, you're wasting your time with me. I can't make a cure."

"No, you can't." Sulawayo smiled. "But you have the ear of the one who can."

Rosie's breath caught. "Pip will never agree."

"I think you could convince him. He trusts you."

"Which is why I'd never ask him to do something he doesn't want to do."

"Are you sure? We are not the Helios he knew." She gave Rosie a pitying look. "Maybe you don't know him as well as you think."

"I. Will. Not." Rosie enunciated each word clearly.

"Yes, you will." Sulawayo sighed and for the first time Rosie saw a crack in her armour. She looked weary, older. "You think you won't do it, but you will because you're a smart girl, Rosie. A compassionate, clever girl, and you know he can't run forever. Things need to change; that's why I'm doing this. You could be part of that change."

Rosie couldn't believe anyone involved with Helios would do something for the good of the world. There had to be something in it for her. Power. Money. Both. God, how could Riley have not known about Sulawayo? It defied everything she knew about him.

Sulawayo was watching her closely, as if she could read her thoughts. "Do you know where Riley is?" she asked.

Rosie jumped. "No."

Sulawayo pursed her lips. "Well, no matter. If he has put his files in that implant, as you think, you can be even more useful to us than I thought."

Rosie felt alone and scared and totally out of her depth. She stared at Sulawayo, reminded even more of Nerita, the pilot on Mars. A thought occurred to her.

"Are you related to Nerita?"

Sulawayo was startled. "She's my cousin. Where did you– Oh, of course, Mars." She shrugged. "We are not much alike. I hear she's become a notorious space pirate."

"Doesn't sound that different from you." Rosie glanced at the door. It was barely a metre away and Sulawayo was still on the chair under the window. If she could move fast enough ... She shifted her weight.

"Nerita was always rebellious," Sulawayo said. "I haven't heard from her for–" Her last words were cut off as Rosie kicked the pack at her and lunged for the door.

"Rosie!" Sulawayo tried to follow but tripped over the bag strap.

Rosie wrenched open the door and flew down the hall to the stairs, almost falling as she jumped down them two and three at a time. Behind her, Sulawayo's footsteps thundered across the flimsy flooring.

"Rosie, stop!"

Six flights of stairs spiralled down to the reception area. Rosie ran like the dogs of hell were after her. She reached the second floor landing and leaped over the banister as Sulawayo's hand reached for her shirt. She

265

heard the woman's frustrated intake of breath as she missed her and Rosie thudded hard onto the floor, biting her tongue. Pain shot up her ankle, but she didn't stop. There was a bin next to the doors and Rosie pushed it over behind her as she plunged outside and sped down the street.

She weaved through the throng of people, not having a clue where she should go. She just ran, pelting down the street, turning down another and another until her lungs were burning and a stitch began to form in her side. Finally, she had to slow. She was struggling to get air into her lungs. She dropped to a walk and looked behind her, but Sulawayo wasn't there.

She'd lost her, or perhaps Sulawayo had given up because she knew exactly where Rosie was going to be at eight am. The Freezone Hotel. Rosie took a good look around, to get her bearings, then headed for the closest shop to ask for directions. She was just going to have to get there first.

CHAPTER 21

They were so close to the city now, Pip could see it on the horizon. They were damn lucky the illegal fuel depot actually had some fuel in it or they would never have made it this far. As it was, there was barely an hour left to get there. An hour to see if Rosie had managed to evade the guards. Fear for her sat in his gut, tight and furious. His hands tightened on the bars of the bike. He knew it was possible that Rosie had been caught. Images of what Helios might do to her went round and round his head, driving him nuts.

"How long?" Dalton shouted over his shoulder against the wind.

"Forty minutes till the city limits," he shouted back. He was pushing the bike as fast as he could. The protective skin was fully extended over their lower legs, the front shield throwing up terrain calculations, speed, wind factor, positioning, you name it. They'd tried to contact Kev again but the com was a cheap piece of crap and wouldn't lock into the signal.

The main road that connected Oak City with Capricornia was empty when they skidded onto it, but feeder roads from the few coastal towns increased the traffic and by the time they hit the outer limits, the four-lane highway was buzzing. Traffic-jammed ring-roads circled the city and there was no AI interface here. It was every driver for themselves in Capricornia and there was no shortage of handmade transports cobbled together from ship parts, jumpers and solar cars, or whatever was to hand, clogging the main arteries.

Without a helmet, specks of dirt, sand and random particles flew into his face and eyes. Pip hunched down behind the bike's front shield to avoid the worst.

They passed high-rises, squat shanty dumps and fully sealed towers all squashed up against each other. Brown rust, cracked walls and windows razed by the sandstorms. Still, it was thriving. People crowded the walkways and there was plenty of trade.

He got off the main artery and headed towards the Freezone, taking the back streets. The hotel was in a run-down area near the end of a cul-de-sac, sandwiched between a seedy Immerse XXX bar and a robotics seller. At the end of the street was the rear of a ten-storey mega mart, and a fenced off construction site took up most of the opposite side. He stopped near a boarded-up shop a block away from the back of the hotel and checked the time.

"Ten minutes to eight," he said quietly. Dalton shifted behind him, but neither got off the bike.

"Looks too quiet," Dalton said. Pip agreed. There were only a few people around and most of them seemed out of it, some just sitting on the pavement staring at nothing and talking to themselves.

The back of the Freezone rose five storeys above the sidewalk, with rows of small dirty windows marking the rooms. The only access was a shallow set of steps and a single door marked fire exit under a rusted overhang. A large square crate was on the sidewalk, one side partially caved in, as if it had been thrown from a great height. The stink of piss and stale beer wafted towards them. No sign of Rosie and no sign of anyone else. Something felt off, but Pip could see nothing to account for it.

"Going to have to check it out," he said.

They got off the bike, coding it so it would only start with one of their thumb prints.

"Where's Kev?" Dalton said. "Inside?"

"Yeah, there's a back room with a side exit." Pip pulled the gun from his waistband and they began walking towards the hotel.

The other people on the street took no notice of them. It was quiet, the sounds of the city traffic and humanity just a dull roar.

"I'm getting a bad feeling," Dalton said.

"You're not alone." Pip's heart rate was spiking, his muscles tensed.

Rosie almost didn't call out to them. She'd been huddled at the table next to the window in the Immerse bar for what felt like hours but was actually less than twenty minutes. The bar had no patrons and was little more than a dark foyer with a few sticky tables, a booth for the attendant and a hallway leading to the Immerse rooms. The androgynous attendant didn't seem to care that she only wanted to sit down. She took another thread of stim to keep alert and tame the implant, but mixed with adrenaline it made her feel like she was plunging through planetfall without a chute. When Pip and Dalton walked past she didn't quite register them.

She saw Pip's dark head then Dalton's dirty blond one and didn't quite believe it was them, even though she'd been hoping so fiercely they'd show. But then her brain clicked into action and she leaped off the stool.

"Pip! Dalton!" She was two steps out the door behind them. They boys spun around, eyes wide with surprise. But before they could say anything another voice shouted, "Get down!" It was not the kind of command to be ignored. All three of them dropped to the pavement as pulse fire hit the building above their heads in a spray of dust.

"Move!" Agent Sulawayo was charging from a gap in the fence over the road, a gun in each hand. She fired towards the Freezone, where two Helios grunts were shooting at them from behind the crate.

Rosie lunged back towards the Immerse, the boys behind her, but met two more grunts who were coming out.

"Rosie!" Pip yanked her backwards. She stumbled, overbalancing. Pip lifted his gun but wasn't fast enough. The first grunt caught Rosie's arm, threw her aside into the street and knocked Pip's gun away as he tackled him. Her head struck the road. All the air left her lungs and specks of light danced in her vision. Pulse fire whizzed and spat off metal and brick and she rolled to the side, dizzy, trying to find some cover. Sulawayo was crouched behind a bin on the other side of the street, firing at the grunts, and both boys were wrestling with others. One of them had Pip against the wall, choking him. Rosie looked around desperately for some way to help. Pip's gun was near the kerb. She scrambled for it, but someone seized her arm and wrenched it up behind her. She screamed.

"That's not for little girls," another grunt said. He kicked the gun away, sending it skittering down the street. She tried to hit him with her other fist, but he inched her arm higher chuckling.

She almost passed out. He was going to break her arm. White sparks made her vision swim, then she caught a blur of motion and a body hit the grunt from the side, throwing him off her. There was a sharp musky scent of leather and she caught a brief glimpse of a man's face, dark skin and the flash of eyes the colour of river mud. Then he whirled towards the grunt who was sprinting away up the street. His long coat billowed as he moved and Rosie saw a knife at his waist. Seconds later the knife was embedded in the grunt's back and he went down. The man then sprang on the grunts tackling Pip and Dalton. He attacked so fast he didn't seem human. His arms sliced the air and the grunt who'd been strangling Pip was on the ground. Then Dalton was left standing as his opponent hit the pavement with nothing more than a startled exhalation. The man bent and stripped both grunts of their weapons. Then he was gone, moving fast towards the Freezone.

Rosie realised then the gunfire had stopped. Agent Sulawayo was out in the street, clutching her side, and another man like the one who'd rescued them was standing over the two other grunts who were out cold on the ground. A third man was with them. It had all happened shockingly fast.

Rosie tried to lever herself to her feet. Her left arm was throbbing and she had to hold it close to her side.

Dalton ran to help her. "You all right?" He was breathing fast and was bleeding from a cut to his mouth, but seemed okay. Pip had collapsed on the sidewalk and was shuddering and sucking in breaths, his head dropped between his bent knees.

"Better than you two." Rosie went to Pip.

"I'm okay," he said hoarsely as she reached him. He pushed to his feet, brushing away the hand she offered. He wasn't steady though and a decent bruise was already forming under his right eye. Rosie watched him with concern. "Quit looking at me like that," he said. "Anyone'd think you liked me or something." A pained smile curved his lips, then he winced and touched his jaw. "Ow."

"Who are they?" Dalton said.

"Yalgu Warriors," Pip answered. "Who the hell is that woman with Kev?" He was watching Sulawayo talk to the third man and the warriors.

"That's Agent Sulawayo," Rosie said. "I thought she worked for Riley, but she's Helios."

"What?" Dalton said. "But—"

"Why the hell was she firing at the Helios grunts?" Pip interrupted. "And how is she even here?" He scanned the ground. "Where's my gun?"

Kev and Sulawayo were heading their way, leaving the warriors to drag the grunts off the streets.

"She was on the train," Rosie said.

"When we got attacked?" Dalton said.

Rosie shook her head. "I don't know. I saw her at Capricornia. I thought she was going to help me. Then she said she was Helios, but that she's part of a breakaway faction. She said that they want to change the way Helios operates. She wanted me to join them." She looked at Pip. "Because she wants you."

"Everyone wants me," Pip rasped. "It's my charm and good looks; I'm irresistible." But his voice was far from even. He'd found the gun now and held it pointed down but ready. He watched Sulawayo approach, something dangerous behind his eyes.

"Pip ..." Rosie put a hand on his arm. A muscle ticked in his jaw and she shared a worried look with Dalton who slowly stepped up to Pip's right side. Sulawayo still had a weapon at her waist and was watching them closely. Even injured, Rosie doubted she'd be hampered.

"You kids okay?" Kev reached them. He was Pip's height, in his thirties, dark skinned, with a face that looked like it smiled often. Just not now. "Rosie, I'm guessing, and Dalton." His gaze took in the both of them.

Sulawayo held onto her injured side, but stood tall. "Pip." She inclined her head at him.

Pip met Sulawayo's gaze. "Kev, Rosie says she's Helios." Kev paused for a millisecond, then his gun was up and he stepped back pointing it at her, his face set hard.

"You said you worked for Riley," Kev said.

"I did." Sulawayo looked at him sideways, still keeping an eye on Pip. "I am also Helios but I'm not with those others."

"You better explain that fast," Kev said.

"She said she's part of a rebel faction in Helios," Rosie said.

Sulawayo acted as if Kev's gun wasn't pointed at her head. Her dark eyes found Rosie. "Changing things from the inside. You could help."

"I don't think so," Pip said softly.

"You can too. Maybe Rosie could tell you how."

"You leave her out of this." Pip's voice had become dangerously low, but Sulawayo only smiled.

"I saved your lives just now. Why would I do that if I'm a threat? We want the same things."

"I doubt that," Dalton said.

She sent him a measured glance. "I'm not sure what you're planning, but my people are going to take over the base in Gondwana Nation. It's probably best you stay out of it, for now. You don't know what you're up against."

"Enough," Kev said. He turned and whistled to get the warriors' attention, then raised a hand and beckoned one of them over. "I don't have time to deal with you now, but my friends here will keep you company – in case you have any ideas about following."

"My people will be here soon," Sulawayo said. "They will outnumber them."

"Numbers don't mean much to the Yalgu."

"We won't give them any trouble – unless they try to stop us leaving."

"That will be between you and them," Kev said.

"I am on your side," Sulawayo said. "Isn't that right, Rosie?"

Her dark eyes glittered and Pip stepped forwards, pushing Rosie behind him. He pointed his gun at Sulawayo. "You don't talk to her." His voice was rough with threat and the gun whined, powering up.

"Pip–" Rosie's heart leaped with fear. Dalton moved like he was going to block him, but Kev stepped between Pip and Sulawayo.

"Relax, bro." He carefully put a hand on Pip's gun hand, pushing it down, and nodded at the warrior who'd reached them. "Take her weapon. Will you keep her here?"

"Until we leave." The warrior held out his hand for Sulawayo's gun. She calmly gave it to him, showing no sign of fear.

Kev spoke over his shoulder to Pip. "You and Rosie take that bike you've got. You know where to go. Dalton, you're with me."

Rosie, tense with fear, looked at Dalton. He was less than happy about leaving her.

Pip holstered his gun and she felt his muscles trembling as he took her arm. "Come on." He cast Sulawayo a hard look as they moved off.

CHAPTER 22

Pip drove the bike to a boarded-up building a few blocks away. Rosie squinted as they rolled inside, trying to adjust to the dimmer light. The air smelled of dust and grease. Three more bikes were lined up near the door. Kev and Dalton were passing a drink bottle between them and Pip pulled up next to them, dropping a foot to the floor. He kept the bike running. The cut on Dalton's lip had dried but his mouth was swelling and he looked pale and exhausted. Like all of them. He handed her the water bottle.

"Thanks." She took a long sip, not bothering to get off the bike.

"Picking up stray girls again, Pip?" a voice said behind her. Rosie jumped and almost choked as a tall, slim blond girl came out of the darkness. "Rosie Black, I presume?" Her cold gaze swept Rosie from head to toe and clearly found her lacking. "I thought you'd be taller."

"Cassie? What the hell is she doing here, Kev?" Pip glared at her.

This was Riley's sister. Rosie stared. She was beautiful, in an angular kind of way, with the same straight nose and brown eyes as her brother, but her mouth looked thinner, harder. Or maybe that was just the way she was looking at Rosie, like she was some kind of unpalatable alien life form.

"She followed me," Kev said. "And we've already had words. You need any more fuel, Pip?"

"No, we're good." Pip was still glaring at Cassie, who looked unconcerned.

Kev got on a bike. "I've got a jumper lined up to get us over the border and back to Worla. But we gotta motor; the border pass expires in an hour."

"What happens if we're late?" Rosie said.

"Border patrol zaps our bird."

"He means the jumper will be externally locked down," Pip said. "They'll electro pulse it so we can't lift off. And we'll be stuck here until tomorrow. Kev will have to clear us again."

"That's about the size of it. Take that one, Dalton." Kev pointed to another bike.

"Any idea where my brother is, super girl?" Cassie

said to Rosie.

"No one knows; he disappeared."

"I wonder why." Cassie's tone implied she thought it was Rosie's fault.

"Cassie, get on your bike," Kev barked. She rolled her eyes as if they were sharing some private joke, but the look in them could have poisoned a viper.

———•◦•———

The jumper was waiting for them on the outskirts of the city, where low bungalows, cobbled together from ship parts and scrap, sat up against apartment towers that had never been finished. Humpies and tents were erected in any spare space and there were lots of people around on the street. Someone had lit a fire and smoke drifted across the road, stinking of chemicals and some unidentified roasting meat.

Kev waved an arm to the right, pointing at a high-rise. A holo sign, glowing red and purple, announced it as the Last Stop Hostel. It looked tawdry, the walls pockmarked with bullet holes and the majority of the windows covered in security grilles.

They followed him into a dark driveway that wound up around the inside of the building to the roof. The jumper was powering up as they appeared. Shaped like a fat bean, it was a converted spacecab, the sturdy short-range kind used to ferry people between space stations or ship to planet.

Pip rolled the bike to a stop next to Dalton. "Looks like a storm coming." He jerked his chin skyward. Overhead was clear, but to the north a line of dark low cloud was gathering.

"Jumper should be all right," Dalton said, but he didn't sound confident.

"Don't look so worried, Curtis. It's all Nation tech. It'll take at least three lightning strikes to knock her out of the sky." Pip smirked.

"Ignore him." Cassie stopped her bike beside Dalton. "You can sit with me, spare you his wit."

"It's not like you to be so considerate," Pip said, and her smile became icy.

"Children, let's go," Kev said.

The jumper had a small cabin for the pilot and behind that were two rows of padded bench seats and a cargo hold.

Rosie sat in the back seat against the hull and Dalton climbed in next to her. Pip cast him a look that was less than impressed and took the seat in front. Cassie sat next to him. She smiled smugly at Rosie as she sat, as if she'd won something. Rosie was too tired to care. Kev took the front bench on the other side and the ship rumbled as it revved for take-off.

Rosie watched through the narrow window next to her as they accelerated away from the roof. They banked hard and Capricornia was laid out beneath them in all its ramshackle glory. Then they were rising higher and levelling out, heading north.

It wasn't a quiet craft. Dalton had to raise his voice to be heard as he leaned over the seat and shook Pip's shoulder. "How long till we get there?"

"An hour, give or take, depending on the weather." Pip twisted around and caught Rosie's eye. "There's a good medical lab there, and Kev's wife's a doctor, a really good one."

The pilot's loud voice came over the intercom. "Strap in everyone; it's going to be a bumpy trip. Storm cell city." He sounded way too happy about that.

They all scrambled to clip themselves in with the seat harnesses. Rosie got hers done up just in time. A massive gust of wind hit them and the jumper lurched sideways. She hung on to her straps, praying they wouldn't snap. Dalton went a paler shade of white. Their eyes met and Rosie grinned and made a terrified face at him. He grinned back.

"They don't have this in simulators," he shouted. Then the rain came and it was impossible to talk. It felt as if they'd gone under an enormous high-pressure hose and the jumper rocked dangerously. She clung to her harness and after a while felt too ill even to be scared. The constant rocking and shaking motion made her want to vomit and she began hoping they might crash just to put her out of her misery. She closed her eyes. *Do not spew on yourself, Rosie Black. Do not.*

Finally, after what felt like half of her life, they began to descend.

"Hope you're all okay back there." The pilot came back over the com, cheerful as ever. "ETA is five minutes. Just hang on a bit longer, and thanks for flying the vomit comet."

Rosie would have shot him if she could. At last, the rocking began to decrease and the engines screamed as they powered down and settled on the ground.

They staggered out. The sky was dark with cloud and it was still raining. The landing site was cleared ground surrounded by thick grass and trees. She'd glimpsed the tops of geodesic dome houses as they'd come down, but not much else.

Kev shouted something and waved towards a road at the tree line. Half bent over by the wind and rain, they followed him as the jumper launched. Rosie ran blindly, following Pip, mud spattering up the legs of her jeans.

They got closer to the centre of the community, but there was no one around, no lights on. The community homes were built along wide streets and spread over quite an area. They looked like parachutes tethered to the earth by stone anchors. The living quarters were in the top half of each dome; the underneath was open to allow flooding and wind to pass through. Rosie glimpsed the door of one dome wide open and banging in the wind, rain washing inside. They passed a cluster of buildings and a few bikes that had toppled over in the mud. A set of deep tyre tracks cut through the road as though a heavy vehicle had been through. One of the bikes looked like it had been run over. They stopped.

"Where is everybody?" Cassie shouted. Rosie saw Pip and Kev exchange looks, then Kev sprinted ahead, followed closely by Pip.

Kev's home was a large dome like the others. Rosie followed Cassie up the stairs, Dalton behind her. The door was broken and Kev's possessions were scattered everywhere. Digi books, coms, and tools were strewn across the floor of a large open living area. Children's toys, clothes and overturned chairs showed the perpetrators had cared little for anything in here.

Kev stood in the middle of the room staring like he couldn't believe what he was seeing. Pip swore as he picked up a broken toy. Behind him, plasglass framed a wide balcony under the protective curve of the dome's roof.

"Where're Lakisha and the boys?" Cassie said, an edge of panic in her voice.

"They've gone to Naru."

Kev spun around, his gun out. A tall man stood in the doorway, dressed in a long coat, like the men who'd helped them in Capricornia. He had on rough trousers and a black T-shirt and his hair was dark and curling to his shoulders. A long curved knife was belted around his waist.

Kev lowered his gun, a tremor in his hand. "They're all right?" he said.

The man nodded. "Our people took both the helis, got out before they came."

Kev exhaled in relief and rubbed a hand over his face. "Thank God," he whispered.

"Helios." Pip said.

The Yalgu man looked at him. The whites of his eyes were very white. "That's right. They were looking for something, or someone."

"What happened?" Rosie asked, then wished she hadn't spoken when the warrior turned his dark eyes on her. It felt like he was looking into her soul and seeing that she knew what Helios wanted, that she was bound up with them.

She thought he was going to berate her, but all he said was, "A team of them came in fast. We hardly had time to get the people out. By the time we came back, this had happened." He spread a hand at the debris around them. "Why would they come here?"

"They're looking for me." Pip said. "They must have figured out where I was staying when they saw me with you, Kev."

"You knew Helios were up here." It wasn't a question and he looked angry about it.

"We've known only for a short time," Kev said carefully.

"You are not the only ones," the man replied. "Omgurri Council gave Helios permission to use their land."

"What?" Cassie said.

He ignored her, speaking only to Kev. "We have come in to end this. To force Helios out. We have given the Council some time to end it, but if they fail, we will act."

"How much time?"

"A day, maybe two if our leaders allow it."

Kev looked shaken. He turned to Pip and Cassie. "I'm going to have to talk to the council right away – and the warriors." He glanced at the man, who stood calm and immutable. "Have you got transport?"

"We have a jumper waiting."

"You all just stay here," Kev said. "I'll be back as quickly as I can. Don't do anything. I'll contact you if possible."

Then he was gone.

Rosie, Pip, Dalton and Cassie stood staring at each other, still dripping on the floor. Outside the rain lashed the roof like it wanted to drown them, and it was getting darker by the minute. Rosie shivered. The boys' shirts were plastered to their chests and she could see a fist-sized bruise on Dalton's ribs through his white shirt. She held her own tank out from her and squeezed, sending a trickle of water onto her shoes.

"What did he mean by 'end this'?" Dalton looked at Pip.

"He means the Yalgu are threatening war," Cassie replied.

"It might not come to that," Pip said.

"What else would it mean?" she snapped. "They said

they were coming to end it."

"And what does that mean exactly?" Dalton said.

"It means they are seriously pissed." Pip glanced between him and Rosie. "Do you know much about the Yalgu Warriors?"

"As much as anyone," Dalton said.

"Which means not much. Look, the Yalgu are like the Nation's military, except they don't really answer to anyone and can overrule anything the councils say if they want to. Which they usually don't. They hardly ever get involved in politics."

"Hang on, I'm confused," Dalton said. "He said Omgurri Council know about the Helios base."

Pip's tone was impatient as he said, "There are nine councils on Nation lands who make the rules cooperatively. Omgurri is just one of them. They must have given Helios permission to be here behind the other councils' backs – which is going to cause one hell of a fight with the other eight. But that's not the main problem. The warriors clearly want Helios out and have given everyone a day to sort it out or they will."

"And I'm guessing their version of sorting doesn't involve much talking," Rosie said.

Pip shook his head. "They're not big on the talking, no. You saw those two in Capricornia. Imagine what five hundred could do."

"What are the chances of the council settling this?" Dalton said.

Pip gave a bitter laugh. "If the Omgurri Council has made a deal with Helios, they're not going to want to break it. Knowing Helios, they probably can't anyway."

"So what?" Cassie said. "The Yalgu can solve our problem for us. Let them get rid of Helios."

"You seriously think it's that easy, Cass?"

"I don't think Helios deserve any mercy, do you?" she said.

"That's not the point!" He ran a hand roughly over his head. "You just don't get it, do you?"

"Get what?"

"I think he's saying it won't end here," Dalton said. His quiet tone made them both pause.

"Exactly." Pip sent a glance his way. "Helios won't take the destruction of their base lying down. They'll come back, they'll bring a full force with them and they'll kill every single person who tells them no. Or if I know them, they'll just make one giant MalX infection bomb and get rid of everybody that way. They made the MalX, I bet they're working on a way to weaponise it."

A MalX weapon? Rosie hadn't thought of that, but now he said it she could believe it. It was just Helios's style. "How many people live in Gondwana Nation?" Rosie asked.

"A million or so."

She felt ill. Even Cassie looked scared. Pip was right. Things would get very, very bad. They were all silent.

"Look," Dalton said finally. "I don't think any of us

are thinking straight right now. Why don't we dry off and get some pain blockers and cell repairs?"

"There's a full kit in Kev's bathroom," Cassie said.

"Good, we're going to need them, and something to eat. Then we can come up with a game plan."

"Can't say I figured a Central for the sensible type," Pip said. At Rosie's irritated look, he added, "But that's not the worst idea I've heard today."

"At least someone here has brains," Cassie said. "I'm having the first shower." She glanced at Rosie. "My room's upstairs. I might be able to find a shirt or something to fit you."

Don't break a sweat with the generosity. Rosie followed her to the curved staircase.

"Curtis, I'm down here." Pip slouched towards a door past the open-plan kitchen. "Meet you back here in ten."

Forty minutes later, Rosie met the boys back downstairs. Cassie had found her a pair of black pants that were too long and a dark red top. It was a relief to be dry, but Rosie felt more tired than ever. Now that a cell repair shot had begun to fix up all her cuts and bruises, all she wanted to do was sleep.

The boys had cleaned up while they waited. Chairs had been righted and most of the detritus picked up. Pip was inspecting the chill unit while Dalton chopped tomatoes.

"Are those real?" Rosie slid onto a stool.

"Taste real." Dalton handed her a piece with a smile.

His hair was damp from the shower, the thick wavy locks brushed back from his face. It emphasised the whopper of a bruise along his jaw.

"Oh my God." Rosie covered her mouth with her hand as she chewed. The slice of tomato was sweet and dusky, tasting nothing like the engineered fruit she'd had before.

"Everything's real in Nation." Pip swivelled back from the cool unit, kicking the door shut behind him. He dumped another mystery container on the bench next to Rosie. "Especially the weather. It's still raining like there's water to spare on the planet."

Rosie looked at the wall of windows. It was dark outside and she couldn't see anything but she could certainly hear it, a constant drumming against the balcony roof and wind scraping past the curved walls.

"Christ, it smells like a cheap boy-toy parlour in here." Cassie came down the stairs. She was wearing a black catsuit that emphasised every curve and made her long legs look even longer. She was pretending not to notice both boys watching her – Pip with a form of admiring contempt like he'd seen this trick before and Dalton with amused appreciation. Rosie hoped she'd trip and fall over, but of course she didn't.

"Hey, Curtis," said Pip. "Be careful of the pretty fruit – they're usually poisonous."

Cassie narrowed her eyes at him. 'Trying to be cute again, Pippy?" She dropped a pack of cell-repair vials and pain blockers on the bench.

"Finally." Pip reached for one. "I was about to bust your door down. And for the record, I don't have to try." He winked at Rosie and skidded a vial across the bench to Dalton.

Pip might be all cheek, but he was grey with exhaustion and his fingers fumbled as he tried to rip open the pack.

"Give it to me." Rosie easily snatched it from his grasp. He didn't protest. She ripped it open with her teeth and handed him the vial.

"Thanks. Nothing like a bit of saliva to help the healing." He gave her a faint, private smile and their fingers brushed as he took it. Her stomach flipped and heat rushed up her neck. She looked away quickly.

"You need a hand?" she said to Dalton, but he was already pressing the vial to the inside of his arm. The self injector made a tiny hissing noise.

"Think I've got it." He was faring better than Pip, but not by much.

"Now we've all played doctor," Cassie said, "what's to eat?"

"Give a man a chance to repair, will you?" Pip said.

"Show me a man and I will." She opened one of the containers. "This looks like some kind of curry."

"Tomato salad and curry then," Dalton said.

Cassie gave him a seductive smile. "Sounds tasty." She leaned on the counter, squeezing her cleavage together.

Rosie was amazed by her subtle-as-a-meteorite flirting. Dalton just seemed amused, but girls probably flirted with him all the time. It irritated her. In fact, everything about Cassie annoyed her.

Rosie's head began to ache again, despite the pain blockers. She rubbed at her forehead. Perfect. *Please, implant, choose now to stick a spike in my brain.* She looked up to see Pip watching her and abruptly dropped her hand.

"What?" It came out more harshly than she meant.

"Nothing. I'll get some plates." He went to a cupboard, but it was obvious he'd noticed her annoyance and drawn some conclusions from it which were all wrong.

Pip heated the curry and they sat around the bench eating.

"First things first," Dalton said. "The reason Rosie and I were coming here was because of the implant Riley put in her brain."

"I'm sorry, what?" Cassie's spoon clattered onto her plate. Rosie realised of course she wouldn't know about that.

"Your brother's idea of a backup plan," Pip said. "He put a cortex implant in her skull to store all his precious information and didn't tell her. He also didn't tell her that little detail of you having to be dead to ever get it out."

"That doesn't sound like him." Cassie frowned.

"Yeah, it does. I keep telling you how he operates, but you don't want to hear it."

"That's because you're wrong. Besides, cortex implants are the safest kind there are."

"Unless they malfunction." Pip shook his head. "Seriously Cass, you gotta knock Riley off that pedestal."

"How do you know it's malfunctioning?" asked Cassie.

"I got too close to an explosion and I think it did something to it. I'm seeing flashes of information, words, numbers, and it kind of hurts," Rosie said.

"Kind of is an understatement." Dalton pushed his empty plate aside. "Rosie, you passed out."

She ignored him. "The point is, we came here because Riley left a message in it that I think was set to activate if he disappeared."

"Saying?" Cassie prompted her.

"It came out disjointed. I thought maybe it meant he would be up here as well, but ..." She paused.

Cassie's expression tightened. "Clearly he's not."

"Are you sure?" Dalton said. "He might think contacting you would be too risky."

"He's not here." Cassie's tone was blunt. "And before you ask, no, I have no idea where he would go. So what did the message say?"

"The gist of it was to come to Gondwana Nation, we think. Maybe because tech up here could decode the implant," Rosie said.

"So it's got to have information about the base on it," said Cassie. "I bet he figured out what they're doing there. It might even tell us where he's gone."

Rosie didn't like the hopeful tone she got at that idea. "I doubt he'd leave any clues," she said. "It's not his style." She glanced at Dalton. "I saw a few other words. Pantheon and Equinox Gate."

Cassie's eyes lit up. "Are you saying he might have figured out who the Pantheon are?"

"I don't know." Rosie pushed her half-eaten meal aside. Her head was throbbing and she had no patience for guessing games. "Look, this is what I know. Riley isn't here. Helios is and nobody likes that. It looks like the best way of keeping a million or so people alive is to get the Helios base shut down before the Yalgu Warriors do it their way, agreed?"

"And what about Sulawayo?" Dalton said. "She said she was going to take over the base."

"It doesn't matter," Pip said. "She's still Helios, whatever she might be trying to sell."

"Who's Sulawayo?" Cassie said.

Rosie sighed and went through a short explanation about how Sulawayo had been a double agent working for Riley and Helios, and had tried to abduct her after the train. "She said she still wanted to work with Riley, that it was her who warned him the rest of Helios had found him, and that's why he ran off, but–"

"We can't trust her," Pip said. "We don't know her

real agenda. Trust me, if I know Helios, it's not all unicorns and rainbows."

Rosie bit her lip. "Still, if Sulawayo's telling the truth, a split in Helios could be an advantage."

"Pip's right; we can't team up with her," Dalton said.

"So what do we do?" Cassie said.

Rosie's head was aching so much it was difficult to think.

"Rosie, you okay?" Pip said.

A faint roaring sound had started in her ears. She tried to respond, but his face seemed to grow longer and wave about like a flower underwater. She pushed her stool out, sensing what was coming, hoping she could get to the sofa quickly enough. Nope.

"Shit!" She heard Pip's low-voiced curse and the bang of a stool hitting a cupboard.

"Catch her!" Dalton said and the planet tilted. Pip's arms went around her, but it wasn't enough to stop the roaring dark, glowing green with words, swallowing her up.

CHAPTER 23

Rosie opened her eyes to a grey ceiling, the sound of rain thrumming on the roof and a low steady beeping. Her first reaction was to be royally pissed off at having fainted again but that was quickly overtaken by resonating pain that spread down her spine to her feet. Even her toenails ached. And then came the realisation she couldn't move. Not at all.

The slow steady beeping rose in time with her frantic heartbeat.

"Don't panic like a little girl; it's only temporary." Cassie's face appeared above her. Her blond hair was wet and slicked back in a ponytail. She couldn't have sounded less comforting.

"Your bedside manner sucks," Rosie said. She'd

intended it to be cutting but she was breathing so fast it came out all high.

"Get a grip, Black." Cassie put a cool hand on her arm.

"Where am I?"

"In the medical lab. We had to bring you here through the rain. Thanks so much."

"Where are Pip and Dalton?"

Cassie made a face. "I sent them out. Useless, the two of them. Pip shouting at me and Dalton shouting at him. It's a wonder I got you stable at all."

"You?" Rosie did not like the sound of that.

"Relax." Cassie passed a handheld scanner over her torso as if she did it every day. "I've been Lakisha's assistant since I was twelve; I know what I'm doing. That's Doctor Lakisha, by the way."

Despite her appalling lack of compassion, Cassie's brusque confidence was making Rosie calmer. "Being an assistant doesn't make you a doctor," Rosie said.

"No, but I will be, one day," Cassie said absently. She put the handheld down and picked up a long wand-like device that hummed. She slipped a hand under Rosie's neck and lifted her head like she was handling a bunch of seaweed — breakable, fragile seaweed, but weed just the same. She ran the wand up the back of Rosie's neck to the base of her skull. "You know, both my parents were scientists, geniuses, and they passed all that brilliance to me. I can be anything I choose, really."

"Can you choose not to be a bitch?"

Cassie took the wand away and smiled. "Move your fingers."

Rosie tried and was filled with relief when she could.

"It will take a while for everything to come back, but it will."

"Why did you paralyse me?"

"You went into a kind of seizure and in their effort to hold you down the boys might have broken your bones. It seemed like the better choice." She looked amused. "Scared the crap out of them. You were almost frothing at the mouth and everything."

Fabulous, bet that looked great. Rosie tried lifting an arm, found she could, and pushed some hair off her face. "Why weren't you scared?" she asked.

"That's not the sort of thing that scares me."

"Can you do anything about the pain?"

"How bad is it?"

"Get someone to drop a jumper on you, that should cover it."

Cassie tapped the wand against her palm. "I don't know if you'll want to do this, but I might have an idea of how to fix the implant, or at least stop it doing this to you."

"And that is?"

Cassie looked the tiniest bit reticent. "There's an imager here in the lab that's capable of accessing the implant. It should allow me to have a go at reprogramming the nanos, stop it hurting you. The only thing is, I've never actually used it myself, but I have worked with Lakisha when she has. I know how it works."

"But?" Rosie winced as a fresh wave of pain washed over her skull.

"I could make things worse. Or, well ..." Clearly, there was chance she could kill her.

This just got better and better, but Rosie knew she was reaching the end of her endurance. "Let's just get it over with."

"I'll get one of the boys to move you. Wait there."

Funny. Rosie tried to lift a leg, but it felt as heavy as a planet.

"Hey, how you going?"

Dalton came in, followed by Pip. Pip looked furious and scared at the same time, his hands tucked up into his armpits.

"Bring her to the chair." Cassie spoke from somewhere behind him.

Dalton picked Rosie up. "Don't worry; I won't drop you."

The pain was getting overwhelming and Rosie couldn't speak. Through half-closed lids she saw a huge room sectioned by long tables covered in equipment and high-tech medical machines.

"This way." Cassie led them through a set of doors.

In the next room was a long recliner with a scanner device suspended above it. One wall was a projection space.

Dalton put her down in the chair and stepped back.

Cassie said, "You might want to put the restraints on her arms and legs, just in case."

"I thought you said you'd stopped that problem." Pip's voice was loaded with apprehension and more than a little anger.

Cassie turned from where she was activating the computers. "It's probably unnecessary, but I'd rather be safe than not."

"Just do it," Rosie said. To her utmost fury she felt tears slipping down her cheeks, uncontrollable now because of the pain.

Dalton stepped forwards, but Pip was faster. "I'll do it." He pushed him back and Dalton didn't protest. Pip gently buckled a set of soft restraints over her arms and legs. She hated the feeling. His hand lingered on her wrist. "Okay," he said.

Rosie stared at him, suddenly terribly frightened. The restraints, the pain – it was all too much. He did something then that was totally out of character. As if there was no one else in the room, he tenderly wiped the tears from her cheeks with his thumb, looking her steadily in the eyes. "It'll be all right," he said softly. "I'll be right here, okay?"

The pulse of fear in her throat dimmed. "Okay," she whispered.

"This is touching, but Pip, you're in the way," Cassie said.

Pip drew back and a faint humming filled the room. The lights dimmed as the device over Rosie's head dropped steadily towards her. It was a circular tube with hundreds of tiny eyelets on it that looked like cameras. It stopped just centimetres from her face and began to rotate.

"Close your eyes, Rosie," Cassie said.

A spike of white-hot light lanced through her retina and she screamed. It felt as if someone was slowly pushing a fine blazing needle through the front of her head to the back. It spread so deep she lost all sense of where she was. Tears streamed from her eyes and the band of agony spread through her skull like molasses, pain oozing through all her nerve endings.

"What're you doing?"

Dimly, she heard Pip's voice and Cassie shouting back, "No, it will stop in a minute. Don't touch her!"

The pain intensified and then suddenly it was gone. She shuddered, trying to draw breath. Then she stilled as something amazing happened. She opened her eyes and instead of seeing the room she saw brilliant colours, a wheel of light and a spiral of circling numbers. It should have been confusing, but it made sense to her. She saw through them to what they meant. She was filled with a sense of euphoria as her brain was flooded with endorphins.

"I'm okay," she whispered. "I'm okay, it's ..." She couldn't describe it. Pip and Dalton were little more than shadows beyond the lights, but she wasn't afraid. She blinked and tried thinking a command to see the files for the Helios base. One of the number sets zoomed towards her and expanded, and suddenly there they were. Plans, information. She knew what Helios was doing up there. Holy crap. She roamed over the information, closed the file, then practised opening it again. Easy.

She went back to the spiral and a long index appeared. File after file. All that Riley had found out about Helios over the ten years he'd been tracking them, investigating everything they did. And there were files on all of them as well. Pip, her, Dalton, even Aunt Essie and Cassie, plus names she didn't know. Then she saw the word Pantheon. She focused on that, tried to open it, but an electric spark shocked her like a slap. She tried again and the shock intensified. She pushed at it and this time the recoil was much, much stronger. A long sharp sliver of pain slipped into her brain. She screamed and a shudder ripped through her. There was a wrenching, pulling sensation, like bone ripped from a socket, and the light was gone, the implant snapping closed. The sharper pain vanished to be replaced by a duller pedestrian ache. She opened her eyes, panting, her pulse running high.

Cassie stood over her, actually looking anxious. Pip and Dalton were at her feet, matching expressions of alarm on their faces.

"She's okay. Her heart rate's dropping," Cassie said. "Christ, Rosie, what the hell?" She glared at her.

"Everything was going well and then you did something."

"You mean I tried to do something." Rosie wriggled her arms. "Undo me."

"Tried what?" Pip began to unstrap her.

"There was an index thing, a list of all the files. One of them was Pantheon, but when I tried to open it–"

"It rejected you," Cassie said. She studied the computer tablet. "That makes sense. I saw this, but didn't ..." She trailed off, staring at the tablet.

"What?" Pip said.

Cassie looked at them, her eyes bright with realisation. "He time coded it," she said. "It's brilliant. The nano work is incredible."

"What?" Dalton said, his tone impatient.

"You mean the information is on a time-release schedule?" Rosie said. Cassie nodded. "So even if I want to access it, I can't."

"Exactly." Cassie said. "He must have wanted you to have the base information first, for obvious reasons, but the rest you'll get access to over time."

"How much time?" Pip said.

"Impossible to tell." Cassie frowned at the tablet. "When she was exposed to that bomb, the magnetic pulse altered something in the programming, so we can't predict what files will be accessible when, but this time coding tells us something really important. Riley put everything on a time delay for a reason. Firstly, to protect Rosie if anyone tried to force the information out of her."

"Why not just kill her and pull it out?" Dalton said.

"Can't." Cassie shook her head. "The implant will selfdestruct. It needs her alive to function."

"Lucky me," Rosie said.

"It also means he must be planning to come back," Cassie said.

Pip raised an eyebrow. "How do you figure that?"

"Because the information is released in some kind of order, probably of usefulness or importance. He must have been betting on Helios getting hold of Rosie at some point, so he put the info in her. It either becomes useful to her if she's not caught, and a life-saving tool for her if she is."

"As in they're not going to kill me if I'm useful," Rosie said. "But eventually the files run out."

"Yes, but he knows how long that will take, and he would have planned to be back before that happens."

"Unless he's dead," Dalton said. "What's the whole time frame? Can you tell?"

"About eight months."

"Eight months!" Pip said. "What was he thinking, that Helios would build her a nice cosy retreat and bring her cakes every day?"

"I don't know," Cassie said. "But he must have been desperate. He wouldn't have done this for kicks."

Rosie tended to agree with her, but Pip clamped his lips together like he was keeping himself from saying something he might regret.

"Let's focus on what we know," Dalton said. He turned to Rosie. "Did you see anything about the base?"

Rosie nodded. "They're building a wormhole just like the UEC has been trying to do. Or at least they're designing the prototype that will lead to an in-space build. They call it an Equinox Gate."

"A what?" Cassie stared at her.

"It's a nifty little number," Pip said. "Bends space and time, allows travel across vast distances in an instant."

"I know what a wormhole is," Cassie snapped.

"No wonder they're keeping it secret," Dalton said. "If Helios have control of a wormhole, they can run — Jesus, everything. They'll control access to Titan's water, the outer planets, the Oceanus colony—"

"And to all future colonies," Rosie said. "How much do you want to bet they have something to do with the UEC's failure to make their own wormhole — and the *Leviathan* disaster."

"They're setting up a reason for the UEC to be forced to accept them running the gate," Cassie said. "If Helios build it first, the way things are now, the UEC would have to agree to their terms of use."

"So," Pip said, "Helios is reaching for universal domination. Hands up anyone who's surprised."

They were all silent for a long moment.

"And I thought the base might be another happy little replica of the Enclave, complete with people dying to create a MalX cure," Pip said. "Literally."

"I'm sure they haven't given up on using you for that," Cassie said. "But maybe you're just not as important as you think."

"Oh, I'm hurt." Pip glared at her.

"Stop it!" Rosie pushed up on her elbows. "Cassie, have you got another tablet? I can trace down the plans for the base."

"Should be one in the other room." Cassie was back to staring at her computer tablet.

"I'll get it." Dalton went out. Rosie swung her legs off the chair. It was fairly high and she had to jump down, but her legs buckled beneath her as she hit the floor. "Whoa!" She grabbed for the chair arm, but missed.

Pip caught her. "You keep confusing falling for me, with falling on me," he said. "Maybe I should explain the difference."

"Just help me up." Rosie was too tired to think of a comeback. He lifted her back up on the chair with a weary groan.

"Think you can stay upright? I'm kind of beat." He leaned on the seat next to her.

Cassie looked up from studying the tablet. "You might be a bit weak for a minute, Rosie, I forgot to say." Rosie cut her an annoyed look, but she just shrugged. "Hey, I helped you, didn't I?"

Dalton came back in. "Got one." He brandished a scribing tablet and brought it to Rosie.

Rosie put the tablet on her lap and closed her eyes,

concentrating on what she'd seen. With great surprise she found she was able to open the file on the base with only minor pain. She could see the details behind her closed lids.

"What is it?" Pip said.

She didn't answer; she just started drawing. It took her ten minutes and four screens of the tablet's memory, but she was able to transcribe the files exactly as she saw them. She'd never had much talent for art, but this was different. It was as if her brain was able to lead her hand to duplicate what she was seeing. By the end of it, she'd traced out a full map of the Helios base, including the security protocols that Riley had found, the number of staff, their names and positions.

"There're more scientific staff than soldiers," Dalton said as he scrolled through her notes.

"They probably think no one but Omgurri Council knows they're there," Pip said. "So, what's our plan? I suggest heading to the base and destroying every goddamned thing we can get our hands on, so they can't make anything more complicated than a soycurd cutter."

"And just how are we going to do that with the grunts there, genius?" Cassie said.

"Haven't you met my trusty friend fry-your-brains?" He pulled the pulse gun from the back of his waistband.

"You can't take them all on with one gun, and I doubt you're that good a shot." Cassie's tone was disgusted. "Why are you carrying that now, anyway?'

"Better to be safe than not. Besides, we've got two guns. Curtis has one." Pip's eyes glittered with a hard light that worried Rosie. The others might think he was joking about shooting the grunts, but she didn't.

"Cassie's right, Pip," she said. "There're only a few, but it's still a few too many for us. We need a plan to get around them."

"And I'd rather not go in guns blazing like some bad Immerse death wish pic," Dalton said.

"What do you suggest then?" A muscle ticked in Pip's jaw and he shoved the gun back in his waistband.

"We need stealth and surprise," Cassie said. "Using Rosie's plans, we should be able to find a way in – quietly."

"Destroying what they're building is a good idea though," Rosie said. "If we can stop them building the gate, it might make them decide to leave."

"Makes sense." Dalton rubbed his eyes, blinking several times, then stifled a yawn.

"But how can–" Rosie had to clamp a hand over her mouth. Soon they were all yawning except for Cassie, who seemed immune.

"I don't think we're going to come up with anything effective without some sleep," Dalton said.

"I'm with Captain Sensible." Pip pulled the disposable com from his pocket. "It's nearly nine. If we sleep till four am, that gives us time to come up with something then start making our way to the base. If we decide to do that."

Rosie could barely keep her head up now, but it was clear from the looks on everyone else's face that they all agreed.

"Can you walk?" Pip asked her.

"She'll be fine now," Cassie said. "Why don't you boys go ahead? Rosie can give me a hand packing up. That's code for girl talk, in case you missed it."

Dalton and Pip looked at each other. Dalton was the first to shrug. "See you back there then," he said and headed for the door. Pip followed him out.

Rosie slid off the chair to face Cassie. Her legs were steady enough now, but she was still way too tired to put up with any more of Cassie's crap. "So what?" she said. "Is this about Riley?"

Cassie stepped closer. "No." Her dark brown eyes regarded her with an intensity that felt out of place. "I didn't want to say this with the boys around. Couldn't put up with Pip's drama act when he heard. It's your implant." She paused and licked her lips, a quick nervous flick. "This type of cortex implant, the one my brother put in you, was designed by Helios."

Rosie straightened up. "What?"

"Yeah, I know," she said. "They just invade every part of your life, don't they? But look–" She smoothed a lock of hair behind her ear. "I was able to adjust the implant to help you access it, but I couldn't do anything about the way it's triggering your pain receptors. You're still going to get the headaches. Sorry, but they are complicated things. It's still functioning and you'll be able to access the data, but over time it's going to start breaking down."

"What are you telling me?" Rosie's heart was thumping scarily fast.

"Basically, the older it gets, the higher the risk some stray nano could affect your sight – or even other parts of your brain."

"Are you saying I could go blind?"

"Yes, or it could affect your motor functions, or worst case it could kill you." She swallowed. "But that's really worst case. It might just disintegrate and dissolve harmlessly. I can't tell for sure, but I just thought you should know. Thought you'd want to. I know I would."

Rosie stared at her. This could not be happening. Sweat trickled down her ribs. Cassie was watching her, not quite calm, but not upset either. Maybe she would make a good doctor. Zero drama-queen mode here.

"But they aren't made to be taken out," Rosie said. "They're permanent."

"Generally." Cassie bobbed a little nod. "But that's because most people don't have the skills. Helios have better doctors and tech than anyone, better even than here in Gondwana. I think they could get it out."

"Think?" Rosie heard her voice go high and struggled to get a hold of it.

Cassie folded her arms. "I don't ..." She bit her lip. "If my brother had known this could happen, he would never have done this to you. You know that, don't you? I mean, he's an obsessive, one-eyed crusader, but he wouldn't—"

"Stop, don't say any more." Rosie swayed away from the chair. "I need to get some sleep." *And when I wake up in the morning this will all be a dream.* She put one foot in front of the other in the direction of the door.

"You don't know how to get back to the house," Cassie said.

"I've got a pretty good sense of direction." Rosie kept going, pushing open the door.

CHAPTER 24

Cassie was snuffling softly in her sleep. Rosie propped herself up on an elbow to check the time display on the wall.

3.25 am. She lay back down and closed her eyes, willing oblivion to take her. Had she even been asleep? She was in a trundle bed on the floor, which was comfortable enough, but she couldn't stop Cassie's words going around and around in her head. She could go blind. The implant could kill her.

She opened her eyes. It was no use. She sighed and sat up. Her headache was gone, but she wondered how long for. She only had two threads of stim left and they seemed the only thing that took the edge off. She pushed back the covers and got up.

She wasn't the only one awake. Pip was at the kitchen bench, bent over the drawing she'd made from the implant, his faded T-shirt stretching across his shoulders. She paused at the top of the stairs and considered retreating, but he glanced up and saw her reflection in the dark windows. She went down the stairs and across the lounge to join him.

"Morning," he said quietly.

"Hardly." She pushed her loose hair back from her face, suddenly very conscious it was a mess. "Um, is there any water?"

"In the cooler."

She went around the bench and rummaged inside until she found a half-full jug. She filled a glass and took a few sips. He'd gone back to the tablet. All the stools were on his side of the bench and she went around and climbed on one, moving it slightly away so he had no chance of catching her morning breath.

It was quiet and still. The hush of early morning filled every corner and there was no sound from outside: no rain, no birds, no wind. Pip kept reading the tablet, not saying a thing. She was wondering if maybe she should just go back upstairs, when she noticed he hadn't scrolled the page at all. She tried to look unobtrusively at his profile.

He needed a shave. There was a shadow of fine dark stubble just visible on his jaw. His thick black hair was ruffled up at the back of his head, short strands falling across his forehead. She liked it better than the dreadlocks, and she liked the way his features fit together. The way the gentle curve of his nose met his lips. His unfairly long, dark eyelashes that flickered up and down as he read, over those blue, blue eyes – that were now looking at her. She jumped, jolting her water glass.

"What?" he said.

"Why aren't you reading?"

"I was." He laid the tablet on the bench.

"Didn't look like it."

"Maybe I'm just a slow reader."

"So what do you think?" she said. "Any ideas?"

"A few." He stared at the benchtop, tapping a finger lightly for a second as if he was thinking. Then he swivelled on his stool, bumping his knees against hers. "Like what did Cassie say to you last night? You seemed upset when you came in."

Rosie's stomach muscles clenched up tight. She opened her mouth to speak but all that came out was a short breath.

"Rosie?" He slid forwards and put a hand on her knee. "What's up?"

She found her voice but it was barely audible. "It was nothing, just … girl talk."

"You're still a terrible liar." His eyes were filled with concern and she could tell she was going to lose it if he kept looking at her like that.

Don't cry, Rosie Black, don't you dare blubber like a

little baby in front of him. But it was no use. Hot tears came anyway, leaking out of her eyes and rolling down her cheeks. She put her hands over her mouth, afraid of the sound that was trying to work its way out.

For a brief second Pip froze, staring at her in alarm, but then he got to his feet and hugged her.

"Jesus, Rosie," he whispered. He rubbed her back awkwardly in little circles. It was enough to break open the flood. She buried her face into the warm skin of his neck and sobbed, trying not to make much noise, the effort shaking her body. Little choking sounds came out anyway and she clung to him like a crash survivor. He sat back down on his stool, pulling her with him so she was half in his lap, her arms tight around his chest.

She didn't know how long she cried; it felt like forever. Finally, she sniffled to a halt, her shoulders jerking up and down for a while. She still didn't want to move though. For the first time in ages, she felt safe, with his arms fast around her and her face pressed against the pulse of his neck, steady and reassuring. She rubbed her face on the neckline of his shirt, trying to wipe the wetness off her cheeks.

"So, she called you names and pulled your hair?" Pip finally said. Rosie managed a shaky laugh that sounded more like a snuffle. He pulled gently back trying to disentangle himself. She let him, unwillingly, leaning against the stool between his legs, so they were still very close. She wiped at her nose, trying to smear snot off herself without looking at him. Her eyes felt puffy, her sinuses heavy with salty tears.

"So?" He was waiting, an anxious, half-amused look in his face.

Rosie took in a long shaky breath. "I, um, I can't tell you." She saw the hurt in his eyes and added, "Not yet, I mean. I can't tell you yet."

"Why not? You did just ruin my third-favourite shirt, so I figure you owe me a little explanation." He was joking but the hurt was there in his voice.

"It's just …" She couldn't even admit it to herself right now. She needed time to think about it. "I just can't." She willed him to understand.

"Is it to do with the implant?"

She paused, not sure what to say.

"It is, isn't it? What did Cassie see, Rosie? Did Riley put something else in there?"

"No." She sighed. "I just need a bit of time to figure it out." It sounded lame, she knew, but it was the truth. He watched her for a moment and she could see the frustration in his face, but he let it go.

"All right. Later, then?" His gaze was keen.

"Yeah, later," she said softly.

Pip had his smile back, but he still looked scared. *You and me both.* He looked down at his hands, loosely holding her wrists. Slowly, he let his fingers drift up past her elbows then down again.

"So …" His fingers were sending little shivers under

her skin and the mood between them suddenly changed.

"Wait." Rosie grabbed his hands before she lost her nerve, and maybe all her focus. "There's something else I need to tell you."

"Is it about how much you missed me?" He pulled her closer, putting his arms around her and nuzzling his face in her neck. *Good timing, Black.* His lips tickled her skin, making her breathless. She closed her eyes. If felt so good … But no, she needed to tell him this now while they were alone, in case there wasn't a chance later.

"Wait." She pushed him away, holding him off with both hands against his chest. "When I was with Sulawayo, in Capricornia, she told me something."

"What?" A frown replaced the teasing, sleepy look in Pip's eyes.

"*She* released that vision of me with your blood in the hospital."

His expression darkened. "It was her fault you were chased?"

"Yeah, but it wasn't about me." Rosie felt him tense under her hands. "She did it to get to you. She thinks she can keep you safe from the rest of Helios and stop the Senate from harassing me."

"She's deluded." Pip's jaw clenched tight.

"I know," Rosie said. "I would never do that. But…" She hesitated, her chest tight with worry. "What are you going to do about the MalX cure if the doctors here can't figure it out?"

"They will. They just need more time, and if that doesn't work, then I'll just start bleeding myself like a stuck pig and export my blood to whoever wants it."

She flinched at the edge of desperation in his words. "Pip, you can't," she whispered.

"Yes, I can. It's my body, my choice, Rosie. Not theirs." His tone softened minutely and he ran his hands up and down her back, pulling her close again. "Or yours." He took in a less than steady breath and said softly, "I can't go back to them. You know that, right? I just can't."

"I know." His touch was sending delicious shivers through her and when she met his gaze she saw the fear in his eyes, but there was something else in there as well. Yearning. He swallowed and his voice was unsteady as he said, "I really missed you, Rosie. You know what I said before was only 'cos I wanted to make sure you were safe."

She pressed against his chest. "I know," she said. Because she did. She knew what he meant because that was how she felt about him. Afraid for him. All the time. "Why do you think I get so mad when you say you'll do stupid dangerous things?" She gave him a smile.

Relief filled his eyes and his lips twitched. "Stupid?"

She let out a tremulous laugh. "Yes, stupid." Heart pounding, she lifted a trembling hand and dared to trace lightly the curve of his jaw. It was rough with stubble. The blue of his eyes darkened as her fingers reached his lips. He took her wrist then, stopping her, and leaned forwards to kiss her.

"Morning." Cassie's overly loud voice rang out. Rosie jumped and turned to see her leaning over the stair railing, a smug, all-knowing smirk on her face. "The kitchen looks so cosy at this hour," she said. "Mind if I join?"

Rosie could have smacked her. Pip was watching Cassie with an expression verging on dangerous, and Rosie stepped away from him as Cassie sauntered over.

"Looks like your face could do with a wash," Cassie said to her.

"Leave her alone, Cass," said Pip.

"No, it's all right." Rosie realised she was probably blotchy from crying and it'd be easier if Dalton didn't see it. "I'll be back in a minute," she said to Pip.

Cassie gave her a penetrating look as she passed, no doubt wondering if she'd told Pip about the implant. Rosie gave the minutest shake of her head, warning her not to say anything.

She washed her face as well as she could, poking through Cassie's things until she found some skin tone coverer that hid the blotching. By the time she came downstairs, Dalton was up and frying eggs, and Pip and Cassie were bent over a map laid out on the bench.

"Hey, Pilot Girl, you hungry?" said Dalton.

"Starving."

After a good sleep he was looking more like his old

Immerse-star handsome self.

Cassie looked up. "Those eggs ready?"

"Coming right up." He turned back to the fry pan and slid the last four eggs onto a plate.

"I think there're tortillas somewhere." Cassie scraped her stool back and rummaged around in a few cupboards.

They rolled the eggs in the bread and were quiet for a while, eating, all of them staring at the map between them. It was an expandable interactive one and Pip messed around with it, tracing routes with a finger and watching the display report the distance and time.

"So where's the base?" Dalton spoke around a mouthful of egg.

"Here." Pip touched a point several hundred kilometres to the north-east and closer to the coast. "The best way to get there is to stick north of the river." He traced a route on the map with his finger.

They were all silent, looking at it. In the dark of the early morning the sober reality of what they were thinking of doing was hitting them. The base was a long way from help, protected by a squad of Helios grunts and their chance of success was slim. Rosie forced the last of her breakfast down a suddenly dry throat.

"We could still try to contact your friend Kev," Dalton said to Cassie. "Tell him—"

"That we think the warriors should back down, that a bunch of kids think they know better than the councils or the Yalgu?" Pip interrupted.

"He's just trying to help,' Rosie said.

Pip exhaled roughly, some of the aggression leaving him. "I know; it just won't work. We're on our own here."

Rosie sat back from the bench. "Look, if you don't want to be part of it, you don't have to, either of you." She looked from Cassie to Dalton. She knew Pip would never think of backing down. "But this is the reason I came up here: to stop Helios. I owe a couple of people that."

"No need to get all heroic on us," Cassie said sharply. "You're not the only one who wants to stick it to Helios. Gondwana has been my home for ten years – there's no way I'm letting those bastards destroy it. We're coming. Aren't we, Curtis?" She looked at Dalton.

"That was the deal. Besides, I've been thinking about how to do this." He moved the tablet with the base plans Rosie had drawn between them. "I was looking at these last night," he said. "I couldn't see any way we could get into the base unseen *and* have time to destroy the gate project in the hangar before the guards got us. And what would we do it with anyway?" He folded his arms across his chest. "What we need are bombs."

"Now that I do like." Pip's eyes shone. "Not bad, Curtis."

"Wait, a bomb?" Rosie said. "But there are people there, scientists who might not really know what Helios is planning."

"But we only have to threaten to destroy it; we might not have to actually do it. Last night you said that the

320

best way to make them leave is to take away their reason for being there. Their reason is the gate project. We use it as leverage. Either they pack up and go home, or we blow it up."

It might work. Rosie couldn't think of any other scenario where a base full of Helios personnel would leave. But still, a bomb ...

Rosie scanned her drawings again, but she didn't need to look too hard to know he was right. None of them did.

"Even if we get past the guards, whoever is running the base might be happy to let us blow things up, then capture or kill us anyway," she said.

"Or they might not," Dalton said.

"It's worth a shot," Pip said. "I vote yes."

"Rosie?" Dalton said. Everyone was looking at her, waiting.

She let out a slow breath. "Let's try it."

"Helios will pick a bluff from a real threat easily," Pip said. "We'll need explosives."

Dalton smiled. "I know how to make them. My old school had chemistry labs, and an engineering department with old ship parts, including weapon systems. A group of us used to mess around. Call it a bored rich boys' club."

"It sounds like you might actually be useful after all." Pip sounded impressed. "What do you need?"

Dalton rattled off a list of chemicals and equipment

that had Pip nodding his head.

"I think we've got most of that. But how big an explosion will it make, and are you sure it'll work?"

"Oh, I'm sure. We used to practise in the old city sometimes — take our boats and go out there and set them on the ruins. You get the mix right and — *boom*." He pushed his hands together and spread them apart fast. "Nothing but rubble."

"Hang on," Cassie said. "We can't just walk into a Helios base with a couple of bombs and say, 'Put up your hands and surrender.'"

"We won't need to." Rosie scrolled through to display the base floor plan. "The gate project is housed in here." She tapped the hangar. "And this vent here" — she pointed out a small square low on the south wall — "is how we can get in."

It took her a little while to go through her idea, and to argue with the boys over who did what, but eventually they grudgingly agreed. She and Cassie would crawl into the hangar and place the bombs while the others kept watch. When they were done, they'd hide in the dense grass that circled the base, just within the range for the detonator signals but far enough away to run back to the bikes if they needed.

"But how do we tell Helios either to leave or we blow up their precious project?" Pip said.

Rosie's mouth went dry. "One of us has to surrender and get taken to whoever is in charge. Have you got coms here?" At his nod, she said, "We each have one so we can contact each other and convince them we're not bluffing."

Pip's expression was all tight angles, his eyes angry. "And I suppose you think you're going to volunteer."

"It makes sense. You can't, and they would be more than happy to put a bullet in Cassie's head, so I'm doing it."

Pip's mouth went so tight his lips lost their colour, but it was Dalton who spoke.

"Actually, it should be me. I'm the most expendable."

Rosie stared at him. "Dalton, no—"

"Good, we're agreed then," Pip said.

"I don't think we are agreed," Rosie said.

"Tough." Pip folded his arms and shrugged.

Cassie said, "Rosie, you've got all Riley's files in your head. He's the better choice."

Furious, Rosie glared at her. "You're not expendable," she said to Dalton. "Not to me, anyway."

"Thanks." Dalton exhaled a sharp breathy laugh. "But I mean it in a purely non-literal way. I don't intend to get myself killed over this."

"There is such a thing as shooting the messenger."

"That's why we set the bombs," he said. "So we have leverage. Besides, we make letting me go a condition of us not destroying their gate. Especially if I tell them who my father is. You never know, that might give more leverage than we think." He gave Rosie a significant look. She knew what he was thinking: if his dad was

Helios, like he suspected, it might work in their favour.

"He'll be fine," Pip said. "Papa Curtis has too much power and influence for them to risk pissing him off. They might be able to use him one day and that's Helios's favourite thing."

It didn't make Rosie feel any better though. It should be her going in there; she had more leverage than anyone, what with the implant … Unless Sulawayo had already told Helios. Maybe she'd lied about everything and they already knew.

"What about Sulawayo?" she said. "She said she was going to take over the base."

"Doesn't matter," Pip said. "She's still Helios and she wants that Equinox Gate as much as they do. She won't want it destroyed either."

He was right, but Rosie couldn't help feeling they should be more worried about Sulawayo.

"Come on, Curtis," Pip said. "Let's get this stuff."

CHAPTER 25

While Pip and Dalton made the bombs, Rosie went with Cassie to scavenge for bio bikes. It took just over an hour to find four reasonable bikes and fuel them up. By the time they got back the sun was up and the boys had a mess of chemicals and parts spread out on the lounge room floor.

"Check the replicator; the coils should be made by now," Pip was saying to Dalton as they came in.

"How many are you making?" Cassie asked.

"Eight," Dalton said from the kitchen.

Rosie looked at the six already constructed. They were small and compact. A short plas tube – a pipe of some sort – was attached to one end of the bomb. Inside was a double chamber where two kinds of liquids were separated by one of the coils Pip was talking about.

"Is this the detonator?" She touched a fingernail-sized receptor that looked like it had been pilfered from a children's toy.

"Yep." Pip didn't look up from the liquid he was measuring. "It'll have a delay of ... what is it again, Curtis?"

"Ninety seconds, give or take."

Rosie eyed the bombs nervously. "Are they going to be safe to transport?"

"The detonator needs a code," Pip said. "They'll be fine. You get the bikes?"

"Best we could find." Cassie headed upstairs. "I'll get some surveillance jammers and coms."

Rosie helped the boys finish making the bombs. Then they packed some food, water and rainproof jackets into light packs. By the time they were ready it was well after seven.

The sky was still clear outside and they rode the bikes through the desolate community in single file. Pip took the lead, Rosie behind, then Cassie and Dalton bringing up the rear. The roads were thick with mud but the bikes were built for rough conditions and ploughed through easily. Pip left the road once they were clear of the houses and struck off into the scrub, following a barely discernible track.

The country was tough going. Long flat open stretches of red earth mixed with sudden outcrops of rock and salt marshes scattered with clumps of sharp razor grass. Crocodiles were not uncommon, and they all kept an eye out for snakes. The air was hot and humid and they were soon soaked with sweat.

It was a ten hour ride to the base, if the weather held out, which was unlikely. Rosie had the remaining threads of stim hidden under her shirt. She felt clearer now, but it might not last. Much as she disliked the way the stim made her feel jittery and hyper, it was better to be alert than dead.

They didn't talk to each other much on the ride and took a break every few hours. A downpour started dead on two pm and kept going for over an hour. It was after seven and dark when they got as close as they could get. They stopped among a stand of trees.

Not far away was the ridge that separated them from the valley where the base was. Rosie's back was aching and her hands stiff from being curled over the handlebars. She stripped off her jacket and got off the bike, taking in a long breath of the warm humid air. Dalton made a low groaning noise, stretching his long body out and Cassie didn't seem to be faring much better.

Now they were so close, Rosie was nervous. Dalton flicked on a torch and checked the bombs stored in his and Cassie's bikes again.

"No problems?" she said.

He shook his head. "Can't see any."

If Pip was stiff from the ride, he wasn't showing it.

His expression was set, ready. They shared the burden of the bombs between two bags, packing them carefully. Rosie was to carry one, Cassie the other. The boys carried the food and water. Overhead, the stars were hidden behind clouds and everything smelled damp and dank, the smell of wet rock filling the air. Distant thunder warned they might be due for another downpour.

It was a kilometre to the base from the ridge across mostly open grassland, but to get to the grass they had to crawl through a narrow, rock-strewn gap in the ridge. Great boulders had fallen from above, creating an obstacle course, and smaller stones underfoot made them slip. The only light they had was the single torch Pip allowed them to use and they groped along single file.

Rosie clambered over a large boulder, sliding down the other side. The bombs shifted in her pack, and her guts twisted into a tight nervous ball. She tried to keep her eye on the faint shimmer of Cassie's hair ahead of her. Behind her, Dalton swore softly as his boot skidded on the rock.

They emerged from the crack into a strip of trees and a few spiked palms. They moved swiftly across the damp red earth. Only grassland lay between them and the base.

They shed their packs and crouched in the dark. Too close now to risk any torchlight being spotted, yet still too light to make a run for it. Pip got out the two pairs of scopes. He handed a pair to Dalton and they surveyed the base. Rosie had the tablet with the plans she'd drawn of the base and put it down in front of her on the ground, matching it to the reality.

"It's huge," Dalton said. Rosie borrowed Pip's scopes and checked it out. It was very different seeing the base for real. Intimidating. There were the five habitat domes, two smaller depot domes and the massive hangar where the Equinox Gate was being created. Behind it was a tower reaching to the clouded night sky. Soft lights lit the perimeter and there were also a few lights on in the windows of the domes. Three helijets sat in a cleared area on the western side.

"Jets." Dalton sounded excited as he spotted them. "I think I just found our emergency getaway vehicle."

"You can fly those?" Cassie said.

"Sure. My dad owns one."

"Poor little rich boy," Pip said absently, staring at the base. "Beats the bikes though. Rosie, do you see any guards?"

"No."

"Doesn't mean they aren't there. Let me see."

Rosie handed him the scopes and studied the tablet.

"I think it all matches up," she said.

Pip tensed. "I see someone. The northern corner of the shed. No, wait … there're two."

"I see them," Dalton said.

Rosie and Cassie squinted to see without scopes. Rosie could just make out two dark figures as they met at the shed corner.

"What info do we have about the guard detail?" Cassie asked.

"Not much. We can get pretty close without being seen as long as the surveillance jammers work."

"We could hide behind that storage dome and work our way around from there." Cassie tapped the screen. "If the guards come, the boys can provide a distraction."

They still had a few hours to wait until most of the personnel should be going to bed. They ate a cold meal of boiled eggs, seaweed salad and nuts, and got on each other's nerves. Cassie and Pip sniped at each other. Rosie sniped at Cassie. The only person who kept some degree of cool was Dalton. Finally, around ten, they all judged it was time.

"I'll carry the detonator," Pip said. They each also had their own com and the boys carried the guns. They'd searched for more weapons before they'd left the community but it seemed Helios had taken any guns that might have been left. Rosie and Cassie slung on the packs with the bombs and they struck out across the grass, navigating by the dim light ahead. The grass reached Rosie's shoulders and it was so thick it was hard to see the lay of the land. She stumbled into potholes filled with water and the bottom of her pants and her socks got soaked.

They stopped about two hundred metres from the base and crouched low. The thrum of energy-producing machines drifted towards them. A wide circle of dirt surrounded the base and there was little cover approaching it, but the night was dark and the lights few.

"Jam the surveillance," Pip said to Cassie.

She pulled the scanner from her pocket and waved it in a slow arc. "It's jammed," she whispered. "We shouldn't be detected."

"Shouldn't?" Pip said.

"Best I can do."

"What are the guards doing?" Rosie said.

"They should be coming back about now." Dalton had been timing the guards' movements. Rosie hoped that only one pair were patrolling at this hour. They had no way of knowing whether there were any in the hangar.

"Let's go." Dalton led them in a sprint to the wall of the storage depot where they stopped. They could hear the faint crunch of boots on earth as the guards completed their circuit on the other side of the hangar. Dalton was watchful. He raised a hand then motioned them all forwards again.

They ran straight for the hangar. Rosie hoped the Nation jamming tech was up to the job of covering them. No alarm sounded as they sped across the short open space between the storage dome and the hangar. They then kept going along the side and around the corner.

"Here." Rosie led them to the ventilation shaft in the back wall. It was two metres up from the ground. Pip squeezed Rosie's hand as they stopped beneath it.

"Remember," he whispered. "If there's any trouble, you bump the connection three times."

"Three times," she repeated. He seemed like he wanted to say something else, but Dalton called him to help get the grate open. Between them they levered it off. Behind the opening a narrow vent ran in both directions along the wall. It was dark and uninviting and a sulphurous smell came from it.

"Okay, one hour," Cassie said and passed Dalton the jammer. As soon as they came back out, Dalton was going to be gone, heading towards the guards and attracting as much attention as he could to get taken to the base leader.

"You can still change your mind about handing yourself in," Rosie said, but he shook his head. She thought she saw a sliver of fear in his eyes, but it was too dark to tell.

"Get going," he said and pushed her gently towards the vent. "I'll see you soon."

Rosie wanted to hug him, but there wasn't time. Pip laced his fingers together. Rosie put a foot into his hands and he boosted her up. It was a tight fit with the packs, barely wide enough to allow her to move through it lying down. She held a finger-sized torch and began to crawl along, fighting an initial wave of claustrophobia. They'd traced a route to an inner grate that would let them into what they hoped was an underused area, but nothing was certain. It might not even be possible to get it open at the other end. She tried not to think about that and waited for Cassie.

"Go." Cassie tapped her ankle. Rosie got moving, following the pinpoint of her torchlight as it bobbed and bounced off the walls. Cassie was close on her heels and they made soft bumping noises as they went.

Ahead, the vent right-angled, and a chute opened up directly above them, taking the dense-smelling air up and possibly out. Rosie curved with difficulty around the angle and kept going. She could hear a faint, rhythmic humming sound coming from inside the hangar now, and they curved around two more turns and slid down a steep sloping section before they made it to their exit point.

Light came through the grate, giving the tunnel a soft glow. Rosie switched off her torch and peered out. They'd chosen well – it looked like a storage area. In front was long shelving, stacked high with boxes and struts. Rosie gave a thumbs up over her shoulder to Cassie, then wriggled the magnetic screwdriver out of her pants pocket. She carefully undid the screws and dropped them into her palm, then pushed her fingers through the grate and shoved it out. It came loose with a sharp scrape. She lowered it to the ground. They were less than half a metre from the floor. She went out head first, walking on her hands until she could get her legs underneath her and stand up in the narrow space between the shelving and the wall. Everything was clean and the air felt fresh and cool. A dull whirring ran through the building like a bass line beneath music. There was no indication anyone was in there. She heard no talking, no footsteps; it felt empty. Cassie slid out and Rosie led the way, keeping close to the wall and peering out from around the stack of metal.

The hangar was massive, and dominating it was a scale prototype of the Equinox Gate the size of a small house. A cube of dark metal formed the centre and surrounding it was a metal halo attached by radiating spokes. A dark tube extended from one side of the square. It tapered to a point and was studded with ridges of raised metal and pulsing green lights.

Cassie leaned over her to have a look. "I thought you said they were making a gate."

"The gate isn't solid. It's a bend in space and time, a wormhole. That machine will create it." She stared at it, momentarily transfixed. "I wonder if they're using exotic matter to stabilise it."

"Who cares." Cassie slipped past Rosie, her boots squeaking on the shining floor.

A row of workstations scattered with advanced coms, tablets, stylos, and bio machines were arranged in a line facing the Equinox Gate and several construction robots stood motionless around it. Stacks of crates took up most of the wall on their left and on their right were four small white tents, sealed up like quarantine areas.

They pulled out the bombs. Cassie began to tape

one under the workstation closest to the machine, while Rosie moved towards the gate. The black tube pointed to a set of doors at the far end of the hangar. One of the centipede-like robots was paused beneath the tube on its back feet with a metal box in its upper graspers.

Rosie approached it, nervous of the bulk over her, and went close to the cube to find somewhere to hide her bombs. The surface was smooth and non-reflective black, with various small mechanisms extruding from it, but it was also raised from the floor. She bent down and slipped a bomb underneath, then moved around it gently, pushing the rest where they hopefully wouldn't be found.

When she was done she jogged back to Cassie, who was trying to find a spot for her final one.

"Hey–" She stopped as they both heard the sound of a door opening. For a second they stared at each other, then sprinted back towards the stack of shelving. They only just made it. A woman came in and headed towards the workstations. She was small, wearing a dark tunic with a Helios insignia, but she was too rumpled to be a guard. Her hair was pulled back in a messy ponytail. She collapsed into a chair with a loud sigh, then muttered to herself as she powered up a com.

Rosie stared at her in frustration. There wasn't supposed to be anyone in here at this time of night. What if they actually had to detonate? The woman didn't look evil, just tired and stressed. Did she have a family? Cassie tugged at her sleeve. She still had a bomb in her hand and was shoving it in her bag and motioning fiercely back towards the vent. "Come on!" she mouthed.

There was nothing she could do for the woman that wouldn't jeopardise them. Feeling terrible, Rosie followed Cassie back into the vent, both of them trying to make as little noise as they could, moving quicker now without the bombs.

They had just come to the last turn when they heard the first shots.

CHAPTER 26

Loud whining explosions were happening outside. Pulse fire. And close. Cassie stared back at Rosie with wide eyes, shadowed by the small glow of the torch.

"Go!" Rosie whispered.

Cassie moved. Rosie was right on her heels.

They reached the outside vent, but the cover was back up. Cassie peered out. "I can't see anyone." Rosie wriggled the com from her pocket and pushed down on the receiver three times. Outside she heard shouts, men calling, most likely the guards, and the sound of running feet, then more gunfire. A scream. They waited, the only sound in the vent their quick breaths. There was no reply from the boys and Rosie was beginning to think they should just push off the grate, when there was a sudden movement outside.

Her heart tried to fight its way out her throat as fingers appeared through the wire. Then Cassie said fiercely, "Where the hell have you been?"

Pip and Dalton. She could breathe again. There was a sharp reply and then Cassie was pulled out. Rosie shuffled forwards and Pip hauled her out by the armpits. Dalton was a shadow watching around the corner of the hangar. Shouts and sporadic gunfire filled the night and bursts of light lit him up in relief as he turned to beckon them frantically. They all ran to the corner.

"What's going on?" Cassie whispered.

"It's the Yalgu Warriors," Pip said.

"What?" Rosie stared at him.

"I know," he said. "I don't know what the hell they're doing here so early. A squad of them just arrived and started attacking the base. Then more grunts came over the ridge, but they went after the base guards, not the warriors. Our plan's shot to hell now."

"Did you see Sulawayo?" Rosie said.

"Nope, but I reckon those ridge grunts are hers and she's making her move."

"And the Yalgu are working with her?" Cassie said.

"Not sure," Pip said. "But this base is screwed either way."

"Did you set the bombs?" Dalton asked.

"Most of them," Cassie said. "We got interrupted. I've still got one in my bag, but what are we going to do with them now? Should we just get out of here?" There was no time to talk though as they heard the pounding of heavy feet close by.

Dalton jogged to the corner to check and came sprinting back. "Grunts. We gotta move."

They all cast about frantically for somewhere to hide.

"This way." Rosie spun around, the others following, running along the back of the hangar towards the habitats. She was desperately trying to recall everything she could about the layout of the base. There were two small storage domes between the hangar and the main habitats. Could they hide there? She paused at the corner, the others breathing hard behind her. Fifty badly lit metres separated them from the storage dome. She couldn't see anyone. Most of the fighting seemed to be closer to the larger habitats. Bright flares of pulse weapons lit up the night and she could hear the whistling snick of bullets.

"Come on." She ran, Cassie at her heels, the boys following.

They were halfway there when a whine of pulse fire split the air past her shoulder. Rosie's insides turned to water. She ducked her head and looked back. Four men were sprinting after them along the back of the hangar. They fired again and dust leaped up around her as the shots hit dirt.

"Run!" Pip roared and he and Dalton shot back, running backwards.

More people suddenly came from their left and opened fire at the grunts.

"Get down!" Rosie pulled Cassie to the ground as a thunderous sound opened over their heads.

The boys were caught in the crossfire and Rosie turned in time to see Dalton fall. Pip was somehow still on his feet, but then a grunt grabbed him around the throat.

"Pip!" she screamed. But he was gone, pushed back behind the hangar.

Rosie tried to go to Dalton but pulse fire and bullets were ricocheting between the dome and the hangar. Cassie pulled her towards the storage dome. Together they lunged for the door, bursting through and slamming it shut as pulse fire hit. Rosie slid the lock across and they cowered on the floor. An automatic light came on and outside the thud and whistle of gunfire continued.

"God, Dalton." Cassie's eyes were huge. Rosie couldn't speak.

"You're hit," Cassie said.

Rosie looked down and saw a rip in her shirt. She felt nothing. Her hands shook as she inspected it. There was a shallow slice on the left side of her abdomen, oozing blood.

"Let me see." Cassie crawled to her, her pack still on her back, but Rosie pushed her hands away.

"It's just a scratch." She let her empty pack slide off. Dalton could be dead. Pip had been taken.

"We're screwed," Cassie said softly, then suddenly laughed, a high, rough squawk that seemed to frighten her. She closed her mouth hard.

Rosie pulled the com from her pocket and tried to contact Dalton. It didn't even go through. She kept seeing him falling down, not moving. A terrible hollow in her chest was making it hard to breathe. *Don't think about it.*

"They've got to stop fighting out there some time," she said. "We wait, listen, then we go out and get him. Okay?"

Cassie didn't reply. She sat silent, her knees pulled to her chest.

"Cassie!" she barked and the blond girl jumped. "Did you hear me?"

She stared at Rosie as if she didn't know who she was, but then blinked and nodded. "I heard. We wait. Get Dalton when it stops."

"Okay." Rosie looked around, checking if there was anything they could use as a weapon, but it was all ordinary household stuff and random tech parts.

"Give me your pack." Cassie let her take it and Rosie took out the bomb and inspected it closely, trying to figure it out. "Do you know anything about how this works?"

"No."

Rosie sighed in frustration but then Cassie touched her arm. "Listen."

The gunfire had stopped. Rosie shoved the bomb back into the bag and, hands shaking, eased the lock off the door and opened it a crack. She couldn't see anyone. The area between the dome and the hangar was empty, apart from Dalton and a few other bodies. Sporadic bursts of gunfire were coming from further away now, and a dull explosion reverberated through the ground.

"Get your pack," Rosie said to Cassie over her shoulder.

She ran out. Rosie's heart was a jackhammer in her chest as she sprinted over to Dalton and skidded to her knees. He was lying on one side and there was blood on the ground and on his leg and ribs. *Oh, Jesus. Oh, God, please don't be dead.* Her throat was tight.

"Dalton?" She touched his face. His cheek was streaked with blood, his hair covered in dust, but his eyes fluttered open and hope slammed right back into her.

"Rosie? I thought you'd left me," he said.

A ridiculous, crazy smile stretched across her face. "Don't be stupid."

Then Cassie was there. She took one quick look at Dalton and, with strength Rosie didn't think she had, Cassie tore Dalton's shirt, ripping off a strip and tying it tightly around his wounded thigh. He gave a soft moan. The wound on his chest was a plasma shot. Rosie didn't want to think what it might have done, but they couldn't do anything about it now. Rosie got an arm under him and Cassie got on his other side, and between them they dragged him to his feet.

"Back to the dome?" Cassie said.

"No, the jets," said Rosie.

Dalton was much taller than them both, and heavy. Rosie's shoulders were aching by the time they made it to the shadows behind the hangar. The jets were on the other side. They shuffled to the next corner in darkness, Dalton breathing in short hitching gasps. On their left was a shadowy impression of high rocks. Ahead was a wide open area, well lit, and across from that were the helijets. There didn't seem to be anyone around. Behind them the noise of fighting continued – muffled shots, cries and explosions. It sounded like the Yalgu Warriors had got into the habitats.

"Ready?" Rosie said. "The closest one." She pulled them forwards.

It seemed to take forever to cross that wide exposed space. Every second Rosie expected to feel pulse fire or a bullet hit her back. She could hardly believe it when they made it. She leaned Dalton against the side of the jet and ignored the pulling ache in her back as she fumbled with the latch. It came open and Dalton swivelled and collapsed on the floor inside with a heavy groan, pulling his legs in. Cassie jumped in after him.

The jet had a small cockpit up front and a roomy cabin. Six flip seats hung from the roof and there was a gun rack alongside the hatch door. Cassie was already searching for a medikit. It rattled as she dropped it on the floor. Dalton's breathing was scarily shallow. Cassie unwrapped an injector of something and pushed it against his neck, then shoved a wound paster at Rosie.

"Put this on," she said.

Rosie held her shirt in her teeth and pressed the paster against the bullet graze. It moulded against her skin, flushing a layer of disinfectant and halting the bleeding.

"Can you fly this?" Cassie looked up from cleaning Dalton's wounds, then frowned. But whatever she was going to say next was lost as the familiar high-pitched whine filled Rosie's head and spiking pain pierced her skull.

She fell against the jet, staggered, then hit the ground. The pain built to a crescendo, short and sharp. There was a bright rainbow light, a spiral, and a single word jumped out at her. *Pantheon.* She was panting, her pulse going a million miles an hour. Names, a list of names. Five of them. Four she didn't know, one she did. Then it was gone as soon as it had come.

Her eyes snapped open. She was on her back staring up at the night sky.

Pantheon. The names.

"Rosie? Look at me." Cassie was beside her. She grabbed her chin, peering into her face.

"I'm okay." Rosie was sweating, her breath short.

"You can see?"

"Yes." She pushed her away. "How's Dalton?"

"Alive, but it's not good, Rosie."

"Can he fly the jet?"

"What?" Cassie stared at her. Rosie ignored her,

getting up into the jet to kneel beside Dalton. Cassie had put pasters on his wounds. He still looked like shit, pale, washed out and scared, but he was focusing.

"What happened to you?" His voice was croaky and weak.

"Just a visit from my friendly parasite. I'm fine."

Cassie pushed another injector against Dalton's neck. He looked at her sideways, then back at Rosie.

"Can you fly?" she said.

His face filled with weary resignation. "You're going back for Pip."

"I can't leave him there. He'd do the same for any of us."

"For you, maybe." Cassie's tone was hard.

"I've got an idea of how I can do it," she said. "I just saw the Pantheon list."

Cassie's mouth went tight. "You're going to try to bargain with them?"

"Whose names were on it?" Dalton said.

"I'll tell you later." She tried not to show her fear. "You've still got the detonator?"

"In my pocket."

"Okay. Cass, got your com?"

"Yeah."

"I'll send you three clicks, and that's the signal to blow the bombs," she said. "If I don't come back, you go." She looked at Dalton. "You fly out of here."

He glared at her. "Three clicks," he said. "But we're

not leaving without you."

His mouth was set. Why did he have to be so bloody noble?

"Dalton–"

He touched her hand. "Get going, Pilot Girl. We'll be waiting."

She shuffled back out of the jet, glowering at him, while her chest worked like there was something too heavy inside it.

"You keep him alive," she said to Cassie.

Then she turned and ran without looking back.

She knew what she was doing was crazy. Her aunt would call it a tied-to-the-wall strategy, the kind you make when you've run out of choices, but sometimes you just had to take that leap. She made it back to the hangar and jogged along the rear to the corner opposite the storage dome. She'd pulled something getting Dalton up and a muscle along her spine ached with each step. The wound on her belly was starting to sting as well and it felt like every part of her had been pummelled. She fumbled under her shirt for the remaining threads of stim, chewed on one and felt the familiar rise of buzz as it hit her bloodstream. Pip wouldn't be happy, but that was tough.

She kept moving, running across to the shadow of the storage dome. The three bodies had been left on the ground but it seemed like everyone else had moved to the main habs. She could still hear gunfire but it was distant. Had the Yalgu Warriors won? She crept around to the back side of the storage dome, keeping low and in its shadow. Beyond it, lighting illuminated the five enormous habitat domes. They were arranged in a triangular shape, with one at the front and four flanking it behind at an angle, and were joined by short pyloflex tunnels. Three men and one woman guarded the front. Rosie was so scared she felt numbed by it.

Were these regular Helios operatives or had Sulawayo got here and taken over already?

She pulled the com from her pocket and wriggled it down the inside of her boot, took a long deep breath, and walked slowly out into the light with her hands held high above her head.

CHAPTER 27

Rosie had gone maybe three steps when they saw her. "Halt!" The woman advanced, aiming her gun. She was well over two metres and was wearing a vest that could project a personal shield. Rosie swallowed and stood very still.

"I'm unarmed," she said.

The woman stopped a few metres away, her huge plasma weapon pointed at Rosie's head. "Baker, search her."

The soldier behind her swung his weapon over his shoulder and strode towards Rosie. He was young, barely more than twenty, tow-headed, with a beaky nose. He patted her down roughly, but it was clear he hadn't done it that many times before, and he stayed well clear of her breasts. She flinched as his hand pressed her wound.

"You're a bit young for a Yalgu, aren't you?" The woman's eyes were suspicious.

"I want to see the boss," Rosie said.

A hard little smile twitched the soldier woman's mouth. "Do you now? How do I know you're not a decoy?"

"Come on, Suma. She's just a kid," Baker said.

"Shut up," Suma snapped without looking at him.

"My name is Rosie Black." Rosie could barely keep her voice level and her mouth had dried right out. "Sulawayo knows me." She was praying this woman was on Sulawayo's side.

Suma considered her a moment, then said, "Baker, call it in."

Baker seemed to be relieved. He whipped a com from his belt. "Team One, this is Baker. We have a kid out here, Rosie Black, says she knows Sulawayo. Instructions?"

After a torturous five seconds, a reply came. "Bring her in."

Suma smirked and shouldered her weapon. "Well, Rosie Black, come on then."

Rosie lowered her aching arms.

———◆———

The habitats were like those built for Mars. Airlock entries, light-green walls and that antiseptic lemon scent she'd come to associate with Helios. It was cool inside and, as Suma led her along the wide main corridor, Rosie saw evidence of a recent firefight. Holes were blasted in walls, rooms on either side were pockmarked with bullet and pulse blasts, and the floor was littered with random unidentifiable objects that might have been equipment. Dull distant explosions shuddered the ground. They passed through living areas and a hallway of bedrooms, going out of the first dome and into another that would have been the eatery. Here tables were overturned and broken, pushed back against the walls. The servery was a mess of shattered crockery and automeal machines blasted black by plasma shots.

Sulawayo was talking to a male soldier. She saw them come in and gestured them over. The soldier took off, running towards the gunfire. She eyed Rosie calmly.

"You can go, Suma," she said. "Take Baker and check the area. She's not here alone."

Suma left and Sulawayo smiled coolly at Rosie. "I see you ignored my advice and came to the base."

"Did you really think we wouldn't?"

"I would have been disappointed if you hadn't. I don't trust people who always do as they're told."

"I don't trust you at all." Rosie looked around at the debris. "So have you taken over here?"

"I am in the process of taking what I need."

"And you've got some of the Yalgu Warriors helping you?" Rosie said with disbelief.

"In a manner of speaking. I faked a message from their council and told a select few of them to make an advance attack against the base. They have been very helpful with assisting in taking out most of the other Helios guards. But my people will have both sides neutralised soon. A potent knockout gas. I don't know why it's not used more often."

Rosie was shocked by how casually she talked about using the warriors. "And what about the rest of Nation? If Helios think the Yalgu drove them out, they'll come back in full force."

"No they won't. I will convince them it isn't worth their while. And I can be very convincing." The way she said it, and the look in her eye, made Rosie's skin prickle. Sulawayo was so cool about it, so calm. What was she getting herself into making a bargain with this woman? She took a steadying breath. "How?"

Sulawayo shrugged one shoulder. "You don't need the details, but Helios will think that their plans for the gate have been lost and they will start working on them again from scratch. The people of Nation will be safe; you have my word."

As much as that was worth. "I hope that's true." She tried to sound confident. "Where's Pip? I've come to get him."

Sulawayo regarded her with dark, measuring eyes. "I told you before, Rosie, it's time he made use of his gift. He can't keep running. I think he's best where he is."

"You also told me you wanted to change things, that you don't agree with how Helios operate. Kidnapping him is exactly how they operate."

"We won't force him to do anything," Sulawayo said. "You will convince him."

Rosie felt they were talking in circles again. "I already told you I won't. Why would I change my mind?"

"Because it's the right thing to do. And that's who you are. You can see the bigger picture, the lives that can be saved."

It was like talking to a brick wall. Rosie shook her head. "So what's your plan? You take control of the Equinox Gate, take Pip and figure I'm just going to fall in line?"

"You've run out of choices, Rosie," Sulawayo said. "That vision of you using his blood to cure your father is out there. Helios knows you are the key to getting Pip back and I can guarantee they're not just going to follow you around any more. They will take you in – that's if the Senate doesn't lock you up first. Agent Whitely isn't one to give up and Riley's not around to help. You're only solution is to trust me. Join with me and I can make all that go away. I can convince Helios that I've turned you to their side and I can protect Pip, hide him from them." Sulawayo's eyes glittered with confidence. "They won't look for him if they think he's dead."

Rosie's heart lurched, her insides turning to ice at the thought. "No," she said, but her voice came out croaky.

She cleared her throat and tried again. "No, that's not how it's going to go."

"It's not?" Sulawayo raised an eyebrow and Rosie licked her lips. Time to see if her plan would work.

"So the gate plans – the only copies are in the hangar, aren't they? And that's the only prototype?" she said.

Sulawayo frowned and her gaze filled with suspicion. "What are you up to?"

"I have a proposal for you." Rosie's heart was pounding as she said, "I have a lot of information in my head on the implant. All of Riley's work. All Helios stuff. That could be useful to you, couldn't it?"

"Are you proposing giving me access to all that?" Sulawayo spoke slowly.

"Yes, and I will join you like you said, but only if you let Pip go."

Sulawayo was silent for a moment. Then she said, "I'm not sure your involvement is worth that. A cure for the MalX is invaluable, and it's not going to happen without Helios tech. If I let him go, how are you going to protect him from the main faction of Helios?"

"You'll still shield him from Helios," Rosie said. "You won't tell them where he is. And you're wrong about the cure. He's going to be able to make it because you're going to give him the tech to do it."

"I am?"

"Yes. Because I know who the Pantheon are," Rosie said. "I've seen the list. And if you want to bring down the powers that really rule Helios, that's what you need. Without it you're just spitting in the wind, and you know it."

Sulawayo was watching her closely. "How do I know you're telling the truth?"

"You don't. By the way, I also have all the plans for the Equinox Gate." She tapped her head.

"I have the gate already."

"You sure about that?"

"What exactly does that mean?"

Rosie took in a breath. "I'm not saying anything more until Pip's here." She was playing a desperate and dangerous game, but she couldn't let Sulawayo know how badly she needed her to accept her ultimatum.

She didn't really want to join their faction of Helios, could hardly believe that she was offering to, but she couldn't leave Pip here, and Riley was gone. Plus Helios tech was her only chance of getting the implant out. Maybe by joining she could play both sides. She could help drive Helios to do some good, and if Sulawayo came good with Helios tech, Pip would have a way to make a real cure for the MalX, and she might not die. She watched Sulawayo, trying not to show anything on her face.

Sulawayo pulled a com from her pocket. "Bring the boy to me," she said. She looked at Rosie. "Happy?"

"When Pip walks out of here, I will be," she said.

They waited in tense silence for Pip to arrive.

"You know what this means, don't you?" Sulawayo said. "To join me you will become part of Helios. We are fighting this battle from within."

"I know," Rosie said.

"And whatever you do, you can't go back on this decision. If you think you can doublecross me, you will be sorry. As will everyone you care about."

"I know," Rosie repeated.

A door opened behind Sulawayo's back and Pip was pushed out by a soldier.

"Rosie?" His eyes were wide with disbelief. Her heart felt like it might explode from her chest and she had to stop herself from running to him. He was across the room in two strides. "Jesus, I thought—" He wrapped his arms tightly around her, lifting her off her feet.

"Are you okay?" She hugged him back hard.

"I am now."

For a moment she felt his heart beating just as frantically as hers, but then he set her down and looked at Sulawayo. "What's going on?"

"Perhaps you should ask Rosie." Sulawayo said.

"What?" Realisation dawned in Pip's eyes. "Rosie, what did you promise?"

"The Pantheon list in exchange for you," Sulawayo said. "Among other things. She's going to join me just as I said she would."

The colour faded from his face and his arm dropped slowly from her shoulders. "Rosie?" He was looking at her like he was begging her to deny it. She swallowed.

"It's not quite how it sounds. I've seen the names of the Pantheon, Pip."

But his lips thinned and he turned back to Sulawayo. "No," he said. "I won't let her. Take me back."

"Pip, don't!" Rosie reached for his hand, but he pulled away.

"You shouldn't have come." His expression was desperate, tormented and her heart wrenched.

"It doesn't matter," Sulawayo said. "I've already decided to accept most of her bargain."

"She doesn't know what she's promising," Pip said.

"I think she does. Not all things are how you remember them, Pip."

"I doubt that." His lip curled in contempt. "I think you've just shown pretty clearly that no apple falls far from the Helios tree."

"I wouldn't be so ungrateful," Sulawayo said. "She put a nice caveat in there for you. I'll be handing over some high-grade tech to your friends here in Nation. Looks like a MalX cure is in your future."

Pip stared at Rosie like she'd betrayed him. "I had to," she said, her throat tight.

"It's all right," said Sulawayo. "I'm sure I can help you distribute the cure. Sorry," she said as Rosie turned to her. "I'm not going to leave that world-saving coup to him. The tech comes with a condition of my own. My people run it."

"I knew you'd do that," Rosie said. "But what's worth

more to you: the cure, or creating the thing that will allow you to control access to everything beyond our planet?"

She frowned. "What are you saying?"

"If the prototype is gone and I'm the only one with the plans for the gate, will you give up the cure then?"

Not waiting for an answer, Rosie crouched and yanked the com from her boot.

"What are you doing?" Sulawayo launched at her, but Pip was faster, blocking her way as Rosie clicked the call button three times.

"What have you done?" Sulawayo shouted at her over Pip's shoulder as he held her back. For about ten seconds, nothing happened.

Then a massive explosion shook the ground and a blast wave shot through the room.

Rosie was thrown off her feet and landed amongst the tables. Her hip smacked hard against a broken top, pain shooting up her side. Table legs jabbed her arms and back. Part of the ceiling smashed to the floor and the air was filled with the crash of things breaking and people screaming. Rosie rolled over in a daze, ears ringing. That wasn't supposed to happen. She was shocked to see Cassie running towards her through a swirl of debris.

"You okay?" Cassie hauled her out of the wreckage. "I think so." Rosie looked for Pip. He'd landed on top of Sulawayo and a bit of ceiling had just missed him.

"Pip—" Rosie stumbled over.

He got up, looking as dazed as her. "I'm good. Soft landing." Dust speckled his dark hair and he glanced at Sulawayo, who groaned. "We better move though."

Rosie hesitated. If she left now she was crossing Sulawayo just like she'd said. "This way." Cassie headed to the door. Pip grasped Rosie's hand to follow, but she resisted.

"I can't leave. What about the deal I just made?"

He turned back, stunned. "Deal? There's no deal, you can't trust Helios."

"But what if this is my best chance to stop them, to save—"

He cut her off. "Don't say me. She wasn't going to help me, or you, or anybody. How many times do I have to tell you before you believe me?"

"I have to try, Pip." Still she hesitated, torn, and his expression became fierce.

"You can't ask me to leave you here. I *won't*." His voice shook.

Rosie's breath caught.

"What's the problem?" Cassie called from the door.

"No problem." Pip's grip tightened on her hand and Rosie couldn't find the strength to abandon him. She followed him out.

The tunnel Rosie had come through earlier had a huge hole torn in the side, opening it to the night, and she realised Cassie must have laid her one remaining bomb right against the outside. The blast had radiated

359

back down either side, smashing through the doors to both domes. The gap opened to the other side of the habitat, away from the hangar. It was dark and people were shouting and running all over the place and a column of fire was shooting up in the night sky from where the hangar had been, small explosions still going off. No one even glanced at them and Cassie led them at a run, away from the base and into the long grass. For a minute Rosie thought she was heading back to the bikes, but then she saw a shape emerging from the dark. A helijet glimmered blackly, reflecting the fires at the base.

Cassie wrenched the side door open. "Get in."

They piled in the back. Rosie was overwhelmed with relief to see Dalton in the cockpit.

"Curtis, you're still alive," Pip said.

He glanced back at them. "That's debatable. You two, strap in. Rosie, I could use your help up here."

Pip and Cassie pulled the flip seats down from the roof and Rosie squeezed through the narrow gap into the copilot seat.

"Here." Dalton handed her an earpiece. His hand was less than steady and he was way too pale, looking almost green in the light from the console. But he was still alive.

"Are you okay to fly this?" she said.

"Gotta be. No one else knows how." He pressed buttons above his head and gave her a pale imitation of his usually dazzling grin. "Besides, I don't want to give up my Prince Charming pretensions just yet."

He took hold of the single control stick and pulled back. Screens lit up in front of them and Rosie tried to make sense of the controls and fail-safes as the jet rose into the air.

At the base, it was chaos. Dalton took them on a curving trajectory well away from it, keeping all external lights off. As they climbed higher, a distant roar came from the clouds and an alarm sounded, lights flashing red on the pilot's deck.

"What the hell?" Dalton held hard to the stick as the jet suddenly swerved as if it had been pushed by an invisible force. "What is it?" Rosie grabbed the copilot controls, trying to help.

"It's the *Cosmic Mariner*!" Pip was leaning forwards, pointing through the side window near Dalton. Rosie swore as the massive bulk of the ship burst through the clouds barely twenty metres from them. The jet shuddered and it was all Rosie and Dalton could do to keep on course as the spaceship passed them in a streak of ion flare, heading for the base. Everything rattled, including Rosie's teeth. Metal creaked and groaned like the jet was going to snap in two.

"Punch the stabilisers!" Dalton shouted and Rosie lunged at the control, swiping it across. For a second she thought they were going down. The jet swerved, dipped and lurched, but then the *Mariner* was gone and they shot forwards into the clouds, levelling out.

"It's okay, okay." Dalton was grey, his hands shaking.

Rosie's fingers were still clenched hard around the stick.

"You all right?" she said.

"Might need a pain shot." His smile was feeble.

"Cassie." Rosie turned back but Cassie was already unstrapping and reaching for the medikit. Rosie met Pip's gaze.

"How much you want to bet that ship was Sulawayo's getaway?" he said.

"Yeah, gotta be." Rosie swallowed, mouth still dry with fear. "Guess she lied about not being in contact with Nerita."

"She's Helios; they lie about everything."

His eyes looked black in the half-light and a hard scared stone sat in her stomach. The set of his mouth was all I-told-you-so, but she still wasn't sure if leaving had been the right thing to do.

"Pain shot." Cassie thrust an injector at her. Pip leaned his head back against the seat and closed his eyes. She turned back to help Dalton, a tight pain pressing against her heart.

"Think you can handle the jet?" he said as she pushed the shot against his neck.

"Hey, I'm Pilot Girl, remember?" She took the co-pilot stick and he smiled wanly, sweat gleaming on his forehead.

"Top of the class." He flicked the main control over to her and she headed them south back towards Newperth.

CHAPTER 28

It was ferociously hot again. Rosie stared out her bedroom window at the pale, almost white sky and the backs of the tower blocks across the street. The constant chaotic hum of the city rose up from below and the climate control in the apartment was barely working again. She could smell the remnants of someone's lunch coming up through the vents with the tepid air.

Behind her, Aunt Essie was making a racket in the kitchen. She'd decided to make a cake the old-fashioned way, instead of using the auto cooker. Rosie was slightly dubious as to how it might taste, but regardless, she'd eat it. It was her aunt's way of declaring a truce and Rosie wasn't about to derail that – especially since it was her fault Essie had been so mad.

Somehow, Essie had found out what had happened and she'd been right there waiting for them when Dalton landed the jet on the beach near his parents' house. Angry didn't cover it. Her leg had still been bandaged and she was walking with a limp but that hadn't stopped her tracking them down. She'd bossed them all around, organised a doctor for Dalton and ordered Pip to lie low at the beach house. Then she forced Rosie into a transport and back to their apartment. That was four days ago and she had barely been able to look at Rosie since.

The injuries she'd got when Riley's place exploded might be healed, but Rosie knew what hadn't was the betrayal Aunt Essie felt for being lied to. There had been a lot of swearing and shouting. Rosie hadn't told her everything though. Essie was having trouble enough getting her head around what they'd done and Sulawayo being a double agent. Rosie couldn't face telling her that the implant Riley had put in her might kill her – or about her offering herself up to Helios to save Pip.

Cassie was the only one to escape Aunt Essie's wrath and that was because she hadn't been there. They'd dropped her off with Kev at Worla Range on the way back. It was too dangerous for her to leave Nation lands, especially now Helios knew Riley was alive. Cassie hadn't been happy about it, but at least she could continue to study medicine up there.

Weirdly, she'd pulled Rosie aside before they left and shoved a wad of stims at her from the jet medikit. "Keep the pain down," she'd said, then made Rosie promise to keep in touch with her about how the implant was going. "Purely for my scientific research of course," Cassie had said. Rosie had been surprised by that and grateful. The headaches had come back and she'd stashed the stims in her room to ration out when they got too much to handle. Maybe she should take one now. She rubbed at her temple, trying to ease the pain behind her eye.

"Rosie," Aunt Essie called. The banging had stopped and she turned to peer through her open door to the kitchen.

"Yeah."

"Come out here. I got a ping from Kev."

Tension made her headache sharpen. They'd been waiting for news on how everything had turned out at the base. The Nation councils had gone in there with full squads of warriors to clean it up but they hadn't heard what they'd found.

She went out and sat at the kitchen bench. It was covered with utensils and mysterious mixtures and Aunt Essie shoved some of it aside while she looked at her com.

"So is Helios—"

"Gone?" Essie interrupted. "Yes. He says the base is completely destroyed and the Yalgu stopped anyone escaping – apart from Sulawayo and two of her crew."

"Do they know where she went?"

Essie shook her head. "No, but I checked. She's here in Newperth. She's gone right back to playing at being a Senate agent."

"But how can she get away with it?"

Essie raised an eyebrow. "Well apart from the few of us, and Kev, no one knows she was involved at all. Her cover is all shiny apples and there's not much we can do about it. Who's going to believe us if we point fingers with absolutely no evidence?"

Rosie digested that. "How many people died?" she asked.

"They found fifty-three bodies."

"Helios grunts?"

Aunt Essie's expression hardened. "And all of the scientists."

"All of them?" That was terrible, but it was also good because anyone who knew how to build the gate was dead, so she really did have the only plans. *Wait a minute.* She was horrified at herself. *Since when is people dying a good thing?* "So what are they going to tell the Senate and UEC?" she asked.

Essie flipped through the message. "Kev says the council is picking some news wavers to allow in to get footage of the remains of the base. They're going to say it's another victory against Helios but no information about exactly what they were building there will get out. They're calling it a secret chem tech lab."

"Right." Rosie felt suddenly very weary. "Still no clues where Riley is either?" Both her aunt and Kev had been scoping every wave and communication since the base defeat to see if he'd messaged them.

"Nothing." Aunt Essie avoided her eye and began pushing around the stuff on the bench again. "So, that car Dalton sent for you should be here soon. You won't stay there too late, will you? I know you're keen to see the boys, but it's not safe."

"I'll be back before dark," Rosie said and Essie nodded. Strained silence fell between them for a minute then Essie said, "Cake should be ready by then … if it's edible." She almost smiled and Rosie was about to tell her she was sure it would be when the door monitor chimed.

Rosie got up. "That'll be the car."

Outside it was as hot as it had looked. Rosie's hair curled in the damp heat, but the AI car Dalton sent had UV-filtered windows and a cooling system and it was a relief to be able to sit for a while without sweating.

The two-hour drive to the beach house gave her a lot of time to think. Too much time. Her stomach was nothing but rattled nerves as the car pulled smoothly down the drive and stopped in front of the house.

"Hey, Pilot Girl." Dalton was waiting for her at the door, barefoot. He pulled her in for a big hug. He felt good and solid and she hugged him back, hard.

"Whoa, don't damage the merchandise." He laughed,

but she just hugged harder. It had scared her, the thought of him not being around any more, much more than she liked. "So you've been worried about me then?" He got out of her vice-like grip and drew her inside, a limp in his step.

"No, not even a little bit," Rosie said.

"You're such a liar, Black." He chuckled and went ahead of her towards the kitchen. "Juice, food, pain blockers?" He spread his arms wide as they entered. "We've got all sorts here at the Curtis mansion. What's your poison?"

"Just juice." Rosie sat at the long table, staring out to the deck and the beach.

"If you're wondering where he is, he's gone for a swim." Dalton put a glass in front of her and sat opposite. There was a funny rueful smile on his face. "That is what you were wondering, isn't it?"

Rosie's nerves fluttered again. She shrugged and sipped the juice. His guitar was leaning upright on the chair at the head of the table. "You've been playing?" she said.

He gave her a look that said he knew she was avoiding answering, but reached for it anyway. "Not much else to do out here. I've even been making up some truly appalling songs about our troubles. Want to hear one?" He grinned and strummed a few discordant notes.

"Maybe later, like when I'm dead," Rosie said.

He nodded sagely. "A wise choice. I shall play them

at your funeral for all the weeping broken-hearted boys."
He began to play a tune she didn't know.

Rosie watched him for a while, then said, "Dalton,
we need to talk."

He looked up at her, fingers still moving softly on
the strings. He wasn't smiling. "I know."

Rosie took in a breath. "You know the deal I told you
I almost made with Sulawayo?"

"Is this the part where you tell me you're thinking
of revisiting that deal?"

"How—"

"Because I know you, Black." He shook his head at
her surprise. "You can't let things go, not where Helios
and Pip are concerned."

Rosie swallowed. "It's not as simple as you think."

"Nothing is." He fingered a few strings "So what?
You're just going to track her down and say, 'Hey, sign
me up.' You really think it's that easy?"

"No, but I still think it's our best chance to bring
down Helios. And I still have the best bargaining chip:
the implant. I'm sure I'm the only one with plans for the
gate now. And the Pantheon list."

His mouth twisted at that last comment and he stared
down at the guitar. "Yeah, the list with my dear dad's
name on it. Jebediah Curtis, traitor to all that's good."
He paused. "Rosie, I get it, I know why you want to
revisit that deal. I know who you're doing it for, but—"

"It's not just for Pip," Rosie said swiftly.

He narrowed his gaze at her. 'What do you mean?"

Her chest tightened. "I ... It's for me. The implant's not working properly."

"Yeah, we know that," he said slowly.

"No. When Cassie looked at it with the machine, she found out it was made by Helios. Special tech of some kind, and it's breaking up. I could go blind or–" She took in a shaky breath. "It could kill me."

"And let me guess," Dalton said softly. "Only Helios has the tech to get it out."

She nodded.

"Are you going to tell Pip?" he asked.

"I can't." Rosie pressed her hands together in her lap.

"You mean you're not going to tell him any of it? Not about trying to remake the deal or about the implant?"

"If I do, he'll try to stop me."

"Do you blame him? What makes you think I won't?"

"Because you're my friend." She gave him a desperate, pleading look.

He let out a humourless laugh. "Friend, sure."

"I'm not even sure I'm going to do it yet," she said.

"Yes you are."

She ignored his bitter tone. "If I do, I need you to promise you won't tell Pip about the implant. Just let him know I'm doing it because it's the best way to stop Helios for good. And make sure he goes north. Don't let him hang around trying to rescue me."

"Sure, anything else?" Dalton's eyes glittered. "Any

other orders before you march yourself off to the firing squad?"

"It's not like that," she said.

"How about you promise me something too?"

"What?" Rosie wondered where this was going.

"Promise that if things go bad you'll find a way to get a message to me and let me help, because maybe I can. Despite what you want to believe, I'm in this as much as you. And I'd really rather you didn't end up dead."

Rosie stared at him for a moment. "I promise," she said. He watched her like he wasn't sure she was genuine, so she offered her hand across the table. "I promise."

"Good choice." He shook her hand, but there was a bleakness in his eyes that worried her.

"You're not going to confront your dad about being part of the Pantheon, are you?"

His mouth twisted as he said, "I haven't decided."

"He might not be as bad as you think," Rosie said. "I'll try to find out. Maybe he's part of the rebellion."

"I doubt it." He began playing the guitar again. "He's a son of a bitch anyway."

Rosie sighed. "Dalton—"

"You should go find Pip," he said. "He'll be waiting for you. He knew you were coming. There're UV parasols in the gym."

Rosie hesitated. "I'm sorry."

"Don't be. I'm a big boy, I'll get over it. Go find Pip." When she still didn't move, he shook his head and half-smiled, but it wasn't a happy one. "Make your choice, Pilot Girl: stay here and console me or go."

She hated seeing him like this. She turned and left, swiping her hand to drop the generated wall of glass, and went out to the deck.

———•◦•———

It was bone-drying hot outside, and Rosie fetched a parasol from the gym before she followed the short path to the beach. The swell was low and the waves minimal, just a gentle wash and fall as if it was too hot even for the ocean to be bothered moving. She spotted Pip's dark silhouette at the water's edge.

He was not long out of the water, and drops still clung to his bare muscled torso and sparkled in his dark hair. He was wearing nothing but a pair of black swim shorts and Rosie tried not to stare. He watched her approach, hands on his hips. His eyes seemed bluer than the sea today, emphasised by the water and the bare darkness of his skin.

"Hey," he said as she stopped by him. "Nice umbrella. Very … pink." His glance was guarded.

"It's a parasol." Rosie held onto it, nervous and hot. "Hold it a minute." She thrust it at him then sat on the sand. She pulled off her boots and rolled up the bottom of her pants.

"Why don't you go for a swim?" he said.

"I didn't bring bathers." She took the parasol back.

"I have no objections to nudity." He tried to smile but it barely curved his lips. He was trying too hard.

Rosie walked into the water, watching it flow over her toes. He stood next to her and she looked at his bare feet near hers. One of the toenails was missing on his left foot.

Everything she'd just said to Dalton kept replaying in her mind. The things she couldn't tell Pip. She took in a quick shaking breath. "We heard from Kev."

She told him what the message had said, how everything had played out. He didn't say anything or even react much to it and she was left watching him, waiting while he stared at the horizon, squinting against the glare.

"So what do you think? What are you going to do?" she said.

"What do you mean?"

"Are you going back to Gondwana?"

He didn't answer right away.

"Pip?" She tried to figure out what he was thinking.

"Is that what you want – you want me to leave?" His voice was tight, quiet and something flinched painfully inside her.

"No, but it's dangerous for you here."

A muscle in his jaw twitched. "Are we really going to pretend you didn't try to make a deal with Sulawayo?

I had to force you to leave."

She swallowed. "It was the only thing I could think of to get you out."

"Don't!" he said with unexpected force and took a step back from her. "Don't say that you did it for me, Rosie." She stared at him, stunned.

He pushed his fingers through his hair and pressed his hands to his forehead, staring down at the water. All the muscles in his torso tensed like he was trying hard to hold something in. "Don't you know how much you scared me?" he said in a rough voice. He lifted his head to look at her. "When they took me, I thought you were dead. I thought all of you were dead. She didn't tell me you weren't. And then there you were, alive, and it was like someone turned the sun on again." His eyes glistened with unshed tears. "Then she said you'd made a deal," he continued hoarsely. "I couldn't believe it, after everything I told you about them."

"I'm sorry," she whispered.

He shook his head, looking away over the ocean. "That deal, those plans for me you came up with – to use Helios tech to find a cure. It was exactly what they did to me, making decisions about what I should do without giving me a say."

He was right. And she hated herself for doing that to him. But it might have kept him safe, safer than he was now.

"I'm sorry," she said again, but he gave a short shake

of his head, like he was shaking off her words.

"I'm just glad we got out of there. I hope Sulawayo doesn't come after you now. Or the rest of Helios."

Watching him, Rosie felt like part of her was breaking open. She'd caused him so much pain. And there would be more, because she was hoping that Sulawayo *would* come after her, and that she'd be able to remake that deal. But she couldn't tell him that. Tears started to work their way from her eyes. She touched him hesitantly on the arm. He looked down at her for a moment, then put his hands lightly on her hips. With a sigh, he leaned towards her.

"You shouldn't have done it," he whispered. "I was so scared they'd take you."

She put her hands on his chest. "I couldn't leave you there."

He drew back. "At least it's over now. We'll try to find Riley, bring them down some other way."

Rosie closed her eyes. She couldn't speak because she was afraid if she did, she'd tell him everything. She felt Pip's hands on either side of her face and opened her eyes to his bright blue gaze. The unguarded emotion she saw made her tremble.

"Pip–"

He cut off her words with a light kiss, barely a brush of his lips over hers. When he pulled back, even though they were still so close it felt as if there was a gulf opening between them that she didn't know how to cross.

She was seized by a terrible fear that if she joined Helios she might not see him again. He seemed to sense something because a sad, worried look crossed his face.

"What is it?"

She didn't know how to answer him, so instead she rose up on her tiptoes and kissed him, harder this time, desperately. For a moment he resisted, then he groaned softly and pulled her close, kissing her back. He tasted like salt water and sweat, like home. She wrapped her arms around him, not caring he was wet, just wanting him closer, wanting to shut out the world until it was only Pip and his breath, his skin. She ran her fingers through his salt-roughened hair, over the hard curve of his back. She didn't know how long they kissed, but the sudden sharp cawing of a seagull made them both start. They pulled apart, breathless.

Pip smiled gently and brushed a strand of hair from her face. "We should get back."

Rosie felt unsteady, like she might disappear. A light wind had sprung up and she looked around for the parasol. It was bobbing upside down in the wash. Pip retrieved it and brought it back to her, trying to flick the water off.

"Here." He held it over her head and put an arm around her, pulling her in beside him under its shade.

Rosie picked up her shoes, tying the laces together so she could carry them in one hand, and they began walking back up the beach. She searched for something to say, some safe ground.

"You know what's weird?" she said. "I don't even know your last name."

He looked down at her sideways. "I never told you?"

She shook her head.

He almost smiled. "It's Ngaru."

"Ngaru." Rosie couldn't pronounce it the same way he did.

"Yeah, I know, it's different. It an old name from wherever my ancestors came from. My dad always said it meant hero, or something like that."

Rosie leaned her head on his shoulder. It suited him, that name. Ngaru. Hero. She turned her face and closed her eyes, letting him lead her along and pressing her lips lightly against his skin. She tried hard to memorise this moment, this feeling of being here with Pip, to tattoo it somehow on her heart, because one day soon it might be all she had of him. One day soon she was going to have to finish what she'd started. Deep down was a terrible fear that after that she might never have a moment like this again.

EPILOGUE

The afternoon sunlight had a brittle harshness that suited Rosie's mood as she stepped from the shuttle station and stared up at the massive building across from her.

Before she'd left, she'd done what she could to ease Aunt Essie's panic at finding her gone. She'd sent a message to Dalton, timed for him to receive it two hours from now, asking him to let Essie know what she was doing, asking him to make good on his promise.

Essie would likely try to follow her, stop her, but it would be too late by then. And she knew she could count on Dalton to keep his word. He'd even keep Pip in hand if he had to.

Pip.

An ache filled her chest as if she felt another invisible scar forming on her heart. She pushed thoughts of him deep down, locked them away. Thoughts like that wouldn't help her now.

Shouldering the pack filled with her clothes, she walked across Aurora Plaza and through the doors of Senate Prime.

Inside it was the same as before. AI ports, people in suits, hard-eyed guards, the cool, temperature-controlled air. Everything so ordered, so … Senate. How many of them knew the kind of people they really harboured here?

"Can I help you?" the attendant on the front desk asked. Holo patches glittered on both his temples.

Rosie swallowed hard, trying to control the rapid beat of her heart. "I have an appointment with Agent Sulawayo."

ABOUT THE AUTHOR

Lara Morgan grew up in the hills outside of Perth, Western Australia but has spent the years since then roaming the world and investigating other hills. She has worked in the arts, at a newspaper and, once, a car wash, but all pale in comparison to being a writer which allows her to work in her pyjamas. She is also the author of a fantasy trilogy called The Twins of Saranthium. The Rosie Black Chronicles is her first series for young adults. She now lives in Geraldton, Western Australia – most of the time. You can visit her online at: www.lara-morgan.com.

ACKNOWLEDGEMENTS

The second book in a series can be the most difficult, because it can sometimes become the stagnant dip in what should be an arc toward the excitement of the third. That this book hasn't suffered that dip is due to the patient, considered cajoling of the recalcitrant author by these wonderful people.

My trio of editors, Chris Kloet, Suzanne O'Sullivan and Sue Whiting, suggested that perhaps leaving a certain part of the book out would be better for the story. Of course they were right. Special thanks go to Suzanne and Sue, whose ideas did much to shape the story and whose support and continued enthusiasm were such a great help. Their patience, gentle insistence and plain hard work have transformed this book into what you hold in your hand. Thanks also to Jess Owen, whose careful reading cut down on the dreaded repetition of words we shall not mention.

Gratitude must also go to Sarah Foster, who helped cut through the muddle I was having over the beginning and reassured me that what I thought in my gut was right, and whose continued advocacy of Rosie's story is such a joy.

Thanks must also go to Amanda Lines, who never tires of reminding me that it's all going to be okay, and my family, who are not above shifting my books to the front of bookstores or talking loudly about them in public. To my husband, Grant, who has always supported me and makes sure I'm not a hermit. And my faithful dog, Jake, who has missed out on many walks for this book without complaint and who will probably not be around for the next one. Hunt well in doggie heaven, my dearly loved scout.